D1011189

Fatal Induction

Books by Bernadette Pajer

A Spark of Death
Fatal Induction

Fatal Induction

A Professor Bradshaw Mystery

Bernadette Pajer

Poisoned Pen Press

Poisoned Pen Press
6962 E. First Ave., Ste. 103
Scottsdale, AZ 85251
www.poisonedpenpress.com
info@poisonedpenpress.com

Printed in the United States of America

To Kelly and Larry, my number one fans.
The pair of you beat a royal flush.

Chapter One

The first indication that Professor Benjamin Bradshaw's life was about to plunge again into chaos appeared in the form of a flatulent horse eating Mrs. Prouty's broad beans over the garden fence, its huge teeth tugging greedily at the vines.

Bradshaw knew wrath was sure to follow, but he felt a certain guilty pleasure in seeing the beans disappear. It had been a long and abundant season, and his digestion could use a rest.

He squeezed his bicycle between his white picket fence and the wagon that was attached to the horse, tossing a disparaging glance at the advertisement blazoned on the square black-paneled side. *Ralph's Redeeming Restorative*, it said, in bold red letters against a bright yellow sun bursting over a distant horizon. In smaller fancy script beneath the sun was written, *The Romany Remedy that Really Works!*

Bradshaw grunted. Someone in the neighborhood was being rooked. Or worse, drugged. Alcohol and opium were the preferred "curative" ingredients of patent medicines, and both were tragically addictive. He glanced down the rutted lane and over the low-fenced backyards of his neighbors, but he saw no one and heard no voices. At noon on a Friday in early September, with cumulus clouds chasing about in a deep blue sky and tinges of orange on the garden leaves hinting at fall, his neighborhood felt deserted. Except for the horse.

He looked at his simple white two-story home and at the firmly shut back door that led to the kitchen. Surely the peddler was not visiting his housekeeper. Mrs. Prouty had more common sense than that. A peddler of patent medicine was more likely to receive the sharp bristles of Mrs. Prouty's broom than pennies from the coin purse she stashed safely in the garments encasing her ample bosom.

As if called forth by the thought, the back door flew open, and Mrs. Prouty emerged with her broom. "Blimey, Professor. Can't you see what that creature's doing!" With lungs like a pair of bellows, a broad open face and wide-set gray eyes that missed nothing and could go from stern to tender in a flash, Mrs. Prouty was a force to be reckoned with. Bradshaw knew better than to react.

He said blandly, "I've no experience with horses, Mrs. Prouty. I leave him to you."

"And what am I? A gypsy? Out!" She waved her broom and rattled the vines under the horse's nose until it blinked and with a shake of its head, backed away. She then reached the broom over the fence and gave the horse's rump a swift thump. It trotted a few steps down the lane before stopping to gaze forlornly at the beans.

"Been out there all morning, it has," said Mrs. Prouty as Bradshaw followed her into the kitchen. He hung his hat and overcoat on the peg by the door. The kitchen smelled divinely of yeasty bread, now set to rise near the blackened stove.

He said, "Someone's bound to claim it soon."

"I didn't see it myself 'til after you'd gone. I sent Justin to see what the wagon was doing out there."

"What did he learn?"

"Didn't say, though he was out there long enough. Found something else to distract him, I've no doubt. He went out the kitchen, and a quarter hour later he's thundering down the stairs from his room. I'll likely find a slug under his pillow."

Bradshaw could well imagine the boy, sent out to investigate a wagon, discovering something else to divert his attention, a glittering rock he thought contained gold, a new form of snail, an empty bird's egg, something he knew Mrs. Prouty wouldn't allow in the house at any rate.

"Someone will soon claim it," Bradshaw repeated, but Mrs. Prouty wasn't ready to let the subject drop.

"It was down the lane a piece when you went out this morning. Dolores said it was there before sunrise when she got up to light the stove." Dolores, Bradshaw recalled, was the Mineos' housekeeper.

"And Martha, across at the Woodworth's, said it was there in the wee hours when she got up to, well—"

"Wee?"

"Professor! You're as bad as Justin."

"Was he home for lunch?" Bradshaw had hoped to be home early enough to see his son. He'd been detained by an impromptu meeting with Jacob Duttenhoefer, the University Engineer overseeing the construction of the new power house. It was Justin's first week of third grade, and Bradshaw hoped the boy was settling in.

"Not that you'd know it. He ran in here with that Paul from next door, ate without using his teeth, then raced off again, shouting something about frogs."

If Paul Dickerson was being referred to as "that Paul," Mrs. Prouty had witnessed or overheard some juvenile misdemeanor. Bradshaw was glad for her oversight, because it reined in Justin's more elaborate schemes. He didn't always want the details. A boy must have his adventures on his way to manhood.

Professor Bradshaw washed his hands at the gleaming white enameled sink, then took his place at the open end of the oak table—the rest of the table being spread with freshly boiled mason jars in preparation for an afternoon of canning—and opened his leather satchel to retrieve the outlines of his class curriculum. Instead, his fingertips stumbled on the contest flyer he'd found this morning when he'd organized his desk, and he read it again.

ATTENTION ALL ELECTRICAL INVENTORS!
The Seattle Grand Theater is looking for ENTRANTS
To their *Musical Telephone* CONTEST.
Budapest, London, and Paris residents have
for many years enjoyed the pleasure of the theater
from the comfort of their homes.
Why should Seattle not boast of our own
modern entertainment device?
Now, residents of OUR fair city shall have
their own Musical Telephone Service.
INVENTORS bring forth your best!
Enter today!
Testing of Instruments and Judging to take place
Friday October 11, 1901.
For more information, see Mr. Fisher.
The Seattle Grand Theater on Second Avenue.

Mrs. Prouty slid a plate of steaming, mushy beans under his nose, then stuck her own nose down to better read the flyer.

"You didn't enter that, did you?"

"Hmm," Bradshaw grunted. The flyer had been distributed last spring. In the chaos of Professor Oglethorpe's death, Bradshaw's copy had been relegated to a bottom desk drawer and he'd only discovered it this morning. One month wasn't much time to create and perfect such a device, and with classes beginning the first of October, it was the worst time of year to undertake something so time-consuming.

Still, he did intend to enter. Better yet, he intended to win. As luck would have it, he'd recently filed a patent on an improvement to a microphone transmitter that would suit this project nicely with a bit more fine-tuning, but it was his habit to batten down enthusiasm, especially in front of Mrs. Prouty who felt he spent far too much time down in the basement. A few years ago, he had become obsessed with a project to the neglect of his small household and his own health, and she'd kept a keen eye on his tinkering ever since. The smell rising from his plate made quelling the excitement of a new project easier. His stomach gave a little clutch of protest.

"Any bread yet?"

"By suppertime," she said proudly. Bread was the only food Mrs. Prouty produced that was light and mouthwatering. It was the food that responded best to her heavy approach, the flour and yeast happily rewarding the aggressive kneading of her large, capable hands. If it weren't for Mrs. Prouty's bread, Professor Bradshaw and Justin would have starved years ago. This past summer, when Missouri had been living in the spare bedroom and sharing the cooking duties, the fare had improved dramatically, and Bradshaw had hoped Mrs. Prouty would retain some of Missouri's techniques. The mushy beans before him were a clear sign she was reverting to her old ways.

He suppressed a sigh and gazed out the window. The peddler's horse was once again dining on broad beans.

Well. It was obvious something had gone wrong. The horse had made off without its owner. Maybe the peddler had taken ill. Could that be it? Was some poor fellow slumped inside the wagon, praying for help, too weak to call out?

Bradshaw marched outside, ignoring Mrs. Prouty's trailing questions. At his approach, and the sight of Mrs. Prouty, the horse backed away from the beans. Bradshaw walked around the wagon, calling out loudly, "Hello! Are you there?" and rapping his knuckles on the side. There was no response.

The covers of the wagon's windows were clamped shut. He tried the door at the back and found it unlocked. He peered inside the dark interior. It smelled of camp living, of cooked food and unwashed clothes, and something sharp and sour he identified with sickness. He made out a bunk bed, a dresser, and a storage trunk, as well as various crates with pots and pans, food staples, and half a dozen boxes of Ralph's Restorative. All was in a state of general untidiness. There was no one, ill or otherwise, inside. He opened the door wider to let in more light.

A bit of shiny clean cloth on the lower bunk caught his eye. A doll, about twelve inches tall and dressed in pink satin so pale it was nearly white. An elegant little thing, it looked out of place, with its lace-trimmed jacket, fur muff, and ruffled hat that surrounded the pink-cheeked cherubic bisque face. He climbed into the wagon and picked up the doll gingerly. Its blue eyes opened and looked into his own.

He poked about the wagon enough to discover girl's clothing. A girl of Justin's age, maybe, or a bit younger, judging from the size.

"Well?" shouted Mrs. Prouty from the back porch.

Bradshaw, still holding the doll gingerly, stepped down and closed the door. "I'll phone the police."

"The police!"

"Yes, Mrs. Prouty, abandoned vehicles fall under their jurisdiction." He handed the satin doll to her, as if presenting her with a real baby. She took it carefully, cradling it, and for a moment was nonplussed. Bradshaw passed through the kitchen to the hall where the telephone resided on a high stand. He lifted the receiver from the hook and heard nothing but the ocean sounds of his inner ear. He jiggled the hook a few times, to no avail.

"Mrs. Prouty!" he shouted. He needn't have. Mrs. Prouty stood just behind him with the doll still cradled. "The phone seems to be out of order. Did the hello girl check in this morning?"

"Melody called at nine, same as usual. Asked if the phone were working, and I said it was."

Bradshaw rattled the hook again and this time heard a breathless young woman, not Melody, say, "All circuits busy, please try again later."

"Fancy that." Mrs. Prouty stood near enough to hear. "What could she mean?"

Bradshaw, not feeling like explaining the possible defects of the telephone system, merely grunted a reply as he replaced the earpiece on the hook. He returned to the kitchen, where he donned his derby hat and overcoat and patted himself down in a habitual check before departing: pocket watch, coins for the streetcar, pen knife, pencil with small notepad, handkerchief, and gloves.

Mrs. Prouty had followed him. She peered out the window. "The phone went out last week when we had that storm. There's no wind today. I'll bet it's those new houses going up. Someone's always knocking down the lines when they put up a new house." She absentmindedly rocked the doll in her arms as she pondered the possibilities.

Bradshaw smothered a grin. "I'll go down to the police station and see what can be done about the horse and wagon." Not giving her time to protest, he hurried toward the front of the house and out the door. He was nearly out of earshot when he heard her bellow, "You've forgotten your beans, Professor!"

Chapter Two

The streetcar was nearly empty, a rare occurrence. Bradshaw had a seat all to himself for the journey downtown, and a clear view of Seattle. The weather couldn't make up its mind. The sun shone on the hills above the city while to the south a line of gray mist revealed coming rain, and down in Elliott Bay, the morning fog had not completely burned away. Dust and smoke from construction and furnaces added to the shifting view, sending Bradshaw's mind thinking of symphony music, and then on to the device he would build for the upcoming contest.

As the car neared Third Avenue, the streets suddenly filled with pedestrians. Mostly men, hurrying, some of them running.

Bradshaw shot to his feet, signaled the driver he wished to stop, and jumped off while the wheels were still moving. He sniffed the air, searching for smoke, fire being his first fear. There was no sign of it. But the air crackled with something strange, some ominous fear he could see in the strained faces.

He joined the hurrying crowd and asked the person nearest him, a young man of about twenty, "What's happened?"

The young man shook his head. "I don't know, I'm going to see where everyone else is going."

As they turned the corner on Second Avenue, he understood they were flocking to the windows of the Post-Intelligencer Building. A sense of dread swam over him. He had to fight a compulsion to turn around and race up to Justin's school to protect him from whatever calamity had struck. Was it war? The thought was a vague, dark dread. War with whom, for goodness sake? There were troops fighting Boxers in China, and soldiers battling insurgents still in the Philippines. But those were ongoing and limited affairs, nothing to send a crowd racing toward the newspaper office.

And then he heard it, among the murmuring voices came distinctly the reason for the fearful crowd: The president. Shot. In Buffalo. McKinley. Shot dead.

Bradshaw stood immobile, a numbing chill prickling his skin head to toe.

Oh, God, no. It could not be! Oscar Daulton was in jail, here in Seattle. McKinley could not be dead. Bradshaw struggled to make sense of what he was hearing. His mind wouldn't work properly. He couldn't get his thoughts past his former student, Oscar Daulton. A young man horrified and altered by his experience in the Philippines, he'd turned to anarchism and plotted to assassinate the president. Last spring. In May. Months ago. Mrs. McKinley had been ill, cancelling the president's trip to Seattle. The president hadn't come, he'd not been hurt. How could he now be dead?

An unseen hand plucked Bradshaw's hat off his head and pressed it into his hands.

Around him, all the men had doffed their hats respectfully and clutched them to their breasts. The buzz continued to swirl, and he picked up fragments. *At the Pan American Exhibition… shaking hands…Buffalo, that's near Niagara…shot at close range…* Bradshaw was bumped and brushed by the crowd. The Secret Service was supposed to protect McKinley. They'd been warned. They knew there were more anarchists out there.

And then from the crowd came a wave of sound, an astonished sigh, moving from those nearest the newspaper office window, rippling out to the street, and a single voice rose above them. "He lives! Shot but not dead! McKinley is alive!"

Bradshaw edged his way out of the crowd. He stood for a moment outside the hum, feeling disconnected from his feet. He wasn't sure what he was supposed to be doing. Clutching his hat, he walked aimlessly for a few minutes until he recalled why he'd come downtown. He then headed up Jefferson Street and within a half block met Detective James O'Brien coming down.

They faced each other silently. The very air was shaking with the buzz of incredulity. He remembered that he'd wanted to see O'Brien, but couldn't think why.

He opened his mouth to confess this, but O'Brien was looking past him, his eyes wide, and he'd taken a sharp, involuntary breath. A pang of fear shot through Bradshaw. He turned to see the crowd on the street below them now surging up the hill. Their voices carried above the trembling atmosphere. Bradshaw felt emanating from them a wave of anger so intense it pricked the hair on his arms and the back of his neck. From the mass of noise came a name, and the name grew into a murderous chant.

"Daulton, Daulton, Daulton!"

Bradshaw and O'Brien exchanged a look that needed no words. Their thoughts were unison: lynch mob.

As one, they turned and ran. Up hill. No easy feat, running up the steep grade of Jefferson. It was like running in a nightmare. After a single block, the effort of lifting an aching leg and pushing off the asphalt to propel himself up and forward seemed impossible, yet Bradshaw did it, muscles screaming.

At the crest of Fifth Avenue, they slowed and gulped air as they hobbled across the intersection.

Bradshaw gasped, "He's safe. In jail." He meant the crowd could not penetrate the County Courthouse down to the basement, through the locked and guarded iron doors, nor the hardened steel cells.

O'Brien shot him a grave look and barked simply, "Hearing."

A hearing would be taking place upstairs, in an open courtroom. There would be a judge, attorneys, a single armed guard. A half dozen unprepared men facing a murderous mob of over a hundred.

They began to run again, and Bradshaw thought it was no wonder this particular Seattle mound had been dubbed "Profanity Hill" by those frequenting the King County Courthouse. If he'd possessed any spare breath, he would have been cussing up a storm. The daggers in his lungs prevented all speech. He and O'Brien staggered up the courthouse steps, down the long corridor, and burst through the courtroom doors, gasping, panting, and dripping beads of sweat. Bradshaw leaned forward, hands on his knees, hoping he wouldn't be sick. Every head turned to stare at them, including the judge at his bench and young Oscar Daulton, pale and gaunt, standing handcuffed beside his court-appointed attorney.

O'Brien found some inner resource to bellow out, "McKinley shot—lynch mob—hide Daulton."

For three full seconds, those in the courtroom were too stunned to move. Their silence allowed the angry, rhythmic chanting of the approaching mob to penetrate the sandstone walls. The judge rapped his gavel. "Hearing adjourned. Get Daulton into solitary."

Bradshaw and O'Brien joined the others in surrounding Daulton as they hurried out of the courtroom into the hall. At the far end, the front doors slammed open, and the youngest and angriest of the mob poured in, the weight of the stragglers pressing behind them. They shouted when they spied Daulton and surged forward with venomous growls, too winded to make coherent speech.

Bradshaw caught a glimpse of Daulton in his cocoon of guards. The boy's thin, pale face glowed like a saint before a vision of God.

"Grab tight!" Bradshaw obeyed his own order, and the others followed as Daulton tried to wrest himself out of their protection. They dragged him down the stairs to the iron doors, startling Jailor MacLeod from his registry book.

The Judge shouted a command that needed no repetition. "Open!"

The jailor shoved the key in the lock and the well-oiled iron door swung silently open. Bradshaw was propelled forward with Daulton into the jail, and the iron door slammed shut behind them.

O'Brien spoke through the bars. "You know him best, Ben. Stay with him until it's clear."

Bradshaw accepted his assignment. Daulton no longer struggled. He allowed Bradshaw to usher him into an empty cell. The door clanked as Jailor MacLeod locked them inside.

For a few minutes they didn't speak. The shouts and threats and scuffling of bodies filled the atmosphere with palpable fear. Great whacks and thumps, like bats hitting wooden doors, echoed with the voices. Several times, something pounded on the outer iron doors sending them ringing. Then the sounds receded. Then nothing could be heard but an occasional cough from other cells.

Bradshaw sat on the one hard stool. Oscar Daulton sat on the bare cot. Meager light came from an electric fixture outside the cell.

"They should have let that crowd have me, Professor. I want to die."

"You forfeited your wants when you took three lives, Oscar, and attempted to take two more."

"They want me to die. Why should they wait for my hanging?"

"Because that's how civilized men dispense justice. And don't sit there telling me you want to die. You want to be made a martyr."

"What's the difference?"

Bradshaw didn't bother to explain. Oscar knew the difference. He was a brilliant young man saddled with a weak nature. Bradshaw had hoped that during his imprisonment he would come to his senses and realize the horror of his actions. It was too late to save his life; Bradshaw hoped yet for the boy's soul. Oscar still believed his cause to be just, still believed the world, and God, would thank him for ridding the planet of the rich and powerful who trampled the poor and weak. The trial, guilty verdict, and sentence of hanging took no more than a day. That final, fatal sentence, however, faced continued delays by appeals from various groups who, driven by their own political and religious goals, hoped to change the hanging to a life sentence.

Bradshaw let Oscar ramble on about the inequities of capitalist societies. He'd heard it all before. His own thoughts avoided the president's shooting and diverted to the waste of Oscar's life.

He'd had such potential. Genius, really. Another Nikola Tesla or Michael Faraday if not for his fanatical passions. The mysterious, potentially revolutionary device he'd invented, he'd used to kill. Its secrets had been locked within a cedar cigar box with screw terminals and two metal rods protruding from the ends. Those rods had held a flaming but silent direct current arc, fueled only by batteries that should not have been able to provide enough voltage to do the job. When caught attempting to stun a fourth victim, Oscar had thrown the device overboard the *City of Seattle* ferry where it sank to the bottom of Elliott Bay.

Had Oscar kept written plans for the device, Bradshaw wondered for the thousandth time? Filed a patent application? He could not bring himself to ask, nor how he'd made it, nor how it worked. The device had killed, but by God it had also pulled off the impossible, seemingly stepping-up voltage, both A.C. and D.C. If it worked as it seemed, if it hadn't been some complex hoax, the possibilities for invention were limitless.

Bradshaw looked at Oscar. The boy, now silent, stared at his hands in his lap.

Even if Oscar were to tell him the details of his invention, could he use it? The moral dilemma boggled. He hadn't much time to sort it out, either. Oscar's mysterious lost invention, mentioned in newspapers across the country, had already drawn curious and less scrupulous inventors to Profanity Hill to try to drag the details from the condemned young man. So far, he'd remained silent. Would the craving for fame and glory crack that silence before the noose stole his voice forever?

An hour later, Bradshaw stood outside the King County Courthouse with Detective O'Brien, a few other lawmen, and a half-dozen courthouse employees. The fog and clouds had blown away, and the city sprawled below them, dearly familiar after today's events. Whitecaps danced on Elliott Bay, but the distant Olympic Mountains hid behind a veil of smoky mist. The angry mob had gone, Daulton was secure, and yet the men did not disperse. Bradshaw's skin felt clammy from his exertion. When he licked his lips, he tasted salt. The buffeting wind sent a chill through him, but he felt a keen and unfamiliar need to linger. He did not want to be alone. The others must have felt the same, because no one wandered off or returned to work. They stood in a clutch at the bottom of the courthouse steps, jackets flapping and hats mashed down, the talk somber.

"Not a pretty world when folks go mad with their ideas," declared a stocky guard with a square face and experienced eyes. He stood with a hand resting on his holstered gun as if expecting another angry mob. "Meredith would be alive today if he'd had the sense to calm down. And Considine wouldn't be facing murder charges."

Before today's catastrophe, the big news had been the summer's gunfight between the Chief of Police Meredith, who'd resigned before the shooting, and John Considine, a Tenderloin business owner with the incongruous reputation of being a family man, teetotaler, and regular church-goer. Meredith had been killed and Considine accused by the coroner's jury of murder. The trial was set for November.

"A man can only take so much," said Patrolman Cox, whether in defense of his former chief or the respected businessman, wasn't clear. Cox was a big man, narrow at the temple, with a bulbous chin and a thick formidable mustache, like a whisk broom that he twirled into points on each end. He had a look Bradshaw recognized, that of someone who put pride over propriety. Old West, not new century.

"No one knows better than a chief that it ain't right to take the law into your own hands." This from a county clerk.

As a debate on the limits of individuals versus the power of the police grew, Patrolman Mercer arrived in a taxicab, pulled slowly to the curb by a sturdy bay, to the surprise and guffaws of his fellow officers.

Mercer, a heavyset and minimally mustached fellow with an air of self-importance not supported by his rumpled uniform, climbed down from the taxi and glared at his audience. "I'm on official business, so leave be, the lot of you." He helped down a young man, a boy really, no more than twenty, with sleek black hair parted in the middle and a delicate face that surely had never yet needed a shave. The boy wore a slim dark suit with an upright collar and a bold tie the color of strawberries. His wrists were trapped in handcuffs, and he limped when Mercer tugged to get him moving slowly up the courthouse steps.

Detective O'Brien, his features as usual unreadable, called out, "Is the matron overwhelmed?"

Mercer growled, "That raid this afternoon put the women's cells over limit, that's why this one's coming here."

O'Brien explained to Bradshaw, "Ordinance violation raid. Matron's cells are full."

Bradshaw's face must have shown his puzzlement. Why would the matron's full cells prevent the boy from being locked up in the men's portion of the city jail?

"I forget how rarely you get about in this city, Ben. Never heard of Nell Pickerell?"

"Should I have?"

"She's been mentioned in the papers on more than one occasion." He nodded toward the captive. "Likes to dress as a man. Calls herself Harry."

"Huh." He glanced up at the limping girl trying to negotiate the steps. "A thief?"

"Nah, not much trouble, really. I don't think we ought to waste time with her. Every so often, someone feels duped when they learn she's not what she seems, and she's hauled in for impersonating a man. I heard last night she was in a fight, but I don't know the details."

Nell "Harry" Pickerell slipped and dropped down onto the steps, nearly pulling Mercer with her. As she struggled to rise, she caught Bradshaw watching her. For an instant, their eyes met, and then an announcement from the guard diverted everyone's attention. "Here comes March. Looks like he has news!"

Bradshaw turned to look down the hill.

"Got a new suit, too, by the looks of it," someone said.

"Tailor made for the golden boy." This comment elicited laughter that felt both welcome and wrong.

The man loping up the hill to them, with enviable ease, was not in uniform. He was handsome and blond with full cheeks and prominent bones and a wide expressive mouth. He wore a stylish felt hat and, as his fellow officers claimed, an expensive tailored light gray suit. He'd recently been promoted to detective and had already proved himself more than capable, or so the newspapers reported. O'Brien hadn't mentioned him.

"Seen the latest placards?" someone called out.

"He's still alive, resting easy. A bullet has been removed."

Comments of relief and hope rippled through the men.

"Who done it?" shouted Cox.

"Man named Fred Nieman from Detroit. Claims to be an anarchist."

As the men discussed this news, Detective March's glance caught Bradshaw's, and his eyes lit with friendly curiosity. "Professor Bradshaw, isn't it?" He held out his hand. "You captured Daulton, our resident anarchist. The nation could use more ambitious citizens like you." The broad smile flashed.

Bradshaw gave only the slightest nod as he shook March's hand. He disliked being congratulated for having discovered a troubled young man had committed murder.

March went on, "And I hear you've been a help with several other cases. I'm glad to finally get the chance to officially meet you."

"Likewise, Detective. You've been successful in your new rank."

"Oh, a mere stepping stone to Mayor, then Governor, then who knows?" He spoke with humor, and his fellow officers laughed.

Only O'Brien refrained, giving Bradshaw a sideways glance. "He means it you know." His usually unreadable gaze held something bitter. Was O'Brien jealous of the up-and-coming detective? Resentful of someone using the police force as a stepping stone into politics?

For a few minutes, the conversation centered around Detective March. He stood like a celebrity among them, shifting the mood, answering their questions with good humor. O'Brien's face turned increasingly sour as compliments and questions flooded March. "Nice work with that pickpocket, he was a slick one...the wife heard your band at the concert last night, wants you to meet her sister...how about my sister? I could use a rich brother-in-law...she thinks the sun rises..."

The image of a rising sun suddenly brought the patent medicine wagon's advertisement to mind, and Bradshaw recalled the initial reason for his trip downtown. It seemed inconsequential now, but still, it had to be dealt with. He turned to O'Brien.

"There's an abandoned horse and wagon in my back lane."

"Not an easy thing to lose. Someone will turn up for it."

"I don't know, it's been there since last night, according to my housekeeper. It's a patent medicine wagon, has 'Ralph's Restorative' on the side panels."

Bradshaw didn't miss the way March, who hadn't been facing them, now turned, eyes wide with interest.

"Did I hear you mention Ralph's?"

"The Professor was speaking to me, Reggie. It's none of your concern."

March took this rebuke with a smile and continued attention on Bradshaw. "You're not a customer of Ralph's Restorative, are you?"

Bradshaw hesitated, trying to sort out the awkward situation. After working with Detective O'Brien last spring at the time of Oglethorpe's death, and this summer on a few electrical incidents, he rather considered James O'Brien a friend. In fact, O'Brien was the only person who called him "Ben" rather than "Professor" or "Bradshaw." He didn't want to be disloyal by disregarding the clear signal he was getting from him, yet here was March, smiling openly at him and it would have been rude, and awkward, to not answer. "You know of Ralph's?"

"By reputation. Word's going round about the tonic down in the Tenderloin. It's making people sick. You said something about a wagon?"

O'Brien tipped back his hat. "The Professor says he's found Ralph's Restorative wagon abandoned."

"Oh? Abandoned? Well, maybe Ralph got wind his tonic was trouble and took off."

Bradshaw, taking his cue from O'Brien who now seemed inclined to speak of the matter, asked, "So there is a Ralph? I mean, usually the names of patent medicines are made up, aren't they? Granny's Goods or Uncle John's Elixir?"

Detective March shrugged. "You might be right. In this case, there is a Ralph, or someone who calls himself that. Don't worry about the wagon, I'll see to it."

"It's in the back lane, behind my house at 1204 Gallagher, on Broadway Hill, although I suppose I ought to get used to calling it Capitol Hill."

March laughed. "Developers and their money, eh? You've got to admit they've done a bang-up job with the paving and sidewalks and new streetcar line. Hard to grudge them the name. I just might snag a lot up there myself before they're all gone. I'll see to that wagon."

O'Brien said, "You're not on duty, March. I can handle it."

Bradshaw sensed again a tension coming from O'Brien.

"No problem, I'd be happy to help out." March flashed a beguiling grin that was met without expression.

"Then take Mercer with you." Without giving Detective March time to respond, O'Brien haled Patrolman Mercer, who'd just descended the courthouse steps, and gave him instructions. Bradshaw almost pitied March, being saddled with the brawny patrolman. There would be no shaking him; Mercer's strength was his stubbornness.

March tipped his hat and strolled off with Mercer clomping importantly behind. Bradshaw realized he'd forgotten to mention finding girl's clothing and a doll in the wagon, but he didn't call March back. The two would no doubt find the owner and thus the child.

O'Brien moved to take his leave, too. "Glad it was you I met on the street today, Ben."

"Yes, likewise, Jim."

One by one, the others peeled themselves from the group until Bradshaw stood alone at the foot of the windy courthouse steps. He didn't know what he should do, where he should go. He didn't even know the time. He checked his watch. Nearly four. Justin would be getting out of school. His heart tightened. He would have to tell Justin.

Chapter Three

Located beneath the Church of the Immaculate Conception in a solid, uninspired four-story box of brick and stone, the Seattle College taught boys of all ages and levels from grammar school through college.

Professor Bradshaw arrived at the corner of Broadway and Madison a few minutes before the bell was due to chime and set the boys free. He wasn't the only parent waiting on the boardwalk; there were a few mothers as well. They were huddled together in somber discussion. He didn't know if this was usual, mothers coming to meet their children at school, or if they came because of today's horrendous news. He didn't usually come himself. Justin walked the one mile with his friend Paul, who lived on their street. In the morning, if they were late out the door, they could take the streetcar along Broadway, but on those days, he knew they preferred to pocket the nickels Mrs. Prouty pressed on them and run.

He saw Missouri's slight figure long before he could make out her features coming up the hill on the Madison Street boardwalk. There was no mistaking her long, graceful stride, the proud carriage of her head above her slender neck. She wore a simple blue wool suit with a skirt of sensible length and shoes of sensible width. He surmised she was coming from the hotel where she worked.

He didn't wonder why she was coming; he was too concerned with battening down the ridiculous joy he felt at the sight of her. Joy was morbidly inappropriate at this moment, when the president's life was in the balance.

But joy he felt. The least he could do to offset this emotion was frown. He frowned. Missouri didn't. She strode silently up to him, placed a slender, gentle hand on his arm, tilted her head to look up into his face, and smiled. An appropriate smile that was a mixture of concern and affection, her amber eyes expressing her full knowledge of today's events.

"I'm so sorry," she said. She knew, of course, about his personal involvement in putting an end to Oscar Daulton's anarchist mission. She knew he would be feeling unreasonably responsible that stopping Daulton had not prevented this tragedy.

He nodded, not trusting his voice.

"The phone circuits are overwhelmed. Mr. Padelford wanted me to stay at the switchboard during my dinner break, but I couldn't see the point."

"You walked off your post? You'll be fired."

Missouri gave a small laugh. "No. Mr. Padelford isn't that sort of man. If he were, I'd have quit long ago. But I will have to return soon. I won't take advantage of his nature. Poor man, I don't think he finds it easy supervising the lot of us, and some of the girls really do push him too far."

He noticed faint dark circles beneath her eyes. "Are you working too many hours? It must not be easy with two jobs."

"Oh, I do so little at Clark Hall, I almost feel guilty getting free room and board from the university. I expect my duties will increase once the fall term begins. The six girls now in residence spend most of their time off campus. But I am tired. I've been studying for the entrance exams."

The school bell sounded. There was an expectant pause, and then the doors flew open and the young boys emerged, a few with wings on their feet, others subdued, or so it seemed to Bradshaw. He caught sight of Paul first, a swaggering boy with black curls and an impish grin always twitching at the corners of his mouth. And then he spied Justin, slim and fair, plodding soberly down the steps behind his friend. It was odd seeing his boy, independent, a small person making his way in the world, armed with nothing more than three small school books strapped with a leather band. A lump caught in his throat. Justin saw him, then Missouri. He didn't smile, although he did approach them.

"What are you doing here?"

Normally, Bradshaw would have corrected such a rude question. Not today. The boy's face was tense, his brow furrowed.

Bradshaw said, "We came to walk you home," and was surprised at the comfort he felt in using that plural pronoun.

"Father McGuinness said someone shot the president."

A pang of relief entwined with regret swept Bradshaw. He would not have to break the news, yet the tragedy was now part of his son's world. "Yes, it's true, but the latest news is hopeful."

Justin's blue eyes remained troubled until he looked at Missouri. His face softened, not quite to a smile, but to something more peaceful. "I mastered the cursive 'r' today."

Bradshaw recalled she had encouraged Justin's penmanship this summer, making a game of it. Her most effective approach had been to have him trace his name in the sand with his finger.

"You did? Oh, that letter gave me fits when I was your age. Always came out looking like a broken chair."

The corner of Justin's mouth lifted ever-so slightly, and he ducked his head.

On the walk home, Missouri remained unnaturally quiet. Bradshaw struggled for conversation, and failed. The news of the abandoned peddler's wagon didn't get them further than a block. All else on his mind, the attempted assassination and Oscar Daulton's grasp for martyrdom, could not be spoken of with the boys in and out of earshot. They ran on ahead, stopped to explore ditches and bird nests and construction sites and other irresistible diversions, and then raced to catch up. Missouri's serenity began to annoy him. By the time they reached Gallagher Street, where Paul waved so-long at his house, leaping over the hedge into his yard, Bradshaw's head ached from not speaking, or rather, from not listening because it was generally she who rambled on entertainingly while he nodded.

At 1204 Gallagher, Justin opened the front gate, and the three of them followed the path round to the back of the house to enter the kitchen where Mrs. Prouty was just finishing washing up. She looked them over, giving a nod of greeting to Missouri, her troubled eyes revealing her knowledge of the attempt on McKinley's life and her decision to not talk about it in front of the boy.

Instead, she said, "Wagon's gone, did you see? The police took it away. Can't say as I like that patrolman. Seemed to think it my fault that horse was eating my beans! Serve him right having to ride behind that gassy beast."

Justin giggled as he slid into his chair at the table and attacked the milk and ginger cakes Mrs. Prouty had laid for him. A silent glance from Bradshaw slowed the boy to a speed not likely to choke. Mrs. Prouty loaded her dense ginger cakes with what she called "wholesome" ingredients, eggs and buttermilk, a dash of this, a pound of that, but not much sugar. Justin thrived on them. Bradshaw used them as paperweights.

He went through to the hall and into the parlor to his desk and found both women had followed him.

"Any news?" Mrs. Prouty asked in a low voice.

"The latest I heard, the president was resting and they'd removed a bullet."

"That's what Detective March said. Nice young man, that detective." Mrs. Prouty slid her gaze over Missouri. "Such a pleasant fellow. And handsome. Wonder if he's married?"

"I'm sure I don't know," Missouri said, her amber eyes wide and her smile deceptively innocent. "Why didn't you ask him?"

Bradshaw turned away from Mrs. Prouty's gasp and pretended he hadn't noticed her indignation. She turned on her heel and marched back to the kitchen. Apparently, she met Justin attempting to leave with loaded pockets. Her voiced boomed back to them, "No food upstairs, young man. I heard mice in the walls today. Big ones. I've set traps in the kitchen and basement, so mind you and that Paul leave them be."

"Yes, ma'am." A moment later, Justin hurried from the kitchen, his pockets turned inside out. He barely controlled his speed up the stairs.

Missouri's eyes followed him tenderly. When she returned her attention to the parlor, her gaze fell upon the doll on the mantel. She went to it and lifted it gently. She moved it, making the doll's eyes open and close, then she ran a slender finger down the elegant clothes.

"This doll is well-loved."

"It looks new."

"It's not. You can see that the clothes have been carefully mended, and the face and hands cleaned often enough that the paint has faded."

He hadn't examined it closely enough to notice.

"The little girl who owns this must be missing it terribly." She returned the doll to the mantel, posing it carefully in a sitting position, and continued studying it. "It's so odd, them disappearing. You said it looked as if a man and child lived out of the wagon? No woman, no mother?"

"Not that I could tell. I didn't do a thorough search." He studied her regal profile. Was she remembering her own mother, who'd recently died of influenza?

She turned her attention to him and he looked hastily away. "I need to get back to work. Mr. Padelford has messenger boys running relay between the hotel and the newspaper office. If news comes in, I'll try to telephone."

"Thank you." He walked her to the door.

"Justin seems to understand today's events."

"Since he was very young, he's had that ability to understand things beyond himself. I wouldn't have. I was a typical child at his age, self-centered and self-absorbed."

He opened the door and stood aside for her to step onto the porch. He followed her as far as the steps, where she paused.

"It serves as protection for children, doesn't it?"

"Yes, indeed. Childhood should be carefree. All too soon they learn the harsh truth of life."

"Oh, Mr. Bradshaw, today's news is harsh, but it's not everything."

He knew she truly meant that. She'd appeared on his doorstep last spring, pale and traumatized from the death of her mother and from her own bout with influenza. She'd come to be with her only relative, her Uncle Henry, only to find he was in Alaska searching for gold. Despite this, she'd awoken the next morning full of smiles and optimism. Full of life and joy. She could see possibilities where Bradshaw saw only threats.

He watched her slim figure disappear down the road.

So many things he wished he could say to her, questions he couldn't, shouldn't, bring himself to ask. *How are you? Do you miss us? Will you please move back home with us?* And questions he would not even allow himself to think, that simmered deep inside and that flared into a small, dull pain in the very center of his chest.

When he returned to the parlor, he found Justin there, reaching up for the doll.

"Justin!" Instantly, he regretted the sharpness of his tone. He was surprised at the protectiveness he felt toward the doll.

Justin dropped his hand with a small jump. "I was only looking."

"See that's all you do. We are keeping it safe until it can be returned to its rightful owner."

"Yes, sir."

Bradshaw waited for a flood of questions and speculation about the abandoned wagon and the child who owned the doll. None came.

"Is Missouri gone?"

"Yes, she had to return to work." He studied the boy's solemn face. Was it today's shooting that worried him, or did he miss Missouri living here and being near?

"I'm sure she'll come visit again soon."

"I know. I'll see her tomorrow."

"Tomorrow? I didn't hear her mention coming tomorrow."

"She comes every day to see me."

"I haven't seen her since she moved out."

"Because she leaves before you get home. Yesterday, she left out the front door when you were coming in the back." The boy smiled, as if it were a game.

"Is she avoiding me?"

"I'll ask her."

"No, no. It's not important."

Justin shrugged, oblivious that the timing of Missouri's comings and goings, her slipping in and out of the house without his knowledge, was stirring a host of emotions in his father. And why hadn't Mrs. Prouty said anything about her visits?

"Can I get something to eat?"

How the boy could even think of food after a plateful of those ginger bricks? Another growth spurt, no doubt.

"Yes, but eat in the kitchen."

"I won't eat in my room." He hurried off.

Bradshaw turned with a weary sigh to the pale pink satin doll. He would have to bring it to Detective March so it could be returned to the wagon, and he felt himself blush at the prospect. Ridiculous. *Uh, detective, I have the girl's doll here...*his headache throbbed. Maybe he'd hold onto it until the wagon's owner and child were found. He went in search of the Bayer Aspirin.

Chapter Four

Professor Bradshaw gave the brass handle of the massive door of the Seattle Grand Theater a tentative tug and found it unlocked. He pulled it open and stepped into the dim, expansive lobby. The floors gleamed, reflecting the sparse light. The air held a faint note of perfume and cigars, floor polish, and some vague scent of wealth. He faced a choice between two sweeping staircases. Using Justin's favorite counting rhyme, "ink, pink, pen and ink, a study, a stive, a stove and a stink," he chose the left. He climbed, crossed a wide carpeted space to one of many velvet curtains and pressed it open. He was at the top of the theater in a box space, looking down on the rows of tiered seats, the orchestra pit, and the curved stage. A few electric lights kept the darkness at bay. Luxurious was the word that sprang to mind, and he felt a faint stirring of long-forgotten anticipation. It had been nearly a decade, a lifetime ago, since he'd entered a venue such as this. His last experiences had been tense, miserable affairs with his wife, yet a part of him remembered earlier events, when attending had been a joy, a night of expectation, laughter, friendship.

Justin had never been to this sort of theater. The boy had seen a few small acts for children at the Emporium and been delighted. At what age did children begin to attend Shakespeare? The opera? His own parents had never been theater enthusiasts. His mother loved home entertainments, and his father attended scientific presentations. They were intelligent people with simple tastes, older than other parents. More than one of his classmates had thought he lived with his grandparents.

Voices carried up to Bradshaw as two men emerged from the wings onto the stage, a rotund gentleman in a well-cut suit and a wiry fellow in shirtsleeves.

"The show is selling out, Victor. Or it was until yesterday." The man in the suit swept his hand around the empty theater. "Can't they delay a week?"

"Not without losing money. They promised Vancouver a two-week run. The Canadians aren't staying away from the shows. It wasn't their president shot."

"Damned anarchists, ruining my profits."

Bradshaw bristled. What were a few days' profits compared to a man's life?

"Will you promise *me* a two-week run when they return?"

"I'll speak to the players. I can likely promise you that. The new troupe is top notch. Your customers won't be disappointed. You've got company." The wiry man pointed, and Bradshaw lifted a hand in a half-hearted greeting.

A few minutes later in the lobby, he shook hands with the rotund gentleman who worried over his profits.

"This really is marvelous, Professor. I advertised my contest in several large newspapers and universities on the West Coast. Only two applicants met my requirements and have committed to participate. I can safely say with your belated entry that we now have three, a real contest."

Bradshaw thought Mr. Daily's failure to offer a financial reward to the winner most likely kept many inventors from entering. The glory of winning didn't pay the cost of equipment or labor. Of course, any patents that emerged might later prove profitable. Mr. Fisher would have no claim on the patents. "Are you sure I meet your requirements?"

Mr. Fisher laughed. "Your reputation not only precedes you, it highly recommends you. Worked for Seattle Light for a time, didn't you, Professor? I like a man of intellect not afraid to roll up his sleeves."

"Do you have time now to give me the particulars?"

"Indeed I do! Come, I'll show you around. Have you seen any of our entertainments, Professor?"

"No, I haven't."

"We'll have to remedy that. Anytime you want to attend, let me know. Can't build a system if you've never experienced our theater, now can you?" Mr. Fisher beamed indulgently.

"A thorough inspection of all elements is a necessity, Mr. Fisher." Bradshaw's somber tone bounced off the jolly manager like the north pole of a magnet encountering another.

"That's what I like to hear!"

Mr. Fisher led Bradshaw into the main auditorium, down the aisle past the gallery seating and into the stalls. There he halted and spread his arms wide. "We've excellent acoustics, Professor. Ideal for our customers, but a challenge for you to capture, or so your rivals have told me. Inside the theater itself, you will respect the other competitors' equipment, and ask me before you cut or drill into the woodwork. You may tap into the building's electric-lighting system for your device if needed, so long as you do not alter the quality of the light by straining the circuit. You must schedule any outages in advance. I don't want darkness to descend unannounced on my players!"

"Of course."

"In a moment, I'll show you my pride and joy, the room that is now my very own central station. You must know that your system should rely solely on telephone lines for distribution to our listeners. We've been given permission from the Sunset Telephone Company, for a fee of course, to use their poles. You may use the equipment in the central station room and install your own, as long as your system can be connected and disconnected on the day of the contest without interfering with other systems. Cover anything you consider proprietary with a black cloth, label it as yours, and don't go peeking under anyone else's. Clear so far?"

"Perfectly." He knew no secrets could be revealed by the lifting of a cloth. Inventors, himself included, were notoriously paranoid. Anything patentable would be securely locked within metal or wood boxes. "Do you have any limitations for the receivers?"

"A subscriber must be able to enjoy the service by listening on a standard telephone headset. That's what would be included with the cost of service for a subscriber."

"Would it be against the rules to provide upgraded equipment that would represent something available for a separate fee to those who desire it?"

"Not at all." Mr. Fisher's eyes twinkled, and Bradshaw knew he wasn't the first to ask. "Mind you, the majority of our subscribers will likely choose to listen on their telephones. This must be an affordable service. And I've never heard a decent quality sound come from any telephone connected to a horn." Here, Mr. Fisher's brow lifted hopefully. Bradshaw remained silent on the superior loud talker he intended to supply, but he was beginning to feel a trickle of excitement despite himself.

"The test will include listeners in one hundred homes who will rate the quality of the sound delivered. One of those listeners will be outfitted with any upgraded premium receiver a contestant provides. In fact, we announced the lucky one hundred last week—we held a drawing, thousands put in their names—and the wires are being strung as we speak."

"You're using a dedicated line?"

"Much easier to control quality. I don't want to be at the mercy of the telephone company. I have big plans if this is successful. I'll start a new business, a newspaper without the paper, just like they have in Budapest, with news and entertainment flowing all day long to subscribers. They'll want a dedicated line for that. In London, subscribers must ring up central and ask to be connected, and then they can't make or receive calls until they ring off."

"You've done your homework, Mr. Fisher. You are familiar with the details of all the services around the world."

"Indeed I am! The way I see it, the telephone is now a necessity of the home, and its many uses shouldn't conflict. No one will be hampered by a subscription to my service. It's a marvelous age to be living in, isn't it, Professor?"

Oh, yes, he did agree, but even with his enthusiasm mounting, he couldn't bring himself to say something so lighthearted on this somber day.

"Might it be possible to have my house connected to the line for testing purposes?"

"Yes, of course, the other two entrants have been given the same. If you win, I will allow you to keep the service free of charge for an entire year."

A lifetime of free service seemed the more suiting offer to Bradshaw, but Fisher's profits were not to be shared, not even with the inventor responsible for them.

Under Mr. Fisher's pleased and watchful eye, Bradshaw took a notepad, pencil, and spring tape measure from his pocket. "I should like to take some measurements and also see your building plans, if you have them."

"Certainly, certainly. Whatever you need. Would you like to hear something from the stage? Miss Darlyrope is in her dressing room. I'm sure I could entice her to perform a number or two. We canceled yesterday's performances, naturally, but we're on schedule today. Unless we hear…has there been any news?"

The smile had vanished from Mr. Fisher's plump face. His eyes crinkled with concern, and even his jowls sagged with sorrow.

"The president is resting comfortably. The prognosis is still uncertain."

"I heard the shooter's name wasn't Fred but Leon, with some foreign sounding last name."

"Leon Czolgosz, I believe." Bradshaw pronounced the last name "chol-gosh" as he'd heard it at the newspaper office. News was beginning to emerge about him. His parents had been found in Ohio.

Mr. Fisher shook his head with a look of disgust. "However you say it, he's ruined my business. No one will want to come as long as the president's health is in question. Who knows how long it will be until our audiences return in full?"

"Damned inconsiderate of McKinley to keep us on tenter-hooks like this."

"You're being sarcastic with me, Professor, but there's truth to what you say. I've no patience for politics meddling in my profits. Well. I'll just go get Miss Darlyrope. She's my best singer, you know."

Mr. Fisher scurried off and Bradshaw got to work sketching and measuring. He'd forgotten about the promised singer by the time she appeared on stage with Mr. Fisher. A tall, full-figured young woman draped in blue fabric that looked suspiciously like a dressing gown, Miss Darlyrope wore her shining black hair piled high like an Egyptian monument. She snatched her hand from Mr. Fisher's grasp. He stepped away with an ingratiating apology and pleaded, "Just a few stanzas, that's all."

The actress' angry gaze swept over the empty seats until colliding with Bradshaw.

"Is that him?"

"Yes, that's the professor."

She took a deep breath and began to sing a familiar tune about lost love. She did have a lovely voice that carried well and filled the air with an angry resonance. Before she was more than a minute into the tune, her anger trembled, her voice cracked. She paused, raised her chin as if to compose herself, but she could not go on. A sob escaped her.

Mr. Fisher came hurrying from the wings, reaching out to her. She rebuffed him, wrapping her arms about herself protectively. "I'm just too upset, Mr. Fisher. Daisy—oh, Daisy!" She ran from the stage. Mr. Fisher climbed down to Bradshaw.

"I'm sorry about that, Professor. One of the chorus girls has taken ill. It's a pity. Has the women all in a tizzy." He tossed up his hands. "I must admit, it's shaken me a bit, too. The poor girl has gone blind."

Was it the girl he was concerned with, or losing her talent? "Scarlet fever?" Bradshaw felt a small prick of fear, thinking of that dread disease and the possibility of his carrying the germs home to his son.

"No, no, it was nothing contagious, thank goodness. It was poison. She'd become addicted to a tonic she bought from a street peddler. You take your life in your hands when you drink any medicine that doesn't come from a trusted chemist."

Bradshaw's fear had not abated. "What was the name of the tonic?"

"Ralph's Restorative."

Chapter Five

"Dad, how does a telephone work?"

Bradshaw handed his son a round metal disc about the size of a silver dollar. "Drop it," he said.

Justin, perched on the three-legged stool before Bradshaw's basement workbench, lifted his hand high and let the disc drop. It hit the cement floor with a clang.

"Did you hear that sound?"

"Yes."

"Know why you heard it?"

"Because I have ears?"

"Yes. And because when that disc hit the floor, the impact carried through the metal, making it vibrate. Those vibrations traveled through the air up to your ear, making the inside of your ear vibrate."

"Oh. But how does a telephone work?"

"Much the same as your ears. There are metal discs, diaphragms they're called, inside of telephones, along with batteries, magnets, coils, and tiny carbon beads. When you talk into a telephone, the sound strikes the diaphragm and causes it to vibrate in and out. Whenever the diaphragm moves inwards, it squeezes the beads. The carbon flexes a little bit, like rubber balls pushed together." He quickly sketched a diagram to illustrate.

"All the tiny contacts between the beads are like electricity valves that slightly open and close. They change in time with the sound waves, which alters the battery's current. Our battery now isn't pumping just any old current, but a very clever current which contains the vibrations of the sounds that created it. That signal travels along the telephone wires you see strung up on poles. At the distant telephone, the changing current is turning an electromagnetic coil slightly on and off. It pulls a metal diaphragm in and out, which then moves the air with the sound waves of your voice."

Justin cocked his head thoughtfully. "But why? Why does that all happen?"

"The same reason flowers grow when you plant their seeds. It's their nature. It's how metal and magnets and electricity interact."

"But this isn't a flower, it's all made up stuff. People made them. How did they *know* to make them?"

"By experimenting. Alexander Graham Bell is the man who experimented and figured out this particular relationship between sound vibrations and electric current. A doctor friend gave him the ear from a cadaver—that's a dead body."

Justin's eyes got huge. "A dead ear!"

"Yes, still attached to part of a skull. Bell examined it and experimented with it to see how it recognized sound waves."

"Do *you* experiment with dead ears?" He looked around the basement, as if hoping to spot a gruesome display.

"No need, thank goodness. Did I ever tell you about the day I met Mr. Bell?"

"Did you see the ear?"

"No, the ear had been buried years before I met Mr. Bell. He lived in Boston, where I grew up. When I was a boy, just a year or so older than you, I went to one of his lectures with my father. That was when the telephone was so new, some people doubted it even worked. I got to go up on stage and put my ear to the receiver and hear a voice coming all the way from New York. That might not seem much to you since you've grown up with telephones, but I'd never heard a live human voice coming from a machine before. No one had. I was amazed. I was so impressed by Mr. Bell, I knew one day I wanted to be an inventor, too."

He looked at his son's eager blue eyes and wondered if the magic of science was taking hold. He didn't want to force his passion on his son, but he secretly hoped the boy would one day share his interests.

Justin jumped down from the stool and ran for the stairs.

"Where are you going?"

"To tell Paul about Bell's dead ear!"

A smile lingered for a good long while in Bradshaw's heart as he began to work. From delight in his son his mood eased into the complete immersion of invention. The news of McKinley had been hopeful. The doctors had operated, and the president still lived, and so Bradshaw felt safe, and guilt-free, in allowing the world and all its troubles to recede. Ideas that had been simmering in the back of his mind came forward to find action in his fingertips, in the drawing of diagrams, the tightening of screws, and the fine tuning of various sensitive devices.

His subconscious had been busy. Actually, he'd been stewing on telephonic ideas since his senior year of college when Edward Bellamy's book, *Looking Backward,* was first published. Oh, he and Henry Pratt had spent countless hours speculating on fantastic inventions that would revolutionize the world. Henry had been, and still was, too argumentative, independent, and impulsive to actually pick up a pencil to draft any of those ideas, let alone build them. His impulsive nature had given a breadth to his educational pursuits, but no depth, and no degree.

While Bradshaw had applied himself purposefully to a degree in electrical engineering from the Lawrence Scientific School at Harvard, Henry Pratt had enrolled in a wide variety of courses that took his fancy, argued with each and every professor, and eventually dropped out to unsuccessfully pursue easy money through very hard labor. Yet he continued to be a happy carefree man, content with a beer in hand, a pretty girl in view, and a good friend to argue with.

Recalling those days, Bradshaw experienced a welling of joy. For an instant, he was filled with the same enthusiasm he'd felt as a boy, a young man, when the world was his to explore, to invent, to achieve. He stood still for a moment, relishing the feeling, breathing in the scent of his basement, metals and oil and the sweetness of cut grass drifting through the transom window. He was almost afraid to move, lest the moment vanish. He wanted to share the feeling. He wanted to tell Missouri. She would understand. He probably wouldn't even need to explain. She would look at him and know.

If only…if only he had met Missouri back in college. Missouri instead of Rachel.

But when Bradshaw was in college, Henry's niece had been a child Justin's age. And without Rachel, he would not have Justin. He could never fully regret Rachel because of Justin.

His smile had vanished.

With a sigh, he cleared a space on his workbench and laid out a crisp, clean white sheet of paper. He sharpened three dark pencils in the steel sharpener clamped to the bench, easing back into the haven of mechanical action. He opened a fine leather pocket case, revealing his German silver drawing instruments: compasses, rulers, ruling pens, and spring dividers.

He stood back and took a deep, expectant breath. The vision of his invention was clear in his mind, carefully crafted, functioning perfectly. He could almost hear the orchestra playing.

Getting this vision to appear in reality would take much work, trial and error and setbacks. He thought of Alexander Bell, a man of wild temperament compared to Bradshaw's conservative nature. But they had this in common, this fascination with invention and discovery. This project before him now, which utilized Bell's most famous invention, gave him a pleasurable feeling of connection.

He divided his sheet of paper into four sections. In the upper corner, he sketched the approximate shape of the auditorium. The theater had been designed to project sounds from the stage and pit out to the audience. He'd noticed that his competitors had already installed devices in the footlights; such placement was typical of other systems. But that location came with inherent problems, including the amplifying of footsteps on stage and the possible drowning of voices by the proximity of the orchestra. The best location for his transmitters would be near the center seats of the dress circle, where all the sounds from stage and orchestra blended harmoniously.

Mr. Fisher would not want to sacrifice any of his best paying seats, and he certainly didn't want any theater-goer interfering with equipment. So why not hang the transmitters above the seats? Suspended from the ceiling. This would have the added benefit of protecting them from accidental bumping while picking up the exciting buzz of pre-show conversation, and thus prove an even more realistic theater experience for the home listener. A few additional microphones could hang above the stage, to be sure every articulation was captured.

A small tingle radiated up Bradshaw arms, a sign that always meant he was moving in the right direction. Already, he'd stumbled upon something he was sure would set his system above the other entries.

In the square adjacent to the theater drawing, Bradshaw drew a rough sketch of his microphone transmitter with the components separated and labeled. The third space, he filled with a map, showing the theater-phone lines leaving Mr. Fisher's well-equipped "central station" room, and carrying music to subscribers' homes. He also added a line to the Sunset Telephone Company's central office. This would provide a backup for Mr. Fisher's service, as well as provide an inexpensive method of delivering a trial service to prospective subscribers.

In the final square, he depicted the inside of a parlor with the horn of a loud-talker centrally located. This was the crucial piece. This was the piece that would put a smile on Mr. Fisher's greedy cherubic face. This was the piece that would change the world. Bradshaw laughed aloud. No, a competent loud-talker with minimal distortion and maximum fidelity would not greatly change the world. However, it would certainly enhance it, and put his system a notch above any other currently in existence. If he could manage, in just one month, to improve the amplified loud-talker he'd been working on intermittently for more than a year.

He drew a neat box in the corner of this section and sketched in the required headphone receiver.

He stood back and analyzed his plan, his brow furled, his heart smiling. The world had disappeared again: his dream was on paper.

He sketched his microphone transmitter, fine-tuned to the specific task of gathering theater sounds, from music to soft human voices, to sound effects and applause. Someday, he hoped to create a transmitter as acoustically adept as the human ear, and a receiver with the musical range of the human voice.

Should he, like Bell, get himself a cadaver ear? Vocal cords? He shuddered, but was intrigued. The human ear was so very small and efficient at gathering sounds, the human throat and mouth so adept at reproducing them. Could a mechanical equivalent be designed?

One major difficulty lay in the distance between the transmitting and receiving devices. The human ear was directly connected to its receiver, the brain, while Bradshaw's electric ear would be many blocks, or miles, away. Those myriad vibrations would need to be preserved in ordinary telephone wire and reanimated into sound waves once they reached their destination.

Well, for now his transmitter would do the job. As with nearly all inventions, he could not claim it to be entirely his own. He'd built upon the knowledge and discoveries of every man before him. Still, his variation of the arrangement of the components, his use of mixed-sized carbon beads to prevent packing, and the internal cone that focused and concentrated every bit of sound were unique enough to qualify as new.

He'd recently filed a patent, but hadn't yet heard if it had been approved. He quelled the instinct to panic. What if someone else was even now being approved for a similar transmitter?

No. He would not let the panic infect him. He no longer played that mad game. The world would not end if someone beat him to the patent office. If he repeated this thought often enough in his mind, he might get his gut to believe it.

Now, the receiver, the device that would require every spare moment of his time. He reached for a small screwdriver and heard the door at the top of the basement stairs open, heard Mrs. Prouty in the kitchen tell Justin to check the mouse traps but mind he didn't touch them, heard the light tap of feminine footsteps coming down the stairs.

He looked at the screwdriver in his hand, unable to think of what he intended to do with it.

"Good afternoon, Mr. Bradshaw."

He cleared his throat. "Good afternoon, Missouri." Mrs. Prouty knew he was down here working and didn't want to be disturbed, yet she hadn't stopped Missouri. He'd taken up this project for just one day, and already she feared the worst.

Missouri came to his side and peered at his drawings. She smelled fresh, sweet, like lilacs. "Is that for the contest?"

Mrs. Prouty would have told her, of course. Or Justin. "Yes."

"So it will work like a telephone?"

"Basically, yes. Only with more transmitters and receivers, and improved sound transmission. That's the key, really, getting good sound quality to the listener."

"I'm not sure why anyone would want to subscribe," she said. He turned to look at her.

"Oh, I meant no offense. I'm sure it's a wonderful invention, but going to the theater is about so much more than just the sounds. It's the excitement of being there with other people, dressing up, seeing the musicians and singers and actors, sharing the experience with someone, surrounded by people who are equally intent on letting go of their troubles and simply enjoying themselves."

It was avoiding all the other people that Bradshaw found so appealing about a home music delivery service. He didn't say so aloud. He didn't need to. Missouri often seemed to know him better than he knew himself. He saw a telltale gleam of understanding in her eye, but ignored the challenge.

"How are your studies? Are you prepared for your entrance exams?"

"I think so." There was a quaver in her voice.

He looked at her again quickly. "Nervous?"

"Well, I've never taken a formal exam before, and this will be a full day of them on seven subjects at a state university. I'm not sure nervous is a strong enough word."

"In which do you lack confidence?"

"Mathematics mostly. And some of the science."

"There are tutors available. Check with the registrar. The library has the texts you'll need, and a practice examination. The university accepts many homeschooled students. You won't be alone." He didn't mean for his tone to be so dictatorial and dismissive, but she thanked him like a good little student and turned to the stairs.

He opened his mouth to say, "Don't go," but then had no idea what he would say next or why he wanted her to stay. She began up the stairs. He said, his eyes on his drawings, "You're not playing the game today?"

Her footsteps silenced. "Game?"

"You come and go without my knowledge."

"Does it bother you?"

"Should it?"

"Yes, at least, I hope it does."

He looked at her then, aware that he frowned while she studied him with a serious calm. "You hoped to annoy me?"

"No, but it couldn't be helped, not if you're thinking of me."

He sat perfectly still, his heart racing as if he were running. "Of course I think of you. You're Henry's niece."

"I'm not *your* niece."

"What are you driving at?"

"I should think it's obvious. I don't want you to think of me as your niece or any sort of family relation. And I don't want all of Seattle thinking of us that way."

"Us?"

"You and I. Oh, really, Mr. Bradshaw, you of all people know how society can be. Once a town gets a notion, it's awfully hard to change. Someone asked me the other day how my Uncle Bradshaw was. You can see how hard it will be to overcome that."

"It's an easy mistake."

"The mistake was my staying here all summer. Now I shall have to undo all the damage."

"Why?"

She looked at him as if he'd just sprouted feathers. "Why? You mind, of course."

"That people think I'm your uncle? Why should I mind?" He was surprised at how easily the lie escaped him. He couldn't look at her. He felt her staring at him. Heat crept up his collar and made his ears burn. He couldn't pretend he didn't understand. Neither could he say what she wanted to hear.

Her footsteps tapped again, then stopped.

"Have the police discovered the mystery behind that abandoned wagon yet?" There was a cold edge to the question, as if it had to push through her anger.

"No."

His own thoughts churned to the abandoned wagon, to the doll with the little bisque face and clothes of silk, to the little girl who, somewhere, was missing her beloved toy. He thought with anguish, *that doll on the mantel haunts me.*

Then Missouri's voice came, softer than it had been, sadder. "That doll on the mantel haunts me." She climbed to the kitchen, her shoes making a delicate tap-tap on the stairs.

Chapter Six

If Bradshaw were asked to name his favorite place on earth, he would be hard-pressed to choose between his own home and the Acme Electrical Supply Company downtown. Conveniently located on Third Avenue between Woodworth's Hardware store and King's Drug, Bradshaw could, and had, spent many pleasant hours poking about and scheming. He'd penciled "Acme" on his calendar for Monday morning, and at ten when the door was unlocked, he was waiting to enter.

"Good morning, pProfessor," greeted Mr. Daily, the owner and fellow electrical enthusiast. A self-taught amateur, Bradshaw respected and admired him.

"Good morning, Mr. Daily."

"Come for the contest, have you?"

The two men sized each other up pleasantly. Mr. Daily was one of his rivals. Mr. Fisher must have spread the word. "Yes. Who is the third man?"

"Phil Smith."

They both smiled. Smith, while an intelligent and capable electrical engineer, had never filed a patent or made an improvement of his own. His entry would work and be reliable, but not extraordinary. Like his name, his work would be common. So. It was a two-man race between friendly colleagues.

Mr. Daily stepped aside. "I'll be sportsmanlike and give you free rein behind my counter. Mind, I can't be blamed for seeing what you purchase, since I'll be tallying the sale."

"You've always treated me fairly, Mr. Daily. And my secrets won't be revealed in my selections today."

A spark of curiosity sizzled in Mr. Daily's eyes. He pressed his lips tight to withhold questions he knew would not be answered.

Bradshaw stepped behind the counter and for a few minutes, as he began to explore the shelves, felt he was circling an abyss. It was a feeling akin to his occasional bouts of vertigo, but beckoning and promising rather than fearful. Alcoholics, he felt sure, knew this feeling as they stared at a bottle of drink. The lure was there regardless of circumstances. When life presented difficulties over which he had no control—such as the fate of President McKinley, the plight of a missing father and child, a troubled young man's soul, and his attraction to a girl he must never pursue—the lure was greater.

He told himself he would not let this contest get out of hand. He could accomplish his goal without neglecting the rest of his life, and Mrs. Prouty's fears would not dictate his life. He reached into a bin of small metal discs, and fell happily into the abyss.

He spent the next two hours in electrical hardware heaven. He began by taking a systematic tour of the store, up and down every aisle in the back room, up and down every shelf. He examined telegraph instrument components, batteries, and magic lanterns. Arc lamps, bells, fans, and rheostats. Wires, magnets, resistors, and connectors. His mind stayed open to all he saw and touched in case some heretofore unknown avenue of invention revealed itself.

He resisted a clever new dynamo and splurged on a fluted oak horn so well-crafted it shone like a piece of art. He would listen to the theater in his own living room with this magnificent piece. For his invention, which was in desperate want of a name, he bought all the components he needed, plus spares, and, to confuse Mr. Daily, a few items he needed for his university classes. He had the box delivered to his home. Mr. Daily looked pleased that Bradshaw's purchases were so ordinary—mouth pieces platinum foil, carbon beads, copper wire—and wished the Professor good luck.

Bradshaw's mind was still pleasurably immersed in the mechanics of invention when he stepped outside and began along Third Avenue. Slowly, sounds began to penetrate his thoughts. The world intruded when he found himself standing before a newspaper boy shouting the headlines.

```
"PRESIDENT MCKINLEY WILL NOT PASS
   THE CRISIS FOR SEVERAL HOURS...
OPERATION IN EVERY WAY SUCCESS-
FUL...ANARCHISTS OPENLY REJOICING AT
   ATTEMPTED ASSASSINATION!"
```

He traded a nickel for a paper, then stood aside to read. Around him, others did the same, their papers snapping as they turned pages. Bradshaw quickly read every word on the president before searching for news on Ralph's Restorative. He found a small notice under Recent Police Cases about the abandoned wagon, but nothing new was reported.

He tried to imagine the events leading up to the abandoning of that wagon, the darkness of night, a peddler and small child, far after the time the child should have been asleep, driving up the hill, turning down the back lane.

He folded the paper and went in search of the police.

He found Detective March just leaving police headquarters on his way down Yesler to G. O. Guy's Drug Store on Second Avenue. He hesitated a moment, wondering whether he should find O'Brien instead, but quickly decided that O'Brien had sent March to deal with the wagon, so March would be the one with answers. The power play he'd witnessed between them was not connected to this particular case, surely, but to professional rivalry.

"May I join you?"

"Of course."

"Official business?" It was at Guy's Drug that the gun fight between former Chief of Police Meredith and John Considine had taken place a few months ago.

March shook his head. "Just going for gum. I've got a Tutti Frutti habit."

Bradshaw fell in beside March, matching his long, loose stride and thinking how very different this felt compared to the dour way he'd unknowingly plodded before Professor Oglethorpe's untimely death last spring.

"Have you found the owner of Ralph's Restorative wagon?" he asked.

March pressed his lips tight and shook his head. "The wagon's at the station, and the horse has been lent to the livery stable in exchange for board. If they go unclaimed, they'll be sold." He lifted his shoulders in a pleasant shrug. "The peddler was probably connected with that band of gypsies that passed through here last week. We sent them on. They're Tacoma's problem now."

Bradshaw was so taken aback by this, he nearly tripped on the paved sidewalk and had to concentrate to regain an even stride. Gypsies? The idea struck him as preposterous and he said so.

"The Romany Remedy that really works," quoted the detective.

Bradshaw had thought that an advertising gimmick.

"*Ralph* doesn't sound like a gypsy name. And why would gypsies abandon an expensive wagon?"

"Name could have been an alias and the wagon stolen."

"Wouldn't you know if it was stolen?"

March smiled and shook his head. "Only if it happened in Seattle. It could have been taken from another city, painted, then ditched when the remedy began making customers sick."

They'd arrived at the corner of Second Avenue and together dodged traffic and dung, paused to let the streetcar pass, then arrived safely on the other side.

"Don't you share that sort of information with other cities?"

March laughed indulgently. "Professor, we've got wanted posters dozens deep tacked to our rogues' gallery. We've got our hands full just tracking dangerous criminals. We don't have the manpower or resources to be looking out for every missing wagon in every city in the country."

No, Bradshaw thought, but wouldn't it be convenient to have an updated organized list to refer to in a time like this? Could something be invented? A telegraph of sorts that automatically recorded key criminal details, separated into categories, and distributed to police stations around the country, or better yet, by region. The records could be filed in an easy to access system.

"...two men in the hospital, and a girl blinded." March's voice brought Bradshaw out of his favored world of invention and to the problem at hand.

"Why not simply leave town when the tonic began to sicken customers? Why abandon everything? The wagon was valuable, and there were personal possessions inside."

"Fear of arrest and imprisonment makes men do strange things, Professor. The possessions will be sold, if not claimed soon. What are personal possessions to gypsies? They take what they want without asking and they leave behind anything too inconvenient to bother with. If a man wants to disappear completely, it's much easier to do so unburdened by possessions. Ralph couldn't hide, even among the gypsies, with that fancy wagon."

The contents of that wagon didn't strike Bradshaw as belonging to gypsies. He hadn't seen the peddler's clothes, but the child possessed calico cotton dresses and bonnets. And that fancy doll. The wagon had been professionally painted. He'd never heard of gypsies going into any sort of permanent business, not even patent-medicine peddling. They sold potions of course, homemade in unlabeled bottles, and trinkets and pots, scarves, and horses. While they might, although improbably, abandon a wagon, they would never abandon a good horse.

"Isn't some sort of license required to peddle wares in the city? Wouldn't the license tell us something about the peddler?"

"Yes, but unless someone asks, who's to know if a license has been bought? That wagon has all the looks of a legitimate business. I doubt anyone bothered to check."

"What about the restorative that was in the wagon? It was poison."

March nodded soberly. They'd arrived at Guy's. As they entered and sent the bell tinkling, March said, "The cases of tonic were destroyed."

March went straight for the oak and glass display on the counter and selected a tin of Adams' Pepsin Tutti Frutti Gum. Bradshaw spied the Cracker Jacks and knew Justin's face would light up with the treat. He bought four boxes for twelve cents.

On the street again with their purchases, Bradshaw said awkwardly, "I found a doll."

March smiled. "Did you now? Taking her out on the town?"

"No, no." Bradshaw felt his face grow warm, "I meant I found a child's doll inside the peddler's wagon. I forgot to tell you the other day. I'd brought it inside the house."

"And?"

"I'm concerned about the little girl. The peddler's child. Everything she owned was in that wagon, too. Her father might be ill, he's certainly in trouble...."

"No need for concern, Professor. Gypsy children are quite resilient. She'll find, or steal, another doll." He slid open the gum tin and deftly unwrapped a bar. When Bradshaw declined the offer of a square, March happily helped himself to the two he'd broken off. The fruity smell was childish, as was the happy grin on the detective's handsome face. Despite his annoyance of March's easy dismissal of the peddler and child, Bradshaw couldn't help but like the man.

How he wished he could approach life in such a carefree manner. His concerns always weighed physically on him, hunching him over. He squared his shoulders and tried to look more youthful.

"Gypsies you say?"

"Tacoma's problem now."

Chapter Seven

The tick of the parlor mantel clock and the crackle of hearth flames kept Bradshaw company at midnight—in the basement. He sat at his workbench wearing his favorite frayed gray button-up cardigan, his feet snug in fur-lined moccasins made by a native Duwamish. The hearth sounds, crisp and clear as if in the room, came from the gleaming oak horn beside him. A telephone wire ran up the wall, along the baseboards of the kitchen to his first test transmitter suspended from the ceiling light fixture in the parlor.

Earlier this evening, Justin had sat at the piano, pounding on the keys and singing in his tuneless way, allowing Bradshaw to hear where the sounds were strong, and where they were weak, allowing him to make minor adjustments to improve the range. The trouble lay in those more vibrant sounds. Tick-tocks came clear and sharp; amplified piano notes held a rough tin edge, and voices a slightly distorted echo-like quality. These imperfections to the sound were far less noticeable with his amplified loud-talker than any other he'd ever heard, but they would not do. He must find a way to eliminate as nearly as possible the distortion and deliver clean, clear, crisp notes.

He now cocked his head, closed his eyes, and listened. A new sound began to emerge from the horn, low, distant, familiar. He realized he was hearing a train, either running down in the city or across the lake near the University, echoing up the hill to his home. He paused to listen. A dog howled in answer to the train. Another joined. A faint clip-clop and jangle grew, then faded. If an actor on stage whispered, his transmitter would relay the sound.

He pulled his attention away from the oddments of sounds coming from the horn and back to the graph on his workbench. Not a graph of invention, but deduction. He was working on what he was calling "The Case of the Abandoned Wagon." The doll on the mantel had driven him to it, its very presence shouting louder than the call to invent. A very loud cry indeed. He needed to discover the girl's fate. He simply could not believe she and her father were gypsies now safely returned to their tribe. The whole situation called to him like a puzzle begging to be solved or a complex trigonometric equation. It annoyed and distracted the outer edges of his thoughts and he knew he'd never fully concentrate on his contest device until he instilled some sense of order.

He decided to approach this systematically like his investigations into electrical accidents and Professor Oglethorpe's death. If he were to find a solution and attain peace of mind, the details required a thorough examination.

He studied the facts, the physical detail of the abandonment. Observed objectively, without knowing motivation, the facts seemed senseless. A man and child had abandoned a business wagon and all their possessions and vanished. Bradshaw was not a man to be discouraged by the unexplained. Observational details of magnetism were inexplicable, if one didn't know about the invisible forces surrounding magnets.

So what could he infer by the facts observed in this abandoned wagon case? What as-yet invisible forces were at work? Because he had no other name to use, he decided to call them Ralph and Child. They lived a vagabond life. They, or at least Ralph, was in trouble because his tonic had sickened, even blinded his customers.

As a traveling salesman, Ralph had expenses that must be met. Besides staples such as food for himself and the child, there would be food and regular care for the horse. There would be upfront expenses for the tonic he sold. Did he make it himself? If so, where did he purchase the ingredients? There were laws concerning the making and distributing of alcohol. Were there regulations on patent medicines? Did Ralph really not secure a license to peddle his tonic? Did Detective March check to be sure? Where were such licenses filed? And if Ralph was guilty of poisoning people with his tonic, as it certainly appeared he was, why were the Seattle police, Detective March in particular, so lackadaisical about it? Why turn the problem over to Tacoma rather than chase Ralph down and arrest him? If it had been the mayor blinded rather than a show girl, would the police be treating this more seriously?

More than likely.

And if the police were being so off-handed about the whole thing, what were the odds they were seriously looking into the welfare of the child?

That thought brought him right back to his graph and the need to find answers.

So. Did Ralph bottle the tonic himself? Where did he purchase the bottles, the boxes, the labels?

What of their final actions before disappearance? Sometime after most of the neighborhood had gone to bed, Ralph had driven the wagon—wait, that wasn't an observed fact, that was an assumption. The horse and wagon had been seen in the back lane late at night, and in the early morning hours, and was still there when Bradshaw returned from the University. It had not been observed being driven or controlled by a driver. The owner and child were missing, true, but there was absolutely no evidence they had been in the vehicle when it was driven into the lane.

Had the wagon been stolen from Ralph then abandoned?

Could the horse have wandered down the lane on its own, Ralph and child, or someone else, having left it alone for so long it grew bored? Drawn by hunger and the lure of Mrs. Prouty's broad beans?

That was often the difficulty in scientific investigation: assumptions could so easily be regarded as facts. Details you never questioned could turn out to be ungrounded or inaccurately understood. A man could know too much and be trapped by his own knowledge. He remembered fondly one of Bell's demonstrations he'd attended as a boy with his father. Bell had said, "Had I known more about electricity, and less about sound, I would never have invented the telephone."

Mr. Bell had succeeded because he hadn't had many preconceived notions about how electricity and magnets should interact. He had not been hampered by assumptions.

So what had Bradshaw assumed to be fact? He looked down his list of detail, underlining those things that were facts, circling those that were assumptions, no matter how logical.

When he came to Mrs. Prouty's testimony, he hesitated. She'd said she'd been told by the neighboring housekeepers the wagon had been out in the lane all night. In the morning, she'd sent Justin running out to investigate and he'd returned with nothing to report.

No. That was another assumption. Justin had gone out, he'd run upstairs, he'd returned to the table and reported nothing. Was that normal eight-year-old behavior? What could have been so much more interesting that he'd forfeited the chance to make friends with a horse or explore a strange wagon? It would have had to have been something more exciting and yet something he felt would meet with Mrs. Prouty's disapproval—why else run around the house to get up to his room? A snail or bird's egg, as he'd previously assumed, would not have been sufficiently motivating. Those were common finds. And why hadn't the boy shown any curiosity in the wagon? Why had he asked no questions? Not even about the doll. Yet he had tried to take the doll down from the mantel. Why?

A chill tingled up Bradshaw's arms.

He pondered his boy. An intelligent, curious child. Private in many ways, like himself. He'd been quiet these past few days, spending a lot of time up in his room even when the sun shone. He had due cause—they all did. President McKinley had been shot. None of them would ever be quite the same. Still, for a child to brood so? Justin was sensitive, but he generally bounced back quickly. Could the boy's mood be connected to whatever motivated him to run secretly around the house and up to his room?

Was he hiding something, feeling guilty? He'd been eating. Usually when upset, the boy picked at his food. Lately, he'd been eating enough for—oh God—enough for two.

The chills now prickled his legs. Then as if on cue, as if the universe were tied to his inner revelations, a sound came through the magnificent horn. The familiar squeak of the fourth step on the stairs from the upper landing down to the hall. Then the soft tap of footsteps.

He dropped his pencil and raced up to the kitchen, his moccasins silent on the wood stairs. He opened the door into darkness, grimacing as the hinges squeaked. He froze, holding his breath, listening. There came a metallic click and a soft thump. The front door closing.

He ran through the kitchen and down the dark hall, his racing pulse and familiarity guiding his way. He threw open the front door to a gray, misty night, and caught sight of a small figure in the street, Justin, fleeing down the middle of the road. He nearly shouted his name, then the child's cap fell off and blond curls came tumbling down.

The girl. Ralph's child.

He gave chase as she skidded, turned to retrieve the hat, then bent for it. She spied him running toward her, gave a small squeak and sprinted away, diving through a short laurel hedge across the street. Bradshaw ran after her, around the hedge, and caught sight of her as she disappeared into the darkness of his neighbor's back yard. He followed, but his moccasins were now wet and slick and he lost traction. He fell, his hands hitting the wet, cold grass that soaked through the knees of his trousers. He scrambled up and hurried on more carefully. But he'd lost her. He stood in the gloomy mist, listening. No sounds of breathing or running came to him.

For a quarter hour, he quietly searched his neighborhood without luck.

He returned home to find Justin waiting for him at the top of the stairs, fully dressed under his robe. Bradshaw left his wet moccasins by the front door, and in bare feet climbed up to the boy.

"Care to explain?"

"Did you catch her?"

"No." Justin got up and led Bradshaw into his room, past his unmade bed, to his closet. He pressed his hanging clothes aside and pointed at the little door to the attic storage space. Bradshaw had completely forgotten it existed.

"You have to get down," Justin explained, and together father and son crawled into the cramped cubby. The space was lit by an electric bulb wired to heavy gravity batteries. It wasn't of Bradshaw's making. Justin must have assembled it himself.

"I knew I'd get in trouble if I lit a lantern in here," Justin explained. "I was going to put your batteries back later."

"Sensible." Bradshaw resisted the urge to praise his son's ingenuity. Now was not the time.

"I didn't eat in my room. I didn't lie about that. She ate." The boy's determined face showed he was still a firm believer in literal interpretations.

He'd made a little nest for the girl of feather pillows topped with blankets. The mantel doll was tucked lovingly into the covers, the long blond curls spread on a pillow.

"She was going to put it back before morning," Justin explained.

Bradshaw tried to get into a comfortable seated position. His head scraped the slanted ceiling.

"Why are you dressed? Were you going to sneak out, too?"

"No. I've been sleeping in my clothes. I couldn't wear pajamas in front of a girl."

"Is she coming back?"

Justin shrugged. "I don't know. She didn't want any grownups to know she was here."

"Has she been here the entire time?"

"She was gone nearly all Saturday, but mostly she's here."

Mrs. Prouty's mice. Saturday, he recalled, Justin had been more his usual self, asking about telephones, running off with Paul.

"What's her name?"

"Emily."

Emily. "Did she tell you her last name?"

"No. Just Emily."

"Where did she go Saturday? Where is she going tonight?"

"I don't know. She says she's trying to get enough money to buy a train ticket home."

"Where is her home?"

"I don't know."

As Bradshaw waited to see if Justin would provide more information, he made the mistake of taking a deep breath. Above the stuffy scent of the enclosed space, above the earthy scent of his damp, grass-stained knees, he got a strong whiff of sour mold.

"What is that smell?"

Justin crawled into the corner of the cubby to a burlap sack. He dragged it to Bradshaw and opened it.

Bradshaw gagged and told him to close it, and to chuck it into the closet.

"She was all wet and muddy when she came. Those are her clothes. I gave her some of mine to wear. She doesn't mind dressing like a boy."

He thought back to the day the wagon had been abandoned, the day McKinley had been shot. Had it rained the night before? He'd ridden his bicycle to the University that day and the roads had been dry, as he recalled.

"Why was she wet?"

Justin shrugged.

"Why did you hide her here?"

"She asked me to. She's scared."

"I imagine she would be. She's far too young to be alone. Why did she run away from her father?"

Justin bit his lip, his fingers picking at the sash of his robe. "She didn't run away from him. It wasn't like that. And she's ten. She's smaller than me, but she's ten."

"How was it then? Where is her father?"

"He's dead." Justin spoke in such a matter-of-fact voice, such an innocent, eight-year old voice, Bradshaw's heart lurched. "She ran away from the man who killed him."

Bradshaw sat silently, the impact of his son's words pressing painfully at his temples.

"Justin, are you sure that's what Emily told you? She told you someone killed her father?"

Justin nodded, staring at his toes. "She saw it happen."

The implication of those simple words stole Bradshaw's breath.

"Oh, son." For a few minutes neither spoke. Bradshaw put his arm around his boy and held him tight.

He struggled to organize his thoughts. He'd been assuming that Ralph was alive. Ill, perhaps, from drinking his own poisonous restorative, but alive. Now Justin was telling him Emily had seen her father being killed. Not dying, killed. He didn't want to ask, he didn't want his son to have to think of it, or say the words. But to help Emily, he needed to ask.

"What happened, Justin?"

"I don't know. Honest, I don't. She just said she saw, that's all. And then she was afraid to get in the wagon because she thought he'd catch her there, so she stayed outside all night."

"Does she know the man who killed her father? Did she know his name?"

Justin shrugged. "She didn't say. She saw it happen."

"Where? Where did she see this happen?" One of his neighbor's homes? It had to have been nearby, otherwise, how had the wagon gotten to his back lane?

"I don't know."

"When did you first see her?" Bradshaw asked patiently. Getting full details from an eight-year-old could be tedious.

"When Mrs. Prouty sent me outside to see what the wagon was doing in the lane. She came out of the laurel hedge by Mrs. Olsen's."

"What did she say to you?"

"She told me to hide her some place because she was afraid because someone killed her dad."

"And you believed her?"

Justin looked at Bradshaw beseechingly. "You would have, too, if you'd seen her."

Bradshaw put his hand on Justin's head reassuringly. "You're not in trouble."

Justin's face trembled as he fought tears. "I don't care about being in trouble, I just don't want her to get hurt."

Bradshaw had never been more proud of his boy. Emily had been safe here, in this nest his son had made and ingeniously lit.

Now Bradshaw had driven her away. Would she return?

"Why didn't you tell me? I would have protected her." He tried to keep accusation from his voice. Justin was wrong not to tell him, but he didn't need the weight of the girl's fate on his conscious. He'd done what his heart told him was right.

"She wouldn't let me tell you. She doesn't trust grownups anymore. And she's kind of a bully."

This struck them both as funny, that the diminutive child with the dainty blond curls was a bully, and they laughed.

"I hope she comes back," Justin said softly.

"If she doesn't, I'll find her. I'll do my very best to find her."

"Now?"

"Yes, now."

◇◇◇

He had to wake Mrs. Prouty to explain why he was going out in the middle of the night. With her gray head in a sleeping cap and her stout frame wrapped in a dressing gown, she scowled with concern as she bustled about the kitchen, insisting on packing provisions just as if he were heading out on a wilderness expedition. In a few minutes, he was laden down with a canvas sack of ham sandwiches and a coffee flask of cocoa. He left Justin and Mrs. Prouty parked at the kitchen table, drinking hot chocolate. As he closed the back door, he heard Mrs. Prouty say, "Now then, young man, you tell me every little thing."

If there were any details to be pried loose from Justin, Mrs. Prouty would do it.

He considered ditching Mrs. Prouty's provisions on the porch, then thought perhaps they'd come in handy if he did find little Emily. He found a short length of rope in the tool shed and tied it in a loop to the canvas sack so he could wear it over his shoulder, lit a lantern, and headed out into the night.

He retraced his earlier steps when he'd been chasing Emily and immediately was struck by the futility of his efforts. A small child, fearful of discovery, could hide in a thousand different dark places. He could have passed her, could be standing a few feet from her, and not know it. He continued on, peering into yards, pausing to listen to the night.

Two streets away, he emerged from the developed portion of his neighborhood to the paved streets with the vacant lots Detective March had mentioned. Expensive lots, fully improved with electricity and sewer and sidewalks, running at about two-thousand apiece. It was rumored buyers were eager to snatch them up, despite the restriction that owners must spend at least three thousand on the construction of their homes.

Most of the vacant lots provided nowhere for a child to hide, but on one stood a small work shed in the inky shadows beyond the street lamp's reach. Some of the shadows, he discovered as he began to explore, were from the early stages of house building that had been halted. A basement had been dug, and a drainage ditch. The ditch was full of water, revealing the reason for the halt in construction. As was the case so often in Seattle, an underground spring had risen to the surface and undermined the builder's efforts. The shed housed a force pump.

His lantern revealed that many of the inky shadows held nothing but mud soaked by the spring. The ground squelched underfoot. The air held the scent of wet earth. That changed as he neared the dark hole of the dug basement. The smell turned sour, but not like Emily's damp moldy clothing. This smell he'd experienced just one place before. The morgue.

He saw the shoe first. His lantern cast a dancing light down into the dug basement over the muddy heel jutting from the cuff of a trouser leg. The body lay face down in the mud. An arm reached out for help that would not be coming. Bradshaw covered his nose and mouth with his sleeve. He had no doubt the man was dead. Was it Ralph? Emily's father? Most likely. That was an assumption even Bell would agree made sense. The child had been wet and muddy when Justin took her in. She'd been here. She'd knelt beside her father and tried to waken him, revive him, after his killer had fled. Had she begged him to open his eyes?

A shudder rippled through Bradshaw. This was beyond his responsibility. The police would come, look for clues, discover the truth. Bradshaw needed to find the child.

Chapter Eight

Where would a frightened child go?

Somewhere familiar.

To someone trusted.

Emily had trusted Justin, another child, to keep her safe. Who else would she trust in the middle of the night? When other children were asleep? What places had she known while living in the wagon with her father? Who did she know?

Ralph's Restorative was sickening customers in the Tenderloin. It was a place of outcasts and criminals, addicts and drunks, actors and miners and adventure seekers. It was a place always open, even in the small hours of the night. It was a place where desperate people would want to believe the claims that Ralph's Restorative could *"Return one to the purity and joy of youth!"*

Emily had been sneaking out this evening when Bradshaw had seen her. It wasn't his discovery of her that had sent her fleeing—although that would likely prohibit her return—she had already been on her way somewhere. Somewhere she thought she could make money.

Where would a ten-year-old girl believe it possible to make money in the middle of the night? Were there mills or factories in town that operated all night? That hired child labor? A child of ten might find work sewing, or washing up, or some other menial task.

She could simply be begging.

It didn't take him long to get to Yesler Way. The newspapers referred to the street as "the Deadline," the northern boundary of the Tenderloin. It marked the beginning of Seattle's wicked district, where decent folks dared not tread. In this part of town, spilling down into the tideflats, music halls and box houses and hotels plied the same trade. Drink, gambling, bawdy entertainment, and women.

He stepped off the streetcar and crossed the bricked road to the gritty sidewalk. The darkness of the night lurked in alleys and peered from upper stories. Here at street level, glowing electric signs, boldly lit windows, and gas lamps pointed the way to the musical entertainments and raucous voices. He stood for a moment, unsure where to begin. Another streetcar passed by, the conductor shouting *last car.*

He began to walk, glad he'd chosen to wear an old suit that had seen better days. He might feel out of place, but he didn't look it. He wasn't the only man dressed shabbily with a burlap sack slung over his shoulder.

Amongst the shabby were the gents in coat tails and top-hats, looking as if they'd just come from a show at the Seattle Grand. Did their wives know, he wondered? Did they know where their husbands went after dropping them home? Were they told tales of business talk, private poker games?

He kept his hat low, his eyes averted from faces, not wanting to recognize any of the better dressed men, hoping only to find a small child with blond curls, her hand out for coins.

On First Avenue, he found scruffy young boys with patched britches and stained caps, playing a rough-and-tumble version of marbles at the entrance to a dark alley. Another boy, no older than Justin, lurked outside the Frontier music hall, and when the door flew open, and a drunk was tossed out, the boy dove to catch anything that flew from his pockets.

None of the boys was a girl disguised in his son's clothing. There were no young girls on the streets at all, although plenty of women hung about in various forms of dress designed to advertise.

On the corner of Second and Jackson, a woman in feathers and face paint, the hem of her dress nearly up to her knees, the neckline plunging deep into territory not usually exposed in public, propositioned Bradshaw in such a bold manner and with such bawdy language he felt himself blush. What a sheltered life he'd been living up on the hill. He could see why Ralph's Restorative had sold well here. In the eyes of many of the women he passed, he could see that the promise of "past transgressions reversed" was a dream yet hoped for.

After two hours of searching up and down the streets, stepping into music halls and theaters to peer around the dim interiors, and questioning those who looked approachable, he knew his search had failed. His burlap sack was empty—he'd given the food and cocoa, flask and all, to a skeletal man he found digging through garbage.

Only as he made his way back to Yesler did he see a policeman. Patrolman Cox came sauntering along, whistling a tune and swinging his club, for all the world like a man on holiday. Bradshaw remembered seeing him at the courthouse. He was the large policeman with the whisk-broom mustache who'd claimed a man could only take so much. It seemed tonight he was pleased with his particular take.

Bradshaw hailed him, putting an end to the whistling and a scowl on the patrolman's face until he introduced himself.

"Professor Bradshaw! If I'd had to bet on ever seeing you down here, I'd have said not on your life, not the respectable professor."

"I didn't realize you knew me."

"Everyone in Seattle knows you, Professor. It was you who put that anarchist behind bars."

"Yes, well, tonight I'm not after anarchists, I'm looking for a missing child. Her name is Emily. Her father's wagon was abandoned behind my house a few days ago."

The patrolman's smile disappeared. His eyes shifted to dimly lit brick pavement, and his whisk broom mustache waggled.

"That would be Ralph Hopper's wagon. I know all about that." He jutted out his chin importantly. "Ralph and the child are gone. Went to Tacoma with the gypsies."

"No, they didn't. And you know him by name? Full name?"

Patrolman Cox thrust his club into its holster and his scowl deepened. "Who told you they didn't go to Tacoma? Of course I know Ralph Hopper's name, I checked his license often enough, just like I do all who sell their wares in my district."

"Detective March thought maybe Ralph hadn't bothered to get a license."

"He accuse me of not doing my job? It's a misdemeanor to peddle patent meds without the proper license, and monthly fees paid. State Pharmacy Board would have my badge. Ralph had a good and valid license, though it don't now look as if he had a good and valid tonic. That ain't my fault."

"No, no I'm sure it's not. I meant no offense, I'm just trying to get information. I, uh, I have a bit of a confession to make."

Bradshaw explained, feeling like a fool, that the child had been hiding in his own home until this evening.

"My son said she's been going out at night. I think she might be coming here. She was wearing his clothing when she fled."

The patrolman seemed to be struggling, not with the information, but with the annoyance of being wrong. "You're telling me she might be down here under my nose? I don't think I much care for this, not at all. I'll have a word with that detective."

"So you haven't seen her?"

"Not a bit. Not hide nor curly hair."

"Can you think of anywhere else, any other part of town a child might go at night to earn money?"

"Rest of the city's locked up and put to bed. Why'd she run away from her father, she say?" His mustache was again dancing as he surveyed the street.

She didn't run away, Bradshaw thought. She ran for her life. He didn't know this yet as fact and he didn't think confessing he'd found a body, possibly Ralph Hopper's, a sensible idea, not here on the street in the middle of the night, with Cox's meaty fist on his baton and his mustache dancing.

So he said, "I didn't speak to her. She didn't tell my son much."

"Well, then. I'd say she'd had enough. Not a fit father in my book." He shouted the words, looking about the street as if to challenge anyone to disagree with him. "I know what the child looks like, Professor. If she's here, she won't get by me."

"Do you know where they came from? Do they have any family?"

"No idea. Down here, folks don't volunteer private details."

"Did his peddler's license show an address?"

"Just the main post office."

"She might be hiding."

Cox narrowed his eyes to hard slits. "I've been a patrolman down here for nearly twenty years. By choice. I could've been promoted, but what would that have meant? Taking my experience off the streets where it's needed most. No, not for me. I know every face down here, and I know the games. That little girl might have come hiding, maybe she knows somebody, but this is my city and my beat, and nothing gets by me, not for long. Now you go on home, sir. I've got another few hours to go, and I'll keep watch. I'll pass the word to the next man on duty."

"Thank you, officer."

Bradshaw shook the patrolman's meaty hand, and they went their separate ways. Bradshaw didn't go straight home. He marched himself up to police headquarters on Third Avenue where he told the sergeant on duty about the body he'd discovered in the vacant lot in the new Capitol Hill development. It was the second time he'd been the first to report the finding of a body. The sergeant, an achingly thin young man with an unfortunate snub nose and intelligent green eyes, lifted his brow, but didn't detain Bradshaw once he'd taken down the information. They knew where he lived.

Chapter Nine

Bradshaw escorted a somber Justin and rambunctious Paul to school the next day to be sure their tendency to make an adventure of the journey didn't lead them to a particular vacant lot where the police might still be dealing with his gruesome discovery. Justin hung back as Paul climbed the steps to Father McGuinness waiting by the classroom door.

"Will you find her today?" he asked, his eyes begging.

"I'll do my best."

"Can I come with you?"

"No, son. You must go to school." He stopped himself from adding that where he was searching was no fit place for children.

He watched Justin climb the stairs and pass safely into the care of the Jesuits, then he pressed his hat down firmly to withstand the marine wind gusting across the hill toward toward Yesler Way.

Sunshine did not improve the district. What had appeared wicked and lively a few hours ago now looked grimy and tired. A few drunks slept in recessed doorways, weary landladies swept away debris from the sidewalk. The music halls were still open, but little music and few customers trickled out.

He again questioned those who seemed approachable. Had anyone seen the child begging? Asking for work? Scrubbing floors or sweeping up? Nobody would admit to seeing a girl named Emily with blond curls who may or may not be dressed like a boy.

When his trudging became fruitless, he stepped into the Queen City Restaurant, a ground-floor establishment in a brick-and-stone business building. The place was clean, noisy with men in cheap suits finishing their coffee at the counter and complaining good-naturedly of bosses and work and wives. He ordered a breakfast he didn't want so that he could sit at a window table with a view of First Avenue. As a plate of eggs and toast turned cold before him, he drank bitter coffee and watched the busy street.

The streetcar made regular passes, freight wagons and delivery carts rattled by. Foot traffic picked up, men with loping gaits, women with defiant strides. These were not the same women he'd seen a few hours ago. These were the wives of the small shop owners, factory workers, maids, domestics.

Across the street from Bradshaw, a peddler set up shop with a few upturned crates and began pitching to passersby. A wiry little man with a self-important air, he reminded Bradshaw of Victor, the Seattle Grand's stage manager. Inside the restaurant, Bradshaw couldn't hear the pitches. It looked like a pantomime, lots of gestures and waving, a solemn hand going over his heart. Nobody stopped, one man waved the peddler off angrily. Then a young man with a slight limp approached. He walked with a cane and was dressed well in a dark suit with a strawberry red tie. No, not a man. Nell Pickerell, a girl in boy's clothing, but not the girl he'd been looking for.

She stood before the peddler shouting angrily. When she picked up her cane and swung it at the peddler's head, Bradshaw jumped up and ran outside. He dodged traffic to cross the street and grabbed Nell from behind, holding her arms tight against her sides.

She shouted, struggling to free herself. "You can't sell that poison!"

The peddler rubbed his arm where Nell's cane had landed. "It ain't none your business, Nellie. Get away from me!"

"The name's Harry, and it's my business when you're selling poison and hurting people I—hurting my friends."

Bradshaw then caught sight of the bottle with the label of a blazing sun on the upturned crate. He didn't loosen his grip on

Nell but turned his own anger on the peddler, who thrust out his chest and clenched his fists.

"Harry's right, you're selling poison. That's Ralph Restorative. It's making people sick."

"There's no proof it's Ralph's making people sick. The people who drink this will drink anything. If they get sick, it's their own damn fault!"

Harry lunged with a growl, but Bradshaw held her tight.

"How many bottles have you got? How much for all of it?"

"I got a dozen bottles. You want it all, it'll cost you five bucks."

"Three, you're selling them for two bits."

"Not to you, I'm not. Five bucks and not a penny lower." He turned away from them and began shouting a pitch to the street. "Tonic here, get your tonic!"

"Stop!" Bradshaw shouted. He released his grip on Harry, and she pulled away but didn't attack. Bradshaw thrust a five into the peddler's grubby outthrust hand, and a full crate of clanking bottles was shoved toward him. The peddler grinned, pried the lid off another crate, and pulled forth several blue-labeled bottles with dignified black letters that said "Dr. Drummer's Proven Elixir."

Bradshaw carried Ralph's to the gutter and one by one opened them up and poured out the contents.

Harry joined him after the second bottle. She winced as she bent to set an empty bottle in the crate.

"Has a doctor seen that?" He nodded at her leg.

"The one at the jail. I saw you outside. You a detective?" Her voice was low, pleasant. Boyish, not deeply masculine.

"No, a professor at the university."

"Yeah? What do you profess?"

Bradshaw laughed. "I profess the wonders of electric power, its theorems and practical uses."

She said, "Well, good for you. I always wanted to know about science and such."

"It's never too late to learn."

"Nah, school's not for me."

"School is for everyone. Do you know him?" He nodded at the peddler.

"Nah."

"He called you Nellie."

"He read it in the papers last year, figured out they were talking about me. Makes him feel big to harass me."

"I know the type."

Bradshaw had the last tonic bottle in his hand. He looked at the label, read again the false promises, then slipped the bottle in his pocket.

"Thinking of ending it all, Professor?"

"Not today."

"Why are you in this part of town?"

"I came looking for a child. The daughter of the man who used to sell this."

Harry looked away, but not before Bradshaw saw something flash in her eyes.

"I'm afraid for her. Her father is missing. He might be dead." He watched Harry for another reaction, but she had closed up and was holding herself very still.

"Until last night, she was hiding in my house. Without my knowledge, my son was sheltering her. She comes to this part of town to find work."

Harry swallowed hard and stared at her shoes.

"If you happen to see her, will you let her know it's safe to return to my house?"

Harry nodded, still not looking at him. She began to limp away, leaning heavily on the cane. She said, "Yeah, sure. If I see her, this girl, I'll be sure to pass that on. I will definitely pass that on. If I see her."

The peddler wasn't having luck hawking his blue bottles. Bradshaw handed over two bits. "I'll take one of those."

"Gonna drink it or dump it?"

"Neither. Where'd you get the Ralph's?"

"Don't see what business it is of yours."

Bradshaw gave the man a five-dollar bill.

"Found it."

"Just like that. Found it. Are you in the habit of taking whatever property you stumble across?"

"Abandoned property is fair game. Finders keepers."

"Where'd you get this other?" Bradshaw skimmed the blue label in his hand. *Dr. Drummer's Proven Elixir. Medical science's most powerful formula to restore the natural balance and ensure health, wealth, and happiness. This powerful tonic has been especially and scientifically created for Men and Women Suffering from Degradation and Despair. A thrice-daily dose will dispel Aches, Pains, Vermin, Disease, Addiction, and Failure.*

He looked up. The peddler had turned away and was waving the bottle at uninterested people across the street. Bradshaw stood silently, patiently. He'd been a teacher for enough years to recognize evasion. He also knew the power of waiting it out.

Five minutes passed, and finally the exasperated peddler whined, "What you want from me? I got it from my usual source, and it's all legit and above board and I got a license from the Pharmacy Board to sell and no you can't see it, you ain't no cop."

"Who's your usual source?"

"You want to get into the business, I ain't helping you. Now beat it, this is my corner, bought and paid for, and you're scaring away my customers."

"How do you buy a street corner?"

"What are you, stupid? Nobody could be that green."

The peddler meant, of course, he was paying the police or some other person of authority to keep competitors away from this spot. "Paying graft for privileges or protection? That's illegal."

"That's business in this part of town, and you'd better learn the ropes if you don't want to wash up on the tide flats."

Bradshaw wasn't frightened. Bluster and exaggeration were as common as mud around here. And yet…the soggy lot on Capitol Hill was far above the tide flats, but a body had washed up there.

"Show me where you found Ralph's." He producd another bill that was quickly snatched.

At the Hotel Eskimo, a modest three-story brick hotel-apartment building, an obese manager with greased hair greeted the peddler warmly and Bradshaw coolly. The last dollars in Bradshaw's pocket were spent to learn that Ralph and Emily Hopper had rented a room several times over the past few months to sleep in a decent bed and have a bath. They'd been expected Friday evening. They hadn't shown. Ralph had left a case of tonic as payment, saying he was short on cash.

"What do I want with some tonic making people sick?" the manager wheezed. "Gave it to Mickey here, see if he could get something for it."

Bradshaw didn't know what to say to a man who valued a few dollars more than people's lives.

Mickey crowed, "Got five bucks!"

"Yeah? Who was fool enough to buy it?"

Mickey nodded at Bradshaw.

"He dumped it in the street."

"Some folks got money to waste."

"He says Ralph's dead and Emily's run away."

"What? No. Went off with the gypsies, that's what I heard. Morning, Miss Darlyrope!"

A gardenia scented breeze wafted behind Bradshaw as the actress glided through the lobby in a long overcoat tailored to her hourglass figure, a festooned hat balanced on her head like a crown. Mickey and the manager nearly bowed, and their smiling eyes followed her to the gated elevator, where a uniformed youth welcomed her warmly before slamming shut the grilled door.

A respectful silence lingered as the elevator ascended, and their eyes followed longingly, then the manager growled. "We done here?"

"Do you know a young actress named Daisy? A friend of Miss Darlyrope?" He saw recognition in both men's wary faces. The manager glanced at the ceiling, up toward where the elevator had risen.

"Miss Darlyrope's roommate?"

The manager frowned. "How much is it worth you to know?"

He didn't need to pay. The question was his answer. "Did you know Miss Daisy is ill?"

"Course I know. I run this hotel."

"You know then that she has been blinded by Ralph's Restorative."

Both men said, "I don't believe it."

"Ask Miss Darlyrope."

They reacted as if he had told them to ask a queen for a dance. And their regret, their fear, for earlier callous remarks about selling Ralph's flashed in their eyes.

"How much is it worth to you to keep your morning's business from Miss Darlyrope? Or shall I tell her you were happily hawking the same tonic that blinded Miss Daisy?"

Mickey's eyes narrowed as he handed Bradshaw the five he'd paid for the case of Ralph's.

Bradshaw didn't take the money.

"If you see Emily Hopper, will you telephone me or send a message? Professor Bradshaw. 1204 Gallagher. I'm on the exchange."

Mickey and the manager didn't speak. They understood he'd offered his silence and the money for information.

On his way home, Bradshaw stopped again at the police station to ask if there'd been any news. The desk sergeant informed him the body from the vacant lot had been recovered and was at the morgue. No one had reported finding Emily.

Detective March, with wide-awake energy and wearing a crisp new suit, emerged from an inner office while Bradshaw was at the front desk, and he walked Bradshaw out to the street.

Bradshaw was glad March had already been briefed; he didn't have the energy to tell the story of finding Emily, and the body, again.

"All this time, hiding in your son's room?"

"My housekeeper thought we had mice."

"Big mouse. You look dead on your feet, Professor. Let me get you a taxi home."

"No, thank you. The streetcar will be here any moment. I'm worried about the child. She told my son that she witnessed her father being murdered."

March's expression was at first blank. He shook his head, as if fending off gnats, then said, "Say again, Professor?"

"Emily saw someone kill her father."

"That wasn't in your report."

"No. I was hoping to find her and learn my son was mistaken about what she told him."

"Did you find her?"

"No."

"What did she see?"

"That I don't know. She gave my son no details, thank God."

"No wonder she's hiding."

"She's trying to make enough money to get home. If we knew where her home was, we could have the railroad and coaches and steamers watch for a child buying fare. And we, or you, could contact the police in her hometown to try to locate her family. Weren't there any personal papers in the wagon? Nothing with a name or address among their possessions?"

"Not a thing. Otherwise we would have tried to find relations, but then, they were living a vagabond life. You don't worry about it anymore. I'll earn my wage and find out all I can."

"I learned this morning that she and her father sometimes took a room at the Eskimo. I don't know if that will help you. Will you let me know if you find anything?"

"Of course, try not to worry. We'll see what the coroner has to say about Ralph's death. You know how children can be. The girl might have told your son she saw her father killed, but she could have been mistaken or even lying. We won't know until we find her. Even then, the truth out of such a child…a child living out of a wagon and forced to sell patent medicine by use of her youthful charm? Well, we can both agree she has not been taught that it's a sin to lie. Most likely the opposite. To her, spinning yarns is just another way of making money."

The streetcar approached, and Bradshaw felt like an old man as he climbed aboard under Detective March's youthful, concerned gaze. The car jerked as it started up the hill, and Bradshaw thought about March's comment that Emily might have been spinning yarns. It was true the child's story had prompted Justin to shake his money jar upside down until all the coins fell through the narrow slit. Mrs. Prouty had heard about that the previous night. The amount wasn't much, one dollar and eighty-nine cents. He'd been saving for a new model submarine kit he coveted, but he willingly shook it all out, and gave it away, persuaded by the girl's frightening story. Was it a true story? Her father was dead. Her clothes indicated she had been in the muddy lot where Bradshaw had found his body. Had she seen him die? Had she seen him being killed? Had the killer seen her?

Chapter Ten

After a hot bath, Bradshaw felt sufficiently restored to hop on his bike and ride up to the University. Had it really only been four days since he'd been on campus, talking to Duttenhoefer about the new powerhouse? It seemed a lifetime ago.

The afternoon sunshine winked off the windows of the Administration Building and set the sandstone glowing white. There was a bite to the wind that swept the lawns and shivered through the narrow branches of the young trees. He went first down to the chemistry lab and presented Graham Nordquist, Dean of Chemistry, with the bottles of Ralph's Restorative and Dr. Drummer's.

Nordquist, a cadaverous man with a hawk nose and ready smile, accepted the bottles with undisguised enthusiasm. His deep-set eyes sparkled with the challenge of discovering the mysteries within.

Bradshaw climbed the wide stone steps to his office, intending to finalize his teaching plan for the electromagnetism and dynamo class beginning on the first of October. Instead, he stood at the window, staring at Mt. Rainier some eighty miles distant, its majestic slopes and snowy crown floating above the low-lying clouds.

This office was new to him. He hadn't wanted it. Neither had anyone else. It was spacious, well-appointed, and provided this most coveted of views. Its last occupant, Professor Oglethorpe, had not been well-liked. And then he'd been murdered. His office bore the stigma of both. With the University bulging at the seams, as it were, and the ground not yet broken for the Science Hall, President Graves had run out of space to assign the faculty. Assistant Professor Tom Hill talked Bradshaw into moving into Oglethorpe's office.

"You're the only one not afraid of the room, Bradshaw. If you move in, you'll break the evil spell."

And so here he was. Distracted by the view, distracted by memories of Oglethorpe and anguish for Oscar Daulton. Distracted by the corpse of a man he'd found face down in the mud, and a child he'd chased from the safety of his home. He wanted to find her. He was not a man to wait patiently, not knowing what was being done.

What if Ralph's Restorative was still being sold? Was March looking into that as well as searching for Emily? Shouldn't somebody? Why not him? He had to do something. Class plans could wait.

Strength and clarity followed his decision. He took a deep, fortifying breath.

Where to begin? How did one trace the maker of a patent medicine such as Ralph's Restorative?

He sat at his desk, pulled the city directory from his drawer, and flipped through the pages to the drug store listings. The first phone call proved to be an education on the business of patent medicines.

"Open any newspaper or magazine, Professor," a seasoned and patient pharmacist explained, "and you will find dozens of advertisements for patent medicines. Those ads don't come cheap, but they do come with contracts. The papers agree to run the ads, and they agree not to say anything contrary to the patent medicine business anywhere in their papers. It's a million-dollar business. We honest medicine makers have to play by the rules. They don't."

"I thought the State Pharmacy Board oversaw patent medicines."

A cynical laugh crackled down the phone line. "They collect fees for licenses, but that's it. Patent meds are exempt from all laws and regulations of pharmaceuticals. They can put anything in their tinctures and tonics, change the ingredients on a whim, make any claim they want on the label."

"Something ought to be done."

"Be my guest! I wish you luck. Hard to spread the word when the newspapers won't print the truth."

A few more phone calls told Bradshaw the local pharmacists knew nothing of Ralph's tonic, other than the rumors about it causing illness. They asked questions of their own: Did the tonic look homemade? No. Was the label handwritten? No. The bottle sealed with a cap or cork? Cap.

He was told it could have come from anywhere in the country. Try the Sears & Roebuck.

Bradshaw found a copy of the catalog up in the library, but Ralph's Restorative was not among the remedies advertised. He decided to hunt down the label maker and returned to his office to dial local printers. His second call proved rewarding.

"Ralph's!" shouted the printer, a Mr. George Fredrickson of Seattle Printing, which advertised its expertise in patent medicine labels. "Where is Ralph Hopper? He owes me money!"

"Is his tonic only sold locally? It's been making people ill, so it's important to find out if it's being sold elsewhere."

"As far as I know, Ralph was only selling it around here. He said he special ordered all the ingredients. Had them sent to his lab where he mixed them himself from a recipe he got from a hundred-year-old gypsy he met in Eastern Washington. You know the sort of story."

"Did he mention where his lab was?"

The printer laughed. "That's the trouble with telephones, Professor Bradshaw. You didn't see me wink. He lives out of that wagon, near as I can tell. I doubt he has any sort of lab."

"Did he really make the tonic? Or just put his own label on someone else's?"

"All I know is he said he'd square with me last month, then it was this month after he sold his latest batch, and I haven't seen a penny. You tell him to get in here."

"I can't. I think he's dead. A body was found last night." There was no need to mention he'd been the one to find it.

"My God."

"His child is missing."

"Little Emily?"

"Are they gypsies?" Bradshaw asked doubtfully. He knew they'd not gone to Tacoma with the gypsies, but he'd forgotten to ask the Eskimo manager if they could be connected to them, or gypsies themselves.

"Them? No! Not from the look of them. He's tall and skinny, fair skinned. Used to be decently groomed, but not lately. Looked like he was ill last time I saw him. And the girl is as blond as they come, with curls and blue eyes. Pretty little thing, but too worldly if you ask me. Sad to see a girl flirting like a woman, and I told Ralph so, to his face. He can't see it though. Thinks the world of that girl, but even so, she belongs in a proper school and a proper home, not selling patent meds out of a wagon. You really think he's dead? And she's missing?"

"Will you let me know if you see her?"

"I will indeed. Good luck!"

When Bradshaw walked into the police station an hour later, the skinny desk sergeant didn't even look up. He'd been here so many times since last spring, his presence was no longer questioned, and they seemed to be taking his finding of another body in stride.

Bradshaw approached the desk. "Where is Ralph Hopper's wagon? Can I see it?"

"Well," said the sergeant, pulling a face that scrunched his snub-nose. "You can see it, but there's not much to look it. It's empty. Got robbed last night."

"Robbed? But isn't it parked here?"

"It was, but we don't have much room in the stable, so we moved it across Jefferson to the vacant lot. We locked it up tight and posted keep-off signs, but…." He put his palms up and shrugged.

"You don't seem unduly concerned, sergeant."

"I'm just glad I wasn't on duty last night."

"Any suspects?"

"Nobody heard or saw anything. Thieves were quiet as the dead."

Bradshaw crossed Jefferson and found Ralph's Restorative wagon. The thieves had been as thorough as they'd been quiet. Not a scrap remained, not even a mattress on the wooden plank bunks.

Bradshaw returned to the station and made his way to O'Brien's cramped office, where a bare bulb spread harsh light onto the detective's freckled face.

O'Brien skipped a greeting. "Any news on McKinley?"

Bradshaw dropped into a chair. "Still the same. You know about the peddler's wagon?"

"I heard. My God, you look tired."

"I just came from the morgue. The body I found last night has been positively identified. It's Ralph Hopper. And he's not a gypsy."

O'Brien's brows shot up. "What made you think he was a gypsy?"

"That's what Detective March said, or rather, that he went off with them."

O'Brien grunted.

"I learned that Ralph Hopper said he made his tonic locally, so there doesn't seem reason to fear it's making people ill elsewhere. Now I'm trying to find out where he and his child were from, and if the girl has other family we can try to locate. She told my son she was earning money to buy a train ticket home."

"I read the report."

"She also told my son she saw someone kill her father."

Bradshaw waited for a reaction. O'Brien fiddled with a capped fountain pen, maneuvering it between the fingers of one hand as if practicing a trick. Perhaps March had told him. Bradshaw said, "That girl has lost everything."

O'Brien remained silent.

"There are two Hoppers in Polk's directory, but neither is related to Ralph. I'm going to the courthouse when I leave here and look at the census records for the state."

"No, you're not."

"I'm not?"

"Go home, Ben. You're tired. You've done enough. We'll take it from here."

Bradshaw stared, but the detective would not meet his eye. He felt as he had last May when he'd been sitting in this very chair in handcuffs being accused of murder. That was before he knew O'Brien.

"What aren't you telling me?"

"Nothing. It's a police matter, Ben. No electricity involved."

"I want to help."

"Not necessary."

A silent moment passed. O'Brien continued to twirl the pen.

"You know. You know about Ralph Hopper and his daughter. I've been wasting my time. Worrying for nothing."

"When is worrying ever productive?"

"When it motivates you do something, like find a missing child. Where is she now?"

O'Brien didn't look up. "I don't know."

Bradshaw stood up so abruptly, the chair tipped over with a clatter. "I thought we were friends."

"For criminy's sake, Ben!" O'Brien threw down the pen and stood, his eyes revealing a depth of emotion Bradshaw couldn't decipher. "Let's take a walk."

They walked in silence up the hill to a small patch of grass labeled "Panter's Park" and a bench strategically placed to frame a view between the brick buildings to Elliott Bay. Those climbing to the county courthouse were given a chance here to catch their breath at the halfway mark.

O'Brien lit a smoke and took a few long drags before he spoke. "You're an intelligent man, Ben, but innocent in many ways. Now, don't take that wrong. I know you've been through rough times, but you still see the world innocently, in black and white, good and evil. It's not that simple."

"I beg to differ, Jim. I doubt I see anything in this world simply. I wish to heaven I did."

"You do see the police as mostly good."

"I'm beginning to see them as incompetent."

"That's not funny."

"Not meant to be. Ralph's wagon was in police custody when thieves helped themselves to everything inside."

"Are you expecting me to defend the department? It was a professional job and we're understaffed. We can't see or stop every crime. Not even ones that take place across the street from the station."

Bradshaw rubbed the back of his aching neck. He thought of the ugliness he'd seen below Yesler Way, of Mickey the street peddler with his corner he'd paid for. He looked out at the buildings and streets and humanity spread before him and knew O'Brien was right. Sixty-odd policemen had no hope of preventing all the crime in a city of a hundred thousand. They were brave to even try.

Bradshaw said, "On the whole, the police do a decent job in Seattle."

"Decent is relative, Ben. That's what I'm trying to explain. A city like this isn't simply managed."

Bradshaw thought again of Mickey and his street corner. The newspapers daily reported graft and corruption at all levels of public office, from the police to the mayor and beyond. "I trust you, Jim. You're not one of the grafters."

"No, not me, and that's my problem. Ralph Hopper's death is tangled in the Tenderloin, and I've been shut out. I can't get information."

"Then why not let me help. I'm not known in that part of town, maybe that would be useful."

"Has it been so far?"

"I can't say it has, no." His attempt to get information had cost much and yielded little.

"As an outsider, you don't know where to begin, or how to ask. Even when you find someone willing to talk, you don't know if you're hearing lies or the truth. You in the Tenderloin, Ben, well, that's like me climbing that pole and trying to unhook that power line."

"With your bare hands? That's energized, Jim, you can't touch it from the pole, you'd need an insulated platform, rubber gloves, and even then, there's danger from leakage…"

O'Brien lifted a hand to stop the explanation. "You see? When you don't know something is dangerous, you can grab hold of it and be dead before you know what hit you."

"Can't you teach me?"

"I can't teach what I don't know."

Bradshaw guffawed. "Ten years with the Seattle police, and you don't know what's up?"

"It's not a fact I live with comfortably. When I joined the force all those years ago, I was an innocent, proud in my brass buttons. Seattle was small-time then, before the gold rush, but the underworld elements were here and I didn't know the rules of the game. I've got an honest streak outsized only by stubbornness. So I took an extended leave and went to Chicago, where it wasn't known I was a cop. I learned the rules on the streets. When I came back, I knew what to watch for, and how to get information without paying for it. I don't go for the small players. I can't change the system. But I can protect the innocent. When crime threatens citizens outside the game, I put a stop to it. Or try to. That's the only reason I made detective. The powers that be knew I'd do my job without stepping on any toes."

"So what's changed?"

O'Brien didn't answer right away. He sat staring at the bay, taking long drags on his cigarette. "Let's just say that I took a wrong step. Bruised a toe I didn't know was there. I know the game, but not the players, not the new ones. Ever since Seattle became the gateway to gold, power's been shifting, and my few resources have been sucked dry. I can't send you to the Tenderloin with any more information than trust no one, and that won't help you find the girl or her father's killer."

Bradshaw thought about O'Brien's resentment of the new detective who'd volunteered to help with the abandoned wagon. "What about Detective March?"

"He's ambitious."

"I mean is he honest?"

"He's welcome everywhere he goes. I've never found that quality completely compatible with honesty."

"Why is he called golden -boy?"

"Didn't you know? He went up north in '97 and was one of the lucky ones."

"Aah." That explained his expensive suits, and maybe the welcoming circles. Folks hoping his luck or his riches would rub off. "Yet he works as a humble officer of the law?"

O'Brien laughed. "There's nothing humble about March. He knows what he's doing. Like I said, he has lofty ambitions."

"Is he involved in this Tenderloin tangle?"

"He knows a hell of a lot more than I do." O'Brien pitched the cigarette butt into the street. "Hell, I'm worried about the girl, too."

"You didn't want March getting Ralph's wagon from my back lane."

"I didn't like how eager he was to work on his day off."

"Did you learn anything from the patrolman you sent with him?"

"Mercer? He's faithful and honest, but not keen on under-currents."

"Why do you think March told me Ralph was a gypsy?"

"I have no idea."

"I need to find Emily. I need to find her before…"

O'Brien met his eye. His fear was understood between them without being said. He needed to find Emily before her father's killer found her.

"Any way I can stop you?"

"No."

They didn't speak for a few minutes, but the silence was companionable.

"There's a new book out you ought to read. *The World of Graft*, by a fellow named Flynt. It'll give you a rough idea of what goes on. Your university book store ought to have it."

"I still want to look at the census records."

"No law against it."

They parted with a handshake and O'Brien's stern warning to be careful.

Chapter Eleven

Professor Bradshaw stood before the picket fence of his house on Gallagher Street and took a moment to compose himself. The sun was dipping low, shadowing the white siding. The gas parlor lamps glowed softly, comfortingly, behind the sheers.

A gust of wind hit him, whistling in his ears and penetrating his clothing. The sign that hung from his mailbox creaked on its chains. Justin had made the sign, carefully burning the words, "Professor Bradshaw, E.E. Forensics Investigator" into the wood with his Junior Wood-Burning Kit.

As Bradshaw stood trying to settle the thoughts and emotions competing in his exhausted mind, the front door opened and Mrs. Prouty stepped out with her broom.

"Any luck?" she called.

He shook his head.

"Bread's fresh from the oven. Best come in before you fall over." Words equivalent to a hug from his housekeeper.

He obeyed.

After bread and beef soup and a large mug of Postum, Bradshaw spent an hour with Justin helping with his math homework and showing him how to add fractions using sweet nuggets of Cracker Jack. It was amusing how quickly the boy grasped concepts when he was allowed to eat the answers.

At nine that evening, when the doorbell rang, both Mrs. Prouty and Justin had gone to bed, and Bradshaw was slouched in his easy chair before the fire reading about graft and corruption in America's biggest cities.

The golden boy stood on his porch. Detective March wearing his handsome suit and carrying two bottles of Coca-Cola, dew drops clinging to the glass. He cocked his head and read the title of the book Bradshaw had absent-mindedly carried to the door.

"*World of Graft?* I don't advise it, Professor. Teaching is a far nobler profession than picking pockets and selling secrets."

"But not nearly so interesting. Do you have news?"

"No, I'm afraid not, but I would like to talk to you."

Bradshaw moved aside and let the detective in.

"I've brought refreshment." March presented the soda pop.

"No, thank you."

"I'll have one, if you don't mind."

Bradshaw brought a bottle to the kitchen and popped off the new-style crown top. He grabbed a glass and returned to the parlor to find the detective examining Emily's doll. The day after Emily fled, Justin put it back on the mantel with a swift, determined glance to Bradshaw that meant, *you chased her away, you find her.* So strongly had he felt the accusation, he'd almost disciplined the boy for being disrespectful.

"This is the child's, I take it? Such a fancy thing. You'd think it belonged to a wealthy girl, wouldn't you? Possessions are deceiving. Pluck a man from the gutter, put him in velvet and silk, who's to know?"

"*The Prince and the Pauper.*"

March lifted his brow.

Bradshaw noted, "Mark Twain's novel?"

"I was thinking more of the illusion, the art of disguise. The pauper might make the better king, but he would never be given a chance. He would always be judged by his rags."

"And the king, stripped of his servants and gold, unable to survive in the mean streets?"

"Most likely. Your son looks like his mother." March had picked up the framed photograph on the mantel of Justin, taken this summer by one of the university students who'd built a camera and opened a small studio business that Bradshaw was pleased to support. He didn't like to have his own photograph taken, but Justin, like his mother, enjoyed posing and seeing the results.

"Yes," Bradshaw said simply.

"You lost her when your son was very young."

Bradshaw nodded, not wanting to encourage this line of conversation.

"Those sort of tragedies never really leave you, do they?" March looked at him, and Bradshaw bristled, seeing a depth of understanding.

"Last week, I was called to something similar."

Bradshaw's stomach tightened. He'd read about it in the *Seattle Times*. In the presence of friends who'd gathered to console her, a distraught woman had swallowed carbolic acid. There were similarities, yes, to the way his late wife had taken her own life. Only his wife had not intended to die, only punish him.

"Say, listen, I'm sorry. I can see I've upset you. I shouldn't have mentioned it."

Last May, the police had learned about his wife's death when they'd briefly considered him a suspect in Professor Oglethorpe's death. O'Brien told him he'd ripped up the file once Bradshaw's innocence had been proven, but not before a few at the station had read the report. Apparently March was one of them.

"My son doesn't know." He gave this warning to anyone who learned of Rachel's suicide. Justin had asked only once about his mother's death and Bradshaw had explained that she'd been ill for a very long time, which was true, and that she'd loved him with all her heart, which was not.

"Of course not. He should never know. It's a heavy burden even for a father to carry."

Bradshaw's throat suddenly constricted. He handed the glass to March, but the detective said he preferred to drink straight from the bottle. They sat before the fire and Bradshaw waited for March to say what he'd come to say.

March jutted his chin at the book on graft. "I've not read that yet. Any good?"

"I don't know, I only just started reading."

"Why this book in particular, if you don't mind my asking?"

"I'm hoping it will help me find Emily."

"She's why I'm here. I wanted to explain. You see, I had it from a usually reliable source that they, Emily and Ralph, were connected with that tribe that recently passed through town. I thought it was a good tip. I should have followed up to be certain. Maybe I'd better get a copy of that," he nodded again at the book on graft, "and study up on how it's done." Despite his admission, he spoke with a teasing confidence. He didn't need the book.

"You could be right about Emily hiding out in our wicked district, and I've come to urge you to leave this to the police. I joke about my sources, but they aren't people I'd feel comfortable with you quizzing. There's a reason patrolmen are armed."

"I understand the dangers, but I'm not going to stop looking for her."

March took a swig of cola, then reached into his pocket and pulled out a waxed-paper pouch of multicolored gumdrops. Bradshaw declined his offer for one. March popped a handful in his mouth and followed with another swig of cola.

It was worse than watching Justin devour ginger cakes. "How can you eat that? Makes my teeth hurt to look at it."

March laughed. "I'm addicted to sweets. Say listen, I've got a lot of friends doing business in the district, and they know what's happening. They hear things. I'm going to use my sources—my reliable sources—and if Emily is in the Tenderloin, I'll find her. You've got to promise me not to go nosing around anymore yourself."

"I can't make that promise."

"Don't make me tell O'Brien."

"What?"

"You're friends, right? He'd be on my side here."

"He's the one that told me about this book."

"Mr. Goody Two-Shoes? Sorry, he's a great chap and fine detective, but O'Brien scorns graft rather to his detriment."

"I think it's to his merit."

March sat forward, his eyes earnest. "Professor, I'm going to be honest with you. Policing a big city is a complicated job, and it's not possible to play it straight when the crooks are playing dirty. Here's an example.

"Last week, a woman was robbed in broad daylight. Thief ripped the coin purse right off her wrist, leaving her bruised and bleeding. A nice woman, a seamstress. She'd just been paid her week's salary. O'Brien was assigned to the case and came up empty. People all over the place and nobody saw anything."

"I thought the people of Seattle were better than that."

"Depends on the neighborhood. This was below Yesler. Now I know someone who's a smalltime gambler, who sees and hears a lot, and he'll pass it on to me if I overlook an occasional roll of the dice where they're not supposed to roll. I paid him a visit and ten bucks later had the crook in jail. Is it right that I let a man charge me to tell the truth? Would it have been right to let that thief get away with his crime? The choice is often the lesser of two evils."

Bradshaw stared at the dying fire. March made sense, and he wondered if O'Brien's strict adherence to honest policing was, in the end, the right way to go if it meant criminals went free and innocent people suffered. Bradshaw was by nature honest himself, and he usually took pride in it. Now, he felt a bit stodgy. And hadn't he done as much? Paid for information? Used the threat of exposure to pressure the Eskimo manager and street peddler to pass on news of Emily? He'd been annoyed at having to do so, but felt not the least bit guilty of wrongdoing. However, he was a citizen, not an officer of the law. He said defensively, "You confessed to grafting."

"More like bribery," March winked. "And I told you because I trust you, Professor, and we both want the same thing. To find little Emily."

"Well, yes, but given your ambitions, I'm surprised how frank you're being."

"In politics, like policing, Professor, frankness saves time, and honesty doesn't always pay. A man has to know the time and place for both if he's to get anything done. It doesn't help either of us to pretend I investigate down in the Tenderloin any differently than any other detective in any big city—except maybe O'Brien. And I'll bet he sent you after that book hoping once you read it you'd be too afraid to go any further."

Bradshaw opened the book at random. He couldn't make sense of the words leaping off the page, "copper-talk" and "bean town" and "unmugged thief." It was like a foreign language.

"I don't know the slant of that book," March said, "but I'll bet it doesn't make any of us look any good. I'll bet it also doesn't offer any decent alternative. You can't change human nature."

"No, I suppose not."

"Don't look so defeated, Professor. If the Hoppers aren't gypsies, they're the next worse thing, and that's professional charlatans, with street smarts and survival skills. The child's disappeared without a trace, and if that's not proof of her ability, I don't know what is."

The next worse thing? The comment didn't sit well with Bradshaw. He didn't know much about the gypsies that occasionally passed through Seattle, other than the fact that the newspapers posted their whereabouts as if providing a security service to the community, and the police made them move along if they stayed more than a few days. Bradshaw didn't like it when entire groups of people were painted with assumptions about their characters.

"If you didn't know anything about the Hoppers until your source misled you about them being gypsies, why did you volunteer to help with their abandoned wagon on your day off?" He met March's eye squarely and the detective smiled openly.

"Being neighborly, of course." At Bradshaw's puzzled look, March added, "The Woodworths? Behind the lane from you?" He pointed over his shoulder toward the back of Bradshaw's house. "They're like a second family to me, didn't you know?"

"No, I didn't know."

"I sit with them at church each Sunday. Haven't you seen us?"

"The Immaculate Conception? I've seen the Woodworths there."

"Yes, we have a family pew. You sit in the back with your son, maybe you never noticed me." March laughed at Bradshaw's embarrassed confusion. "I have to apologize for my ego, Professor. I assume everyone knows me on sight, and it's my nature to put a name to everyone I see. I'm glad that wagon provided the chance for us to properly meet, because I've been an admirer of yours for a good while now."

Bradshaw felt ridiculously flattered.

March stood, leaving the full bottle of soda on the side table and pocketing the empty. "You quit worrying now, Professor. I'll find the girl."

Bradshaw met the detective's confident eyes. If anyone could find her, this ambitious and intelligent man could.

"What if she's not even in the Tenderloin? What if she went somewhere else?" He was suddenly overwhelmed with the notion that she could be anywhere in the city, in the state.

"It's not so easy for a child to get about on her own unnoticed. I've put word out at all the usual places someone goes to find transport. So far, she doesn't seem to have left town, so there's a very good chance she's burrowed in somewhere close. Now, try not to worry."

When the door had closed, Bradshaw went to the mantel and propped the doll upright. The little blue eyes opened. He didn't think of Emily. He thought of Justin and the faith he placed in Bradshaw's ability to find the girl. What if he failed? If he gave up his search? The doll slipped sideways, and the blue eyes closed. Bradshaw's chest and throat tightened, and he turned away.

Chapter Twelve

Sleep was impossible, Bradshaw discovered, when a child was missing, and inaction impossible when one's son had put his faith in his father's promise to find her.

At one in the morning, he gave up the effort, climbed from bed, dressed quietly, and left a note for Mrs. Prouty.

The raucous Tenderloin, bathed in artificial twilight, was no longer unknown to him on this third visit. He was beginning to recognize faces and remember the names of the music halls and theaters, saloons and hotels. The names told an oddly accurate tale of Seattle's history. The Settlers Bar, Lewis & Clark Music Emporium, the Duwamish Hotel, and the Klondike Saloon. He found that the rougher the name, the more honest. The Klondike was filled with scruffily dressed men drinking hard liquor and swapping tall tales. The Queen City Hotel was an ugly two-story clapboard building filled with "cribs," rooms no larger than closets. He'd heard of such places, of course, but it had still shocked him, when he entered the dim lobby to make his inquiry, to see the long hall, the curtained doorways, and to hear the unhindered sounds of activity within. The smell was best not described.

He asked few questions at each establishment. In some places, he spoke not at all. The book on graft had taught him that much. His questions would not be answered, not with truth. It was better to watch and listen, to become someone who belonged and blended with the regulars. He was keenly aware when eyes slid his way, assessing him, that Ralph's killer might be on the same mission, visiting the same places.

He ducked into a bar when he saw Patrolman Cox come whistling down First Avenue. He'd learned that from the book, too. He could be seen giving the patrolman money, not shaking his hand.

From bar to music hall to vaudeville theater, he made his way through the district, leaning against walls in dark corners, listening with his head bent over a drink that never touched his lips. He heard things he'd never known and wished he still didn't. But nothing about Emily Hopper.

At six, with the sun not yet risen, he took the Capitol Line streetcar back up the hill, slipped into his house, took a long hot bath, and dressed for a day at the University. When he gave his pockets a habitual pat, he found them empty, so he dug into the jacket he'd worn all night to retrieve his notepad and pencil and tokens.

His fingertips felt something in the lining of the jacket, square and stiff. No, he thought, not the lining, the inside pocket. He opened the jacket to reveal the small secret pocket designed to safely stash money. It had a button closure. He'd never before used it.

He unfastened the button and found inside a slip of paper folded four times into a neat square. He unfolded it to reveal unfamiliar handwriting.

This is not your business. Unless you want your boy to be an orphan like the girl.

He stood immobile, a cold numbness washing over him.

He'd not felt a thing. His thoughts raced back over the past few hours. Not once had he been close enough for someone to reach inside his coat. Had he bumped shoulders with anyone in one of the bars or dance halls? No, maybe. To reach inside his jacket, unbutton that small pocket, how? Did it matter? Whoever had done it knew how best to stop him. They knew he had a son. They knew about Justin.

The room began to spin. He sat heavily on the edge of the bed, his face in his hands. And the room went black.

When light returned, it was the wrong color. Not early morning golden, but soft full light, filling the room. He was fully dressed, minus his shoes and jacket, in bed, under the covers. His bedside clock said 9:30. He'd been asleep, or unconscious, for over two hours. He felt immensely refreshed. He sat up.

And remembered the note. He looked at his empty hands, shook the bed clothes, and lifted the pillow. Where was the note? He checked the floor, the nightstand, and then spied his jackets—the good one that went with the suit he was wearing, and the old one he'd worn during his search of the Tenderloin—hanging on his clothes rack. He didn't remember putting them there, or taking off his shoes, though they were sitting neatly under the rack. On his dresser he found his notepad, pencil, tokens, and the note, partially folded. He opened it and read again. The threat had not been a nightmare.

He let go of a corner of the note, and the creases of the paper pulled it partially closed, hiding the writing. He folded it completely and shoved it deep in his trouser pocket.

Mrs. Prouty sat at the kitchen table, her feet up on a stool, reading the morning paper.

"So you've decided to rejoin the living," she said. "I wasn't fancying calling up the morgue."

"Is there any coffee?"

"Just the dregs. I'll make a fresh pot." She began to rise, but he waved her down.

"Dregs will do. Any news on the president?"

"The doctors say his blood cor-puskle count is good."

"Corpuscle," Bradshaw corrected, as he helped himself to two thick slices of bread and slathered them with butter. He was suddenly ravenous. "It means they believe no infection has set in."

"Says here his temperature is 100.4. He's fighting something."

Bradshaw trusted Mrs. Prouty's instincts. She knew before Justin did when he was falling ill.

"Let's hope the doctor's prediction is right."

He joined Mrs. Prouty at the table with his breakfast. There was a note in her handwriting held down by the sugar bowl. It said simply, "Prof. Hill."

"Professor Hill telephoned?"

"That's right. He asked where you wanted some new measuring meters to go. Thomas Mack or some such."

"Thomson-Mascart electrometer? He's eager. I told him I'd be there this morning to sort the new equipment."

"That was yesterday morning, Professor, and I told him you were sleeping and not to be disturbed."

"No, no, today. It's on my calendar for Wednesday."

"Today's Thursday. Didn't you know?"

Bradshaw stared at her, his mouth full of bread and butter. Thursday?

"Professor, you've been asleep for twenty hours, near as I can tell. I don't know when you went down, but when I went in to clean your room and found you dead to the world, it was about noon. Yesterday."

He continued to gawk. It was disorienting to think he'd been hard asleep, not for two hours but for an entire day. He swallowed as the implication of her words sank in. She'd taken off his shoes. He imagined her swinging his legs up onto the bed, tucking him in, putting a palm to his forehead, then his chest, feeling for the rise and fall of his breathing. She'd hung up his clothes. Laid his pocket contents, and the partially folded note, on his dresser. Had she read the note?

"If you don't believe me, look." She handed him the paper and there was the date in bold black print. Thursday, 12 September, 1901. He read, not because he didn't believe her, but to give himself time to try to divine if she'd read the threatening note. He couldn't ask without alerting her; she couldn't say without admitting she'd read a personal note without permission, but he knew she would find a way of making her opinion known.

He relinquished the newspaper, and tried to lighten the mood. "Call me Rip Van Winkle."

"What do you expect, staying up round the clock for more'n two days."

"You're worried about the girl, too."

"Course I am, but you ought not put yourself in the grave trying to find her."

That was her second reference to death. Were these intentional or just her usual practice of exaggerating? Her tone was blunt, not leading, and she met his eyes squarely.

"When the detective and patrolman were here to take away that peddler's wagon, what sort of questions did they ask?"

She put down the paper to look at him with narrowed eyes. "What is it you're up to, Professor?"

"Just asking."

"Last time you asked a lot of questions and poked your nose into something, you found yourself nearly going over Snoqualmie Falls."

"I promise not to go near the Falls. What was asked? What was said?"

"I wish you'd not let Justin make that sign out front, announcing to the world you're now an investigator."

"I'm not an investigator, I specialize in electrical forensics, and that has nothing to do with this."

"I don't care what you call it. You nearly get yourself killed with your nosing about, and all summer that O'Brien comes round to drag you into police business…" *Uh oh, now O'Brien was being classified with 'that Paul'* "…and now you've found that poor man dead and you're obsessed with that doll on the mantel—" Her voice choked, and she pretended to cough, then set her jaw tight.

"I'm trying to picture what happened the night Emily and her father disappeared. Sometime that night, they were in their wagon, they came up to our neighborhood. Why? They came down our back lane. Why? They got out of the wagon. Why? They disappeared. Why?"

"It don't make sense."

"No, it doesn't."

"Nobody around here was buying their potions, not in the night."

"Why else would they come, if not to sell something?"

"Not to go visiting. Nobody knows them from Adam."

"Are you sure?"

"Course I'm sure. I talk to the other housekeepers, don't I?"

She did, and though he was sure she kept his household gossip, minor as it was, to herself, she gathered tidbits from the neighbors' help with professional thoroughness. "And what have they to say?"

She heaved an enormous sigh of defeat. Something she would not do had she read the note. He breathed a little easier. "Nobody remembered hearing nothing. And when that handsome detective come by with that oaf who accused me of feeding the horse beans, well, we didn't have nothing to say. Martha wouldn't have heard a train if it plowed through the house, o' course, she's dead to the world when she sleeps. That's why she could never work in the nursery. Not even a squalling baby can wake her. She saw the wagon, though, out the window, in the wee hours," she shot him a look, warning him not to make a crude pun, "and it was a bit further down the lane when Dolores got up to light the stove."

"Don't the Woodworths also employ a man-of-all-work? Did he see anything?"

"That'd be Albert." She made a face that let Bradshaw know Albert did not rate her approval. "He told us all to mind to our business and quit gossiping like geese, so I don't know what he saw or heard. Nothing, I'll bet, or he'd be finding a way of lording it over us. He's nothing like his brother."

"His brother?"

"Detective March, the handsome one, not that awful patrolman. Of course, they're years apart in age, nearly twenty, I reckon. Always been jealous, and it's made him bitter."

"But he didn't see anything? Has anyone recalled anything more?"

"Nothing to do with the wagon. We all wondered if the driver had some relation hereabouts, Seattle being that sort of city, with all and sundry mixed together, you never know what life your neighbor might have led before settling here. None of us could think who it might be, and there's been no talk upstairs, if you know what I mean. Only Millie, Mrs. Olsen's housekeeper, had ever heard of Ralph's Restorative. She'd seen the wagon last week on First Avenue, when she was on the trolley, and only noticed because of the child. Cute as bug, she said she was, with a head of golden curls, sitting up by the driver. Millie said it was like looking into the past and seeing herself as a girl, and it gave her such a happy feeling until she got home and caught a look at herself in the glass and saw an old woman looking back."

Millie was nearly as old as the widow she cared for.

"She never saw the wagon in the lane. She did hear something, she doesn't know what. It woke her up."

"Does she know the time?"

"Roundabout a quarter past eleven. There was thump or a clump or a bump. The sound woke the widow, too, and they couldn't get back to sleep, so they warmed some milk and read for a bit, the widow to Millie since Millie's eyes tire so easily these days."

"They heard nothing more?"

"Just Mr. Woodworth coming home, 'bout midnight. He'd gone to some business affair in the city. Albert always comes down the back lane so Mr. Woodworth doesn't have to climb the steep stairs to the front porch. His knees trouble him. He goes in through the kitchen, and there's only the two steps up. Mrs. Woodworth never goes to those dinners. She gets bored with all the shop talk, and I think she's been feeling poorly."

Bradshaw thought of the top-hatted men in the Tenderloin district whose wives were oblivious to their actual whereabouts. Had Mr. Woodworth truly been at a business dinner? The Woodworths were the only family on the lane with a carriage, a specially designed private coach with *Woodworth's Tools, Seattle's Finest* in elegant script on the side panels.

"Was the lane free or blocked? Did they hear any sort of commotion?"

"Must have been blocked, they said, because they heard Albert a few minutes later prodding his horse backward. There's nowhere wide enough to turn round, as well you know. I'd say that Ralph couldn't have been in his right mind, abandoning that poor child. Intoxicated on that remedy of his, I've no doubt."

The bells of the telephone pealed. Bradshaw rose to answer, chewing his last bite of buttered bread as he padded down the hall. He was still starving.

It was Dean Nordquist on the line, with his chemical analysis.

"The Dr. Drummer's contained grain alcohol, sarsaparilla, grape juice, a few herbs. Nothing curative, nothing dangerous either. The bottle of Ralph's? The only thing that stuff can cure is the habit of breathing."

"Was there wood alcohol?"

"Yes, your suspicions were right about the show girl's blindness. I ran two separate tests, one of them just published. Tedious and time-consuming, but worked beautifully. They both confirmed methyl alcohol. You'd be shocked to learn how much foodstuff is adulterated with methyl, medicines, too. I've been running tests all summer for a group trying to set purity standards. A tip: Bradshaw, tell your housekeeper to stick to fresh lemons and ginger. Much of the bottled stuff is toxic."

"Good grief."

"Methyl's used as an extract. Quite a number of fatalities have been reported, mostly back East, with a product called Jamaican Ginger Beer."

"Was it included intentionally, do you think? In Ralph's, I mean?"

"Not by the tonic maker, not unless he wanted to sabotage his business. The percentage wasn't high, and not everyone is susceptible to blindness, but even small amounts will sicken just about anyone. Methyl's just the first of the toxins, Bradshaw. I also found phenol—that's carbolic acid."

Bradshaw's grip tightened painfully on the receiver.

"Sorry," the dean said. That simple word, genuinely spoken, revealed much. The dean was another who'd learned about his wife's suicide last spring and promised his silence to Bradshaw. Missouri knew. The night they'd spoken of it haunted him still. In the parlor lit only by the fireplace embers, he'd told her the story of his courtship to Rachel and their miserable marriage. Missouri had held his hands, her amber eyes aglow with tenderness, and he knew that he'd never be the same.

"Bradshaw? You still there?"

"Oh, yes, go on."

With considerable gruffness that was essentially tact, Dean Nordquist said, "The phenol I found simply by odor, it's unmistakable, even in this concoction. I ran a few tests—a definitive one is needed—and I'm as close to positive as I can be. The final poison is a pharmaceutical. I wouldn't have thought to look for it, but there were white crystals at the bottom of the bottle. It took me a few tests to narrow it down. It's acetanilid. That's a fever drug. Not used as much now that there's phenacetin and Bayer aspirin around. In large doses or too frequent use it seems to damage the blood and liver. None of these poisons was in high quantity. Looks to me like the intent was to sicken consumers, not kill them. Those ingredients certainly weren't added to provide any sort of cure."

"Thank you, Dean. Could I trouble you to send your results to Coroner Cline?"

"Already done. Will you be up to the university today?"

"I don't know yet."

The dean laughed. "Doesn't your calendar say?"

Bradshaw's strict adherence to his calendar was legendary, but he didn't like being accused of inflexibility.

"I've made other plans. Thank you, Dean."

Bradshaw dropped the receiver onto the hook. He hadn't made other plans. Yet. He inspected his calendar, and yes, he had scheduled himself to be at the university. Was there anything critical pending? His class preparations were far enough along that he could get by the first few weeks of term without trouble. Assistant Professor Hill could handle the organizing of the new equipment. He crossed out his entry with a pencil but added nothing else.

The plans he would make for today were not for public viewing. Or Mrs. Prouty's.

He changed out of his rumpled good suit into fresh and comfortable work clothes before going down to his basement workshop, taking the threatening note with him.

He read it again carefully. The writing was unfamiliar, yet certain elements gave him information. The flow was unsteady, the vertical lines wobbled, and there was no forward slant. The writer had used a nondominant hand, a right hand most likely because there was no smudging of the ink, which was very difficult to avoid when writing left-handed. The paper was of standard weight, clean and white, sized four inches by five, and slightly uneven. The edges were sharp. This had been cut with scissors from a larger piece of paper.

The folds were as precise as could be given the slightly imperfect cut, the creases pressed firmly and smoothed. The creator of the note had a careful and methodical nature. But the creator need not have delivered it. Only a professional, seasoned pickpocket could have slipped the note inside Bradshaw's buttoned inner pocket without his noticing.

As best he could with a memory fogged by the exhaustion he'd felt and the interceding blackout of sleep, he reviewed his movements the night the note had been slipped to him. Only in one place, the Occidental Theater, did it seem remotely possible. A noisy place, with a piano player plunking out ragtime melodies, and women on stage in what looked to him like frilly undergarments, bouncing to the tunes. He'd crossed the crowded room to get to a corner table near the doors to the backroom in order to steal a look into the kitchen to see if Emily was there scrubbing or peeling. He might have bumped, or been bumped, along the way. Yes, now that he thought of it, he'd been jostled, and someone had said "pardon" just as a waitress had approached him and asked him his pleasure in a way that seemed unrelated to drink. He had no memory at all of who had jostled him.

He folded the note, tucked it in a small cardboard box of brass screws, and set it on a high shelf above the workbench.

O'Brien and March had been right in warning him. The Tenderloin was dangerous. He'd been aware, of course, of immediate dangers, crooks, drunks, suspicious types who didn't like outsiders asking questions. He'd known he might become a victim of a random attack of violence. It had never occurred to him he would be targeted like this. He didn't regret searching for Emily; he would not stop searching for Emily. He regretted only that now his identity was known, he couldn't return to the streets to search for her. Besides being a foolish risk, it would be a waste of time. If O'Brien had bruised a toe, well, Bradshaw had broken a foot.

He heard Henry's voice in his head as clearly as if his old friend were standing beside him. "Don't let the bastard win."

"No," Bradshaw said aloud. "No, Henry. I won't."

So. He must be more clever than the criminal he was up against. More adept than the criminal's associates. What did he possess that they did not? What were his weapons? He looked around his basement. He had science. In particular, immediately before him on his workbench, he had transmitters and receivers. Mechanical ears and mouths. Could these be put to use?

If the music of the theater could be brought to his home, why not simple conversations? Could he listen from afar to places he now dare not tread? Not to everything said in every joint in Seattle, no, but one or two specific places? Where? That was the real problem. If he knew where to listen, where he might hear news of a child hiding, or trying to earn money, he wouldn't have had to walk the streets and stir up this threat. The odds of overhearing a discussion about Emily or her father were miniscule. And setting up such a system would take a ridiculous amount of subterfuge. He'd have to go in disguise, make up some legitimate-sounding excuse to the business owners for installing the wire and hardware. Oh, it was absolutely impossible. It could never happen.

Yet the visionary dream beckoned. Small listening devices secretly installed, bringing to him all the whispers of the dark corners. His transmitter was sensitive enough, he was sure of it. For a few minutes, he indulged the dream. He imagined his devices hidden in walls, disguised in lamps, sending the secrets through a private cable to his basement. And then? How to manage the dozens of conversations ceaselessly flowing? He couldn't sit down here twenty-four hours a day listening to them all simultaneously. He'd need a team of listeners. He only had himself, and limited time. He looked again around his basement. What device could take the place of many human listeners? What device not only listened but saved sound?

The Graphophone and Phonograph, of course, recorded sound onto revolving cylinders of wax or tinfoil. Could he record conversations using one of them? Would the sound have to be played from a horn to be recorded, or could he bypass the horn and get the stylus of the recording instrument to move in coordination with the receiving components of the telephone? That's how a new invention by a man in Denmark worked. Poulsen was the man's name, and he called the device a Telegraphone. Poulsen had figured out that by replacing a telephone receiver with an electromagnetic assembly in which a length of steel wire streamed from one spool to another, a magnetic recording was made upon the wire. This recording could be played back by placing the electromagnet in series with a telephone receiver and spooling the magnetized wire through. It was an ingenious device, not yet perfected, but oh, so full of possibilities!

Wax cylinders could only hold two minutes worth of sound, while spools of wire held the promise of much longer recordings. But even then, when would he have time to listen to what he recorded? He needed to find a way to filter out the useless conversation. Find a way to hear only something that might lead him to Emily.

What if he could find a way to selectively record? Automatically. He'd need to be able to distinguish the important conversations from all others. If he were listening in person, how would he know he was hearing something that might lead him to Emily? He would hear her name, or Ralph's name, maybe the tonic's name. How could he get his listening devices to be selective? Could he develop an auditory closure that completed the circuit only when certain sound waves triggered it? Maybe the selection could take place at this end. Could a recorder be set in motion by certain auditory signals? Record two minutes of conversation, then reset itself? That was within the realm of possibility.

Bradshaw spent several hours completely absorbed in designing this eavesdropping system he knew he would never be able to install in the practical world. There were aspects that would, if he ever undertook them, challenge him to the core. The auditory closure and the telephone recording device taunted him like the concept of a practical flying machine taunted others. He *knew* it must be possible, but *how*—that was the money question.

The process invigorated him, focused his attention on minute details, and gave him a feeling of control he didn't possess when pondering Emily Hopper's whereabouts. He didn't consider his work a waste of time. Past experience had taught him the value of turning away from a puzzle completely. Direct confrontation could obscure vision and narrow approaches. By looking away, often the answers would slip in sideways.

He wasn't aware when he heard Detective O'Brien call his name and heard his footsteps descend the stairs to the basement that an answer was slipping in sideways. An answer, and the chance to turn his far-fetched invention into reality.

Chapter Thirteen

"The coroner has completed the autopsy. Ralph Hopper drowned. A small stream runs under the lot, makes the ground swampy. That's why building has been delayed." As O'Brien spoke, he stood beside Bradshaw at the workbench, his eyes on the drawings depicting the elaborate eavesdrop system.

Bradshaw's own vision had turned inward, to the image of Ralph Hopper face down in the muck, unable to lift his head, unable to breathe. He swallowed an instinctive gulp of panic.

O'Brien picked up the outer shell of a telephone transmitter from which the internal workings had been removed. "Mrs. Prouty told me you took a long nap."

"Mrs. Prouty blames my association with you."

"She told me that, too." He swapped the outer shell for a bar magnet.

"Was Ralph ill or drunk, did you learn? I spoke with Dean Nordquist this morning. He sent Cline his findings from examining a bottle of Ralph's Restorative."

"Those results coincided with the autopsy findings. Ralph was consuming his own tonic. A few witnesses have said he began drinking it heavily to prove it was safe. There's no conclusive signs of physical restraint. It would seem he was unable to lift his head, but whether from weakness due to drinking his poison, or obstruction, it's not clear. He appears to have died where he fell, face down. There's dried mud on the back of his head."

Bradshaw imagined a chase, Ralph weak, stumbling, falling, his pursuer standing over him, lifting a foot and setting it down. A small weight able to suppress what little strength Ralph had left. And Emily had seen. It was assumption, yes, but logical and likely, and supported by that threatening note.

"Is there bruising or other evidence of force?"

"Nothing conclusive."

"Will there be an inquest?"

"Yes, but the outcome is likely to be cause of death accidental drowning, or at best, undetermined. It depends on the jury, of course. It's a fact of life that we judge death by our feelings about the victim. Many will feel Ralph Hopper got what he deserved. We need a witness." O'Brien set the magnet down with respectful care and at last looked at Bradshaw.

Emily was the only witness.

"That's it then?"

"Unless more evidence comes forward. We're still looking for Emily, but we can't search every home and place of business in the city without cause and search warrants. It's hard to find someone who doesn't want to be found."

"She's afraid of her father's killer. Isn't that enough cause to search every inch of this city?"

"Hearsay, Ben, from a child, and she implicated no specific person or place." The words were in a tone of apology.

O'Brien lifted next a length of silk-covered copper wire with his left hand. What percentage of the population was left-handed, Bradshaw wondered? He glanced at the shelf above the workbench, at the box of brass screws where the threatening note was hidden and decided it was not a likely candidate for the detective's restless hands. Should he show him the note? To what end? O'Brien had already warned him the Tenderloin wasn't safe. He didn't want to hear I-told-you-so. Yet the note might contain clues the detective could decipher.

Before Bradshaw could make a decision, O'Brien asked, "What did you learn at the courthouse?"

"Nothing. I barely made a dent in the records."

"It's not a filing system designed for investigation. You have to know names and dates and counties to find anything. And if you knew all that, you wouldn't be searching records. This is a beauty." He was looking covetously at the polished oak horn.

"It's for a contest."

"Music and frivolity piped into your parlor. Listen in leisure," quoted O'Brien, revealing his knowledge of the contest. "I hadn't realized such magnificent horns would be part of the system."

"Horns will be available for an extra fee, but not ones as fine as this."

O'Brien chewed his lip, rubbing a restless hand over his closed mouth. Bradshaw had spent the past eight years of his life in a self-imposed social vacuum, but from within that protective sphere, he'd watched others, he'd studied them. And he now recognized that revealing gesture. O'Brien was struggling with information he was unsure of revealing.

At last, his hand dropped, and he cleared his throat. "Ralph— well, he bought his supplies on the cheap, from a supplier that makes a lot of money selling what it doesn't have. You tell this supplier you want food-grade alcohol for your tonic, he gives you a crate of bottles labeled grain alcohol. The contents could be anything."

"Was this a fight, then? Ralph against his supplier?"

O'Brien didn't reply. He picked up the transmitter Bradshaw had been working on earlier. It was about the size and shape of a large round tin of shoe polish, with open slots for admitting sound to the diaphragm. "Is this the contest transmitter? How sensitive is it?"

"I'll show you." He attached one end of a length of silk-covered wire to the transmitter, the other end to a telephone headset which he placed upon O'Brien's head.

"You stand there." He directed O'Brien to the far corner of the basement by the door, while he went with the transmitter and a dry cell battery to Mrs. Prouty's shelves of pickles on the opposite wall, trailing the cord between them. He opened a wooden floor chest and set the transmitter and battery inside, nestled between rubber hoses and garden tools. He closed the lid and moved as far from both O'Brien and the transmitter as he could get.

He whispered, "Can you hear me?"

"Ah! Crystal clear! Is that thing picking up your voice from inside the chest? Whisper something else."

"Is the drug supplier operating in my neighborhood?"

"No, I still don't know why Ralph came up here, or died up here. Maybe he was being chased, or followed. He could have come up here to camp in Volunteer Park for the night. It's quiet and safe. It's not permitted, of course, but tramps do it all the time."

"And then what? Was he so ill he became lost? Turned down my back lane by accident? It doesn't seem likely."

"Only because it was your back lane, Ben. You could accept a random abandonment anywhere else." O'Brien pulled off the headset with a satisfied smile, and they met again at the workbench.

O'Brien asked, "Where will you position that at the theater? How far away can it be from the stage?"

"Suspended above the seats in the fourth row, and above the stage. Emily couldn't be alone where she's now hiding. Someone must be helping her. Why haven't they come forward for protection?"

O'Brien rubbed his jaw and mouth again, but his reply came quickly enough. "She could be with people who are as leery of the police as they are afraid of her father's killer."

"You know who it is? Or have an idea?"

O'Brien nodded at the transmitter on the workbench. "That's why I'm here."

"What? The Seattle Grand? Emily's at the Grand? But that's above Yesler. You said Ralph's death was, how did you put it, 'tangled in the Tenderloin'."

"It is. The Seattle Grand sits north of the deadline, but that's an arbitrary line. Emily's not there, Ralph's supplier…listen, Ben, your dean of chemistry's report told me more than it told Cline."

He paused and met Bradshaw's gaze squarely. "If I make you privy to something that must remain secret, even from your household, that puts you at risk, are you willing to know?"

"Will it help us find Emily?"

"It's our best shot."

"Then yes. Of course, yes."

O'Brien took a deep breath. "Sit down."

They sat on stools, side-by-side, at the workbench. O'Brien lowered his voice.

"Ever heard of phenacetin?"

"What? The fever drug? Yes, of course."

"Have some in your medicine cabinet?"

"I don't know. Mrs. Prouty gets prescriptions for Bayer aspirin now."

"Hmm, so does my wife. If you have any phenacetin, throw it out. A few weeks ago, I was approached by the Feds and a German whose name you don't need to know. This German works for Bayer, the firm that holds the patent to phenacetin."

"Something wrong with it?"

"Most likely. It was introduced into the United States ten years ago and took over the market. It's now in something like eighty percent of all prescriptions. It's only supposed to be brought into the country through official channels, duty paid. But more than half of the phenacetin circulating in the country doesn't enter legally, it's smuggled in."

"To avoid custom fees," Bradshaw said.

"I believe in patents, Ben. Folks ought to be rewarded for their hard work and ingenuity. But I don't think patents have any place in medicine, and I especially don't like a German company forcing Americans to pay more for a drug than is necessary."

"Yet you told the Germans you would work on their investigation."

"A federal investigation for the United States. For three reasons. Duty taxes on imported phenacetin keep our fighting boys armed and clothed and fed. Second, the smugglers don't care about saving lives. It's all about profit, and they double their profit by cutting the smuggled drug with other cheaper drugs. They usually mix phenacetin with acetanilid."

"That's the crystal residue the dean found in Ralph's."

"Exactly."

"He said it was a fever drug."

"It's a lot like phenacetin, reduces fever and pain, only it's far cheaper, and far more toxic. When I give my daughters a drug to bring down a fever, I want it to work safely, not hurt them."

"And the third reason you said yes to this investigation?"

"The same as your own. To help Emily."

"Did Ralph Hopper sell smuggled phenacetin?"

"There was none in the wagon, but I believe when he bought supplies to make his tonic, he stumbled on the phenacetin smuggling ring. I believe he learned more than he was supposed to, so someone laced a case or two of his tonic with poisons they had ready to hand with the intent of ruining his business. Methyl alcohol and carbolic acid are common, sold everywhere. But acetanilin is only sold by prescription. The smugglers have it, and I think they used it. And I've discovered that they're operating out of the Seattle Grand."

"Mr. Fisher?" Bradshaw thought of the manager's concern for profits.

"Possibly, but I'm almost dead certain it's a few of the traveling players and the stage manager."

"Why poison Hopper's customers?"

"To threaten him so he'd be scared silent, leave town. He didn't go, and I think he wasn't silent. He threatened their business, and so they followed him, and silenced him."

A chill ran up Bradshaw's arms. "Emily saw him silenced. And Emily knows what her father knows."

"If we find the smugglers, we find Ralph's killer."

"And Emily?"

"With her father's killer behind bars, my hope is she'll feel safe enough to come out of hiding."

Bradshaw reached up to the box of brass screws and his fingertips found the folded note. He handed it to O'Brien, saying,

"This might provide clues." He watched O'Brien read, braced for recriminations.

O'Brien's expression went blank. He refolded the note and tucked it into his watch pocket. "I hope you plan on heeding this warning." He avoided eye contact, for which Bradshaw was grateful.

Chapter Fourteen

O'Brien's idea had been not only to task Bradshaw with poking about the theater, but also to listen in at the Seattle Grand using his contest invention and a secret wire strung to O'Brien's personal listening station.

But that was impossible. The components of Bradshaw's contest entry would only be hooked up for testing and the competition itself, and the transmitters would only be in the main hall. What was needed was his far-fetched eavesdropping device, portions of it anyway, with sensitive transmitters placed secretly throughout the theater. O'Brien had been thrilled with the idea, and together, they'd developed a plan.

Hidden telephone lines would bring the overheard sounds to the building adjacent the theater where O'Brien was now renting a room for the purpose. He also was hiring three stenographers and swearing them to secrecy. They were to work in shifts, selectively noting every bit of conversation unrelated to a musical production. The task would be challenging, with the stenographers having to make intelligent choices when multiple conversations were relayed. They might also hear conversations unsuitable for a woman's ears. O'Brien was looking for women over forty who were either married or widowed, and so less likely to be shocked by rough language.

There was no time to develop any sort of mechanical recording scheme, and hiring the stenographers made recording unnecessary. Efficiency and the need for speed trumped invention.

Bradshaw set right to work, and that evening, when Mrs. Prouty shouted down the stairs that dinner was ready, Bradshaw heeded the call, but he didn't join Justin at the dining table. He piled his plate with fricasseed chicken and stewed vegetables, tried not to be affected by the sight of his boy looking so small and alone at the big table, set a stern face for Mrs. Prouty as he passed through the kitchen and plunged down to the basement again.

Twelve hours later, Justin came down the stairs dressed for school and bearing the morning newspaper. The plate was still full, the chicken congealed in its sauce, the vegetables looking dredged from the compost.

Justin climbed on a stool and cocked his head. "Did you stay up all night long?"

"I slept a bit."

"Mrs. Prouty says your bed's not been slept in. And you're supposed to come up for breakfast."

"Mmm. Are you ready for school?"

"Yes. Do you want me to read you the headlines?"

This was a favorite morning activity for Justin, begun the year before when his reading skills took a big leap.

"Sure," Bradshaw said, although he didn't.

"*Friday, 13 September*—hey, it's Friday the 13th! Bad luck today."

"Superstition. It's no different than any other day."

"*President McKinley Takes a Turn for the Worse,*" Justin continued. Bradshaw felt a twinge of alarm. The news had been so good yesterday, he'd begun to believe the president would survive. "That's in great big black letters. That sounds like bad luck to me. Is he going to die?"

"I don't know son. The doctors are doing all they can for him."

"*Heading Home: Steamship Seattle to Return from Skagway. $150,000 in gold dust reported aboard.* That's not so much."

If he hadn't been so tired, he knew Justin's remark would have made him laugh. "You've been spoiled by reports of millions coming down. That would buy nearly a hundred houses like ours."

"The money doesn't belong to just one miner, it says that's how much about two hundred of them have altogether. That's just…" the boy paused, screwing up his mouth and looking at the ceiling, "seven-hundred fifty each, right?"

Bradshaw paused, doing the math in his own head. "Right." Pride penetrated his grumpy mood.

"Uncle Henry's kit cost more than that, didn't it?"

"More than double, I expect, with passage and the cost of setting up a camp at his claim."

Justin shook his head like a wise sage. "Not worth the trip, it seems to me. Do you suppose Uncle Henry is having better luck?"

"Knowing him, no. Now off you go, young man."

"OK, but you better come up for breakfast. Mrs. Prouty is awful mad."

Bradshaw trailed up behind Justin and a few minutes later stood on the front porch with a mug of coffee steaming into the cool air, watching the boy join Paul and race off down the street with a wave.

He'd hoped to avoid a confrontation with Mrs. Prouty by returning to his workshop through the basement door at the back of the house, but she'd guessed his intention and stood waiting inside.

"I won't stand for it, Professor."

"I'm in no mood, Mrs. Prouty. Please go upstairs."

"You keeled over, dead to the world for a full day after searching for that girl."

"And she's still missing."

"Burying yourself in the basement to win a stupid contest ain't doing her any good. It's a sickness with you, Professor. Obsession! You get a notion and can't let it go until it about kills you. You told me you'd not do it again and here you are like a mad man."

"It's either me looking for the child on the streets, or down here working on this contest. You should be glad I'm home."

"You ain't home, you're gone. Your mind's gone from your home and family, you're gone from the dining table. You're even gone from the university, and what good would it do any of us if you were to lose your job?"

"Leave me be, Mrs. Prouty! Your interference is not welcome. Get upstairs and do your job and leave me to mine!"

He grabbed a penciled list and his old hat hanging by the door.

"Where do you think you're going dressed like that?"

He was going downtown for parts, and he was in no mood to answer to her like a schoolboy. He was so tired, he'd forgotten he was in his grubby clothes, but he didn't want to please her by going upstairs to change. He smashed the hat on his head and marched out.

◇◇◇

He went first to Acme Electric Supply, where his appearance was noted but not mentioned. Mr. Daily himself had been known to appear tattered when in the throes of invention.

Next, he ducked into Woodworth's Hardware for a new set of clamps. The bell jangled pleasantly as he entered, and the white-aproned clerk behind the glass-case counter, busy with a customer, lifted a hand in greeting.

The walls of the store were lined floor to ceiling with shelves loaded with labeled boxes, bins, drawers, and crates of various hardware items for sale. Bradshaw was known here, although not so well as at Acme, and he didn't have backroom or behind-the-counter privileges.

Bradshaw strode to where he knew the vise clamps to reside, and stood before the glass-display counter examining the selection as best he could from a distance.

"Professor Bradshaw!" Mr. Woodworth emerged from behind the black cloth of the backroom. A handsome man of around sixty years, with silver hair and a fit physique marred only by a slight favoring of one leg, Woodworth radiated an aura of intelligence, discipline, and kindness.

"Good morning—no make that afternoon, Professor. For neighbors, we see far too little of one another."

"Yes," Bradshaw agreed without apology. He saw just as much of his neighbors as he wished. "I only stopped in for a vise clamp. Anvil model that swivels." He pointed at the shelf. Mr. Woodworth put down the paper to retrieve the vise anvil.

"This?"

"Hmm." Bradshaw lifted it, testing its weight for sturdiness. He set it down gingerly on the glass and spun the lever to see how tightly the jaws fastened.

"Mr. Daily tells me you and he are competitors at the Seattle Grand. I've got a wire coming to my house. My wife is looking forward to all the entertainments." He nodded at the vise. "Is this for your invention?"

"Hmmm." Being evasive was a habit for Bradshaw when it came to his inventions.

Mr. Woodworth took no offense. "Say, I hear you found the owner of that peddler's wagon dead not far from our street. What happened, do you know? Reggie says it's official police business, and I interpret that to mean the case isn't yet solved."

Bradshaw looked up from the vise.

"Reggie? Oh, you mean Detective March." What had March said? That the Woodworth's were like a second family? "He's some sort of relative?"

A glowing pride suffused Mr. Woodworth's demeanor. "I'd call him 'son' but that would be disrespectful to his parents, who are also very dear to us. Reggie's father was our driver and gardener when we lived in San Francisco, and his mother was our cook. Their other son was fully grown when Reggie came along. A surprise baby, as they say. He grew up in our kitchen, and the rest of the house for that matter. My girls treated him like a little prince. Spoiled him a bit, but it didn't do him much harm. Bright boy. I paid for his education, and he came up here to work with me in the family business."

"Oh?" It was hard to imagine Detective March working behind the counter, selling clamps and door locks.

"Well, you can guess the rest. He was bit by gold fever and lure of excitement up north. I knew it would be a good experience for him. So I financed his kit. He left a boy, although past twenty, and came home a man. I never expected he'd come home a rich man."

"Did you see the wagon yourself, the night it was left?"

Mr. Woodworth paused, seeming unable to quickly transition away from his golden boy.

"Why, no. I got home from a business dinner at about midnight. That one there, as a matter of fact." He scooped up the newspaper and handed it Bradshaw. A quick scan of the front page article, "Seattle Business League Annual Meeting," told him Mr. Woodworth had indeed been in attendance until very late at the Butler Hotel, discussing Seattle's future.

"I didn't notice anything. Was it there then?"

"It seems so. And the child."

"Child?"

"The peddler's child, Emily Hopper. She was hiding in the lane all night." Mr. Woodworth's mouth gaped. "Didn't Detective March tell you?"

"That's like him, not wanting to worry me or my wife. I wouldn't have known about you finding the dead peddler if I hadn't read it in the newspaper. I've got to admit, I sleep better at night not knowing the sort of things Reggie must deal with on the streets. He did tell me you're now a sleuth for the police department. Says you're invaluable."

"No, no, I only advise on electrical matters."

"I'll ask Albert if he saw the wagon, if you like, when he comes for me." Mr. Woodworth checked his pocket watch. "He's out back now to take me to lunch. I'd be pleased if you joined me."

"No," Bradshaw said without thinking. "Thank you for the invitation, I have to get back to work, and I'm not dressed." He held out his arms to show off his shabbiness.

"I did wonder, but you inventors have a reputation for eccentricity. We'll dine another time. Do come talk to my driver and see what he remembers."

Woodworth's handsome coach stood in the back cobbled alley. The driver climbed down when they approached. He wore the collar of his black uniform turned up against the wind and spitting rain that had swept in since Bradshaw left home. Bradshaw had seen Albert a few times over the years, although not recently, and he couldn't recall if they'd ever spoken. He was a man nearing fifty years, with graying hair and a serious manner that he knew Mrs. Prouty found irritating. In his tidy uniform with brass buttons, something about him struck Bradshaw as familiar. The full cheeks, the thick hair, the blue eyes. He was an older, faded, somber version of the golden boy.

"I understand you're Detective March's brother." Bradshaw extended a hand.

"I am," Albert said wearily, but his handshake was firm, his palm rough.

Mr. Woodworth chuckled. "Albert took over when his father retired and is invaluable to me and my wife. We almost lost him. He went up north like Reggie for a year or so, but his bad luck was our good fortune." He gave Albert a firm pat on the shoulder. Albert turned his head away and stared down the cobbled alley. "The Professor is wondering if you noticed that abandoned peddler's wagon in the lane the night before McKinley was shot. Or a child. Seems the peddler's child was in the lane all night as well! Where is she now, Professor? I trust she's been returned to relatives or an orphanage?"

"She's missing." Bradshaw watched Albert's unflinching profile. "Did you notice anything?"

Albert lifted his chin and took a breath before turning a somber, almost defiant face to Bradshaw. "I did indeed." His pleasant tone contrasted with his glare. "After I saw Mr. Woodworth to the door, I went down the lane to tell the driver to move along and let me by. There wasn't anyone in sight. I had to back out and my Sally doesn't like to back out. Coaxed her with sugar lumps."

He'd heard as much from Mrs. Prouty, but he thanked Albert for the information and let Mr. Woodworth get on to his lunch. He headed for the streetcar with his new table vise nestled in straw in a small wooden box, body bent against the blowing rain. Maybe O'Brien was right. Maybe the only reason he was mystified over the location of the abandonment of the wagon was because it had been in his own back lane.

Chapter Fifteen

The slap of the newspaper hitting the porch awakened Bradshaw's hearing before the rest him could struggle up from the blackness of sleep. Birdsong followed, and the metallic rattle of the newspaper boy's bicycle chain. He lifted his head from his arms where he was slumped over his workbench and rubbed his stubbled face. His brain was a muddled mess, his neck ached, and he couldn't shake the edge-of-sleep image of the newspaper hitting the porch. There was a ghostly quality to it, both urgent and hopeless.

He climbed the stairs to find Mrs. Prouty standing in the middle of the kitchen, clutching the newspaper. Her stricken face told him even before the bold black headlines. President McKinley was dead.

He pressed a hand to her shoulder. She patted it, shaking her head, her lips pressed tight. Her eyes dashed to his, full of anguish. He swallowed the lump in his throat, only to find it brought his emotions closer to the surface. He pressed Mrs. Prouty's shoulder again.

A moment later, he stood before his son's closed door. He turned away, and went into the bathroom to wash and shave and brush his teeth. Only then, after he'd changed into clean clothes and looked the image of a steady and reliable father, did he tap on Justin's door.

The boy was awake, still in bed, flying a model of Dumont's cigar-shaped airship over a fleet of pirate ships. For a moment,

Bradshaw was distracted by the sight, the mix of technology, past and futuristic, which existed side-by-side now, at the dawn of the twentieth century. It was an exciting time to be alive, to be a child.

Yet today came also with terrible troubles.

Justin brought the airship in for a landing, then sized up his father. "You going to work?"

"No, son. The newspaper's just come with some very serious news I wanted to talk to you about."

Justin cocked his head. "Did the president die?"

"Yes."

"Who's gonna be president now?"

"Theodore Roosevelt. He's a bright and brave man."

"He was a Rough Rider."

"That's right." Bradshaw sat at the edge of the bed, and Justin moved closer to lean against him. He picked up the airship again and held it on his lap.

"What if someone shoots Mr. Roosevelt?"

He wanted to deny the possibility. To assure his son that the new president was safe, that the world was safe.

He couldn't. "It's not likely to happen. He will be well guarded. I thought we'd spend the day together. Don't you have a new puzzle? A thousand pieces, isn't it?"

"Five hundred. Aren't you working on your invention?"

"I'm taking a break."

"Paul and I are going dig a hole in his backyard today."

"Why?"

"To see how far down we can get. Carter, he's in the fourth grade, he said if you dig down deep enough you can see China."

The teacher in Bradshaw wanted to explain the absolute impossibility of such a feat, about the diameter of the earth, the layers of granite, the debate over the composition of the earth's core, as well as the fact that even if you could dig straight through the entire planet, you would find not China, but the South Atlantic Ocean.

The little boy yet lingering in Bradshaw remembered doing the exact same thing. He'd dug alone. He hadn't had a best friend across the street when he was growing up. With the memory came the feel of the shovel in his hands and the thrill of anticipation. One more shovel-full, he'd kept telling himself. When he'd finally given up, the hole had been over his head and his father had taken into him town for ice cream to celebrate his effort.

It could be that such faith in foolish dreams as a child, the willingness to slave over something in order to achieve an impossible but coveted goal, was what helped boys become men, and men become inventors.

"You'll have to wait for next Saturday. The Mayor has asked everyone to be quiet for the next few days, as a way of showing our respect."

"Digging isn't loud."

"Even so, let's work on the puzzle today, shall we?"

Justin reluctantly nodded.

Mrs. Prouty changed her plans as well. She said it wouldn't be proper to spend her usual Saturday with her cousin, lunching at Frederick & Nelson, and they couldn't take in a show at the Third Avenue Vaudeville even if they wanted to because all the theaters and places of entertainment had been asked to close. She stayed home, puttering in the kitchen, baking batches of bread that filled the house with the comforting smell of warm yeast, and joining Bradshaw and Justin at the dining table where they'd spread the puzzle pieces and began to lock together the outer edges.

That night, for the first time in perhaps two years, Justin asked to sleep in Bradshaw's bed. The boy slept well, but his limbs were active, as if in his dreams he ran and played as he had been prevented from doing during the day. Bradshaw slept very little. He lay watching his son, memorizing the lines of his face, the curve of his cheek, the shape of his nose that was beginning to hint at what he would look like as an adult. This was a moment in time that would never happen again.

He recalled other such moments when he'd taken time to focus exclusively on the most important person in his life. Justin as an infant, as a plump toddler. Those versions of his son were gone. On this somber night of the president's passing, it felt to Bradshaw like those versions of his son had vanished completely, as if death had stolen them.

He thought of Emily, alone in the world. Where was she sleeping on this night? Was she with adults she felt safe with? Was she unsettled over the death of the president? After losing her father, witnessing his death, could anything as distant as a political leader's assassination touch her? On the night her father died, she'd been completely alone. The next night, she'd been warm and dry and safely snuggled in the cubby in Justin's room. His son had provided what she needed: shelter, food, and companionship.

Bradshaw reached out to his son and gently touched the boy's warm hand. He didn't wake, but his small hand curled into his father's and held tight.

Chapter Sixteen

Bradshaw stifled a yawn and sat up straighter. Beside him, Justin sat quietly, his head resting on the back of the pew, gazing dreamily at the dust moats high in the rafters.

"…and so as we gather today," continued Father McGuinness, "united in faith, united in grief, I ask you to consider the experiment of this great nation. An experiment in freedom that is surely mankind's destiny, and yet with freedom comes risk, and the opportunity for those with evil intentions to carry them out."

Bradshaw frowned over the priest's use of the term "experiment." Everywhere he turned, it seemed, the word appeared. It was being used in the most inappropriate places to indicate modern trends and change. Bradshaw especially didn't like the use of the word 'experiment' in regard to social conditions. Experiments included, of necessity, expendable components. Failure was a precursor to success. When the components were human, who had the audacity to use them, lose them, toss them away?

As the sermon unfolded, William McKinley's life and achievements were honored, his eternal soul prayed for, and the dark destructiveness of anarchy and its practitioners condemned.

"What evilness lurks in the hearts of men like Leon Czolgosz?" asked the priest, mangling the assassin's last name. "He was a timid boy who became a disgruntled man. He chose violence and destruction, but not with the bravery and self-sacrifice of a soldier. No, this assassin acted upon his own immoral weakness.

His stepmother said of him, 'Why, he was the biggest coward you ever saw in your life.'"

Bradshaw's chest tightened. The priest could have been describing Oscar Dalton. The quote from the stepmother had been in the newspaper earlier in the week, and Bradshaw had read with a clenched jaw. He didn't want to know the details of the young man's life, about the poverty of his childhood, his brother serving in the Philippines, his timidity and cowardice and obsession with socialism and anarchism. He'd finally thrust the paper aside, the details too similar to Oscar's own to bear contemplating. He wanted Leon to remain a stranger. Let someone else ache for the horrific tragedy of Leon Czolgosz.

It was enough for Bradshaw to feel this anguish over Oscar. He understood the forces that had driven Oscar to murder, but understanding was not condoning. Neither was it condemning. Oscar was troubled, disturbed, and yes, he'd committed mortal sins and would pay with his life. But evil? The sort of evil that deserved eternal damnation? No. That he couldn't see. And if he, who'd nearly been one of Oscar's victims, could see humanity and goodness yet within him, surely there was hope for his soul.

When the service was over, he spotted Detective March with the Woodworths as they rose from their pew and began down the aisle. The detective's brother Albert was not with them. Why? Mrs. Prouty didn't attend with Bradshaw and Justin only because she and her cousin belonged to the Episcopalian church, but he knew in some households lines between family and the help were more strictly observed. He glanced toward the back of the church, and there was Albert already at the door with a few other drivers in uniform. Did he resent his position, Bradshaw wondered? Relegated to the back pew while his favored little brother sat up front with the family?

He pondered the question briefly as he and Justin walked home, glad of his own small household and their simple routines. After breakfast, he set out again on foot to the King County Courthouse. A handful of silent protestors held picket signs that read, *Hang Daulton! Hang the Anarchist! Death to Anarchists!*

He averted his gaze and passed them undisturbed. A few minutes later, he was locked with Oscar inside his cell, wondering why he'd come.

Did he hope to find the words to get the boy to understand he'd done wrong? Find some way for him to redeem his soul before the inevitable hanging? He had failed in his attempt to appeal to Oscar directly. Perhaps he could use his sideways method to find a way into what remained of Oscar's humanity. The boy loved invention. They had that in common.

"If you wanted to increase the output of a telephone receiver so that it could be heard distinctly in a room without losing sound quality, what would you do?"

Oscar didn't speak for a few minutes, he barely moved. The news of McKinley's death was affecting him differently than Bradshaw expected. He'd thought he might find the boy elated. He was instead despondent. A moment passed with the electrical question hanging, before Bradshaw noticed Oscar's tension give way, his jaw and shoulders relax, and his thoughts turn inward to electrical matters.

"I'd amplify the signal," he finally said.

It was the obvious reply, like saying he'd make it louder. The calm pleasure in the faraway look in his eyes, however, told Bradshaw he was thinking of how to do it. Bradshaw's own approach, an electromagnetic amplifier, was a big improvement on existing devices and full of limitations. "What about distortion? How would you minimize it? Improve the fidelity of the sound?"

Oscar shook his head. "Go for a dive, Professor. You'll find what you need at the bottom of Elliott Bay."

Bradshaw was taken aback. Was Oscar provoking him? Or was he serious? Could that mysterious invention of his, now rotting in salt water, have telephonic applications?

"It's not too late for you to do some good in the world, Oscar. You have the talent to do great things in your remaining time."

Oscar's eyes went blank. "They set the date for my hanging. I'll be dead in three weeks."

Bradshaw looked away from the emptiness of Oscar's stare, a vise gripping his heart. He swallowed, willing his emotions to settle. When he felt he could stand it, he looked at Oscar again and caught a glimpse of fear, of confusion, before the blank mask returned.

"Even more reason," Bradshaw said, his voice gravelly, "to admit you made grievous mistakes, and in your remaining time, give what you can of your talent." He had never meant anything more sincerely and less selfishly in his life, but Oscar took his words differently.

"Never thought of you as greedy, Professor. You're becoming one of them. I can't empower my enemy."

Bradshaw flinched, and anger flared. His efforts had been rewarded with rejection.

The guard came to let Bradshaw out. After the door clanked shut, Oscar said quietly, "Here's a hint, Professor. What I used for protection will soon be my eternity."

As he walked the few miles home through a misty rain, the coil of anger began to dissolve and Bradshaw pondered Oscar's hint. Protection could mean what he used while making his mysterious invention to keep from touching dangerous components. Or it could mean the material he used to insulate his components. In the small space of the cigar box, he must have used an insulating material able to withstand high temperatures and high current without breaking down or catching fire. His eternity? Did he still believe his murders had been for the greater good and that his eternity would be spent in comfort and glory? Or did he now understand the horror of his actions, and mean that his eternity would be spent in fire and brimstone?

Brimstone.

The bright yellow crystalline solid found at volcanic vents. The stuff of biblical hell. The element known as sulphur.

He turned his mind back to last May when Oscar had briefly displayed his invention at the canceled Electrical Exhibition. Bradshaw's hands had picked up a strong, offensive odor. The memory was powerful, as odor memories can be. In his mind, he relived seeing the mysterious cigar box connected to a collection of batteries, the steady blue arc at the terminals, Oscar's beaming pride, shaking hands with him, and then going down to the laboratory with President Graves. It was there he'd noticed the smell on his hands, and he'd thought it was a chemical reaction from all he'd touched upstairs and in the lab looking at various projects. Now he knew it wasn't.

Pure sulphur, powdered or in flakes or "flowers," smelled subtly of lit matches. When working with sulphur, the scent, meaning invisible traces, transfers to the hands where it then begins to react with the oil and sweat and natural bacteria on the skin, forming a new, organic compound that reeks like rotten eggs.

Sulphur had a high melting point, and slightly higher burning point. It was an excellent insulator and could withstand the intense heat generated by electric current. Oscar's mysterious invention inside the cigar box had been encased in molten sulphur.

"...dripping for a week, and I know you don't like working with the plumbing."

Bradshaw blinked. He was standing in his kitchen beside Mrs. Prouty, looking into the white sink. A drop of water formed at the end of the brass spout, swelled, then plopped into the enamel.

"Do you want to fix it or shall I get a plumber?"

"A plumber," he mumbled, then turned the hot and cold taps and began to scrub his hands with Mrs. Prouty's bar of lemon soap. Washing away the sulphur stink that was there only in his mind. He tried to recall walking home from the courthouse, crossing streets, entering the house and couldn't.

"It wouldn't take you long," she said, and he knew it annoyed her that she had to call someone in when an engineer lived in the house. He'd tried to explain that water and electricity were entirely different. An expert at one could fail entirely at another. He'd studied water pressure, of course, and current flow, and hydraulics. Water, being visible and tangible and easily measurable in all its states and movements, aided the understanding of the more nebulous electricity.

But knowledge of hydraulics wasn't the same as mastering the mechanics of pipes and washers and fittings. He shut off the tap, watching for the drip, thinking of pressure and leakage. He twisted both taps open, closed, open, closed, thinking of pressure control, switching mechanisms, electric current, and methods of transforming voltages by first altering frequency. On and off. On and off.

When he next came to an awareness of his surroundings, he was in the basement with the door wide open to let the volcanic fumes of melting powdered sulphur escape and Mrs. Prouty was calling down in a voice subdued by yesterday's tragedy that she didn't think the smell made a good accompaniment to her Sunday roast but he was to come up to dinner anyway.

He washed, changed clothes, and joined Justin and Mrs. Prouty at the table. He didn't head again to the basement until Justin was tucked snugly in bed, a chapter of Kipling's *The Jungle Book* read, and Mrs. Prouty had retired to her room for the night.

He hadn't foreseen her returning to the kitchen in her bathrobe and nightcap. He had the basement door open, and the light filtered up to the dark kitchen, revealing her silent, disappointed face. It hurt him more than any amount of shouting. He wanted to explain, to tell her it wasn't obsession over invention driving him now, so soon after the president's death. It was the need to help Emily.

He couldn't say it. Besides his promise to O'Brien, he knew telling Mrs. Prouty meant endangering her.

He stepped down the stairs, pulling the door closed behind him.

The sulphur, which had been a deep amber the color of Missouri's eyes when melted, had hardened into a golden yellow block. He longed to start experimenting. He knew he hadn't time. He shouldn't have taken the time this afternoon to melt the sulphur, but it hadn't been a decision he'd made consciously.

He stood immobile for a full minute, physically battling what Mrs. Prouty so feared, obsession with invention. Two directions cried out to him; a third spoke with the innocent voice of a child.

Oscar's revolutionary invention would have to wait, and he couldn't take time to improve his amplified loud-talker. His contest components worked, they would have to do. Quality must be sacrificed. For Emily. If he lost the contest, so be it.

It went against every fiber of his being to set aside both a compelling new idea and perfecting one he would be making public. In a foul mood, he spent the next several hours, gathering and partially assembling all he would need for his contest entry.

It was three in the morning when he was done. He piled the crates of components at the foot of the stairs, disgusted because he knew the loud-talker was flawed. He barely resisted the urge to give the crates a brutal kick.

Chapter Seventeen

Trust no one, O'Brien had said. Bradshaw, flat on his back on a hard rafter in the dark, dusty crawl space above Victor's back stage office at the Seattle Grand, thought about those words and marveled at how easily he had accepted them. He marveled at how easily he had accepted this entire, insane scheme. Obsessed with finding Emily, obsessed with the idea of testing an idea in the real world, he hadn't thought through the consequences.

As a result, here he was, trapped above Victor's office, unable to so much as twitch without revealing his location. Sweat trickled down his temples. He could hear Victor's muffled voice below him, but not clearly enough to distinguish words. He could have been outlining the entire smuggling operation, for all Bradshaw knew. The microphone transmitter in his hand was capable of hearing, but he'd not yet connected the receiver, and the wires ran far out of reach to Mr. Fisher's central station room.

He strained to hear. The room below was silent now. Had Victor left? He hadn't heard the door. He remained still. The theater was closed to the public until Friday, on orders from the mayor. Victor was here, a few musicians, and the company of players rehearsing a new show. A lively act was under way now, the sounds carried faintly to him. Had Victor gone out to oversee?

He had no way of knowing. The man could be sitting at his desk directly below him. How would he ever explain why he was stringing wires up here if he were caught?

It wasn't just this investigation and Emily's safety at stake, but Bradshaw's reputation. He was spying on the people of the Seattle Grand. Neither Mr. Fisher, nor the University president nor the Board of Regents would find that upstanding behavior. If he were caught, he would lose his job.

Why hadn't he thought of that before now? Was it even legal for him to be doing this for O'Brien? If he could have risked making the noise, he would have groaned.

He listened again. Silence. He would wait another few minutes. His installation was nearly complete. Mr. Fisher had made his task so easy, eagerly agreeing to have a loud-talker wired in his office so that he could hear rehearsals and productions from there, delighted with the idea of a loud-talker in the back-stage hallway for the actors to hear their cues. Both of those installations had given Bradshaw the opportunity to install the secret listening devices. Mr. Fisher had balked, at first, at his request for a cable line to be strung to Bradshaw's own house. He hadn't told O'Brien he'd be making the request. He was fairly certain O'Brien wouldn't approve.

Mr. Fisher had said, "I've already agreed to connect you to the theater line."

"Yes, and that will allow me to hear exactly what your subscribers will hear. A separate cable would be composed of several wires bringing me individual sound components that I can analyze and determine where improvements can be made." He'd been surprised at how easily the lie had formed. "I will pay all expenses."

"The copper wire doesn't come cheaply, Professor. And you'll need, what, two or more miles? You're up on Gallagher?"

"Yes, but the investment is worth it to me. I have several other projects that could benefit from what I learn."

"A new invention? Something revolutionary?"

"One can always hope."

"Very well, then. I'll take care of it straight away."

He'd left to do Bradshaw's bidding, and all had gone well until Victor returned to his office while Bradshaw was above it.

Well. He couldn't stay up here all day. Soon, his whereabouts would be questioned, someone would see his ladder propped under the attic access panel in the hall and come looking for him.

He made a few tentative moves, then stopped to listen. When no shouts came, he inched a bit more until he could position the microphone on its support bracket. He began to back up, slowly and quietly at first, then as he sensed he was above hall space, with more speed and less care. He was halfway down the ladder, breathing a sigh of relief, when a shout nearly toppled him from the rungs.

"What the hell are you doing up there?"

He gripped the rung, heart racing and vertigo threatening with a nauseating clench of his gut.

"Vic, that's our Professor. He's installing his wires for the contest."

He looked down to find Victor glaring and Miss Darlyrope smiling up at him.

"The other two didn't go poking around up there. I heard you clear down the hall!"

"The other two didn't install a loud-talker, Vic. Look at this, we'll be able to hear what's happening on stage from back here. I won't miss any entrances."

Bradshaw stepped off the ladder, feeling clammy and sick, as Miss Darlyrope showed Victor the horn projecting into the hall from its wall-mounted base.

"I'll believe it when I see it," grumbled Victor. Miss Darlyrope, several inches taller than Victor, smiled down at him and rumpled his hair, and he strode off with a swagger "to see what those idiots on stage thought they were doing with the chorus number."

She turned a flushed face and anxious eyes to Bradshaw. He wished he could thank her for distracting Victor, but "trusting no one" included Miss Darlyrope. He wiped his face with his handkerchief and concentrated on breathing calmly. What if Victor decided to climb up later to inspect Bradshaw's work? There was nothing he could do to prevent it. Even if Victor did climb up and see the wires strung in all directions, would he understand what that meant? Most people had little idea of how anything electrical worked, but it didn't take an engineer to understand that wires led to electrical devices. If he followed the wires to the microphone…well, Bradshaw could only hope that Victor's blustering was territorial bravado and not a true suspicion that Bradshaw was up to no good.

Miss Darlyrope apologized for being so angry toward him when he'd come in the week before. "I was upset about our Daisy. I had no right to turn that against you."

"I understand. How is Miss Daisy?"

"Oh, it's dreadful. The doctors say if she hasn't recovered by now, she'll be blind for life. I'd be tempted to kill that Ralph, if he weren't already dead."

"He was drinking his own tonic, Miss Darlyrope, I doubt he was aware it contained poison."

"He should have known. He was selling it, making money off of innocents like Daisy. Who else is there to blame? Oh, let's please not talk about it or I'll be too upset to work. What do you think of the new show?"

"It sounds lively."

"Mr. Fisher said audiences will be ready for a good laugh when we reopen, and I daresay he's right. The name is certainly catchy. *The Folly on the Trolley*."

"Featuring Miss Darlyrope. Sounds like it was written for you."

Her expressive face flashed secretively. "Might have been."

"You don't travel with the rest of the players? I was under the impression you were all going up to Vancouver."

"They went, that was the Pacific Players Touring Company. Now we have a visiting company from Portland. They're actually quite good."

"You sound surprised."

"Well, they're new, not much experience. I'm a regular, the star attraction you might say."

"And Mr. Fisher says."

"He'd better." She gave him a wink that was full of teasing, that held him, for a moment, spellbound and admiring. He thought of her floating through the lobby of the Eskimo Hotel, the manager and peddler's rapt attention, and he knew he currently looked as smitten.

"Does Victor have a brother?" He was recalling how much that peddler looked like Victor, right down to the bravado.

"Might have." She shrugged as if she didn't much care. "Daisy was my understudy, such a little star she was becoming. Such a lovely, pure voice."

"Losing her sight is a tragedy, but not the end of her singing, surely. Think of Helen Keller. Born deaf and blind, she has learned to speak, goes to school, and is much admired by the entire world."

Miss Darlyrope's red mouth dropped open. "Why Professor, I hadn't thought of her. I suppose there might be a way for Daisy to perform again. She might even have a certain tragic appeal. You've given me hope." She hugged him fiercely, and he was enveloped in her perfume and pressed against her soft flesh. She laughed at his flushed face as she pulled away.

Late that night, armed with his canvas tool bag, Bradshaw met Detective O'Brien in the alley beside the darkened Seattle Grand.

"How did you get on today?"

"Fine."

"No trouble with the installation?"

"No."

"Learn anything?"

"New company of players from Portland."

Together they dug a ditch and buried an insulated cable across the alley to the building where O'Brien had rented a room on the third floor. They brought the cable up the shadow-line of the decorative trim, and finally through a small window overlooking the alley.

Inside the room, O'Brien had supplied a desk and two chairs, and Bradshaw had supplied two telephone headsets and a desktop switchboard he'd adapted for the purpose. He explained to O'Brien, who would explain to the stenographers, how to listen to all five lines at once—the four secret and the one from the performance hall—or one at a time, flipping between one location to the next, searching for potentially important conversations.

The next afternoon, Bradshaw returned to the theater to complete the installation. By four o'clock, the time he'd set with O'Brien to run a test with one of the stenographers ensconced at her post, his work was complete, and he was ready for Mr. Fisher's unwitting help.

Mr. Fisher sat behind his desk in his luxurious office and, as directed, flipped the switch beneath the polished horn. Miss Darlyrope's singing filled the room. Bradshaw pasted a grim smile on his face, while every crackle and warble distorting the young actress' voice made his skin crawl.

"...and when he jumped on the trolley, my true love saw his folly, too late to keep..."

"My dear, Professor, that is indeed marvelous. It's as if I'm right down in the seats. Marvelous, marvelous!" Mr. Fisher's pleasure was genuine, but it didn't erase Bradshaw's disgust. Yes, it was better than any other loud-talker currently available, but it was not what he'd envisioned, not what he was capable of.

"...why would he go and do a thing like that? When he knows that trolley is bound for..."

"The volume can be adjusted here." Bradshaw demonstrated by twisting the knob. Mr. Fisher imitated him, delighting in the rise and fall of the sounds.

"Will you assist me in testing the backstage horn?"

"Indeed, I will!"

"You'll need your keys. I'd like to be sure the horn can be heard from the dressing rooms and offices."

Without hesitation, Mr. Fisher pulled his large key ring from his top drawer.

Once backstage, Bradshaw stood in the hallway beside the wall-mounted horn, the base open, a screwdriver in hand as if prepared to make adjustments. The sounds of the rehearsal, with Victor calling out curtain and lighting adjustments, poured from the horn.

Mr. Fisher, eager as a schoolboy, unlocked one room after another and stepped inside leaving the doors ajar. He hummed as instructed, under the impression he was judging the horn under everyday conditions when the rooms would have humming and chatting actors.

"Yes, I can hear!" He would call out after humming, then move on to the next room. He moved to Victor's office, and Bradshaw joined him. The windowless room held a desk, filing cabinets, a couple wooden chairs, and all manner of papers, scraps of costumes, crates and boxes stacked haphazardly. Colorful posters of past musical shows plastered the walls. Nothing obviously incriminating revealed itself, not even a single bottle of aspirin, and Mr. Fisher seemed unconcerned by Bradshaw's poking about.

"What are you looking for, Professor?"

"Oh, just ways to improve my system." He lowered his voice and whispered, as if divulging a secret, "It has uses beyond the stage."

He paced to the back of the room, mumbling under his breath, while Mr. Fisher beamed on him indulgently.

They moved to the prop room, over which the last of Bradshaw's transmitters sat listening. Victor was more meticulous in his care of this room. It was like walking into the well-organized attic of a compulsive packrat. Furniture of every style and type was stacked floor to ceiling. Tables, chairs, and bedsteads. Boxes labeled "curtains" and "dishes" and "candlesticks." Other cases indicated costumes for men, women, children, there was even one marked "dogs."

A tall wardrobe stood against the far wall before a door.

"Mr. Fisher, that wardrobe blocks a door. That could be a fire hazard."

"It only leads to the basement, Professor. No one goes down there but spiders."

Bradshaw gave the wardrobe a push and found it moved easily.

Mr. Fisher didn't flinch. "It's on rollers, Professor. It's a prop we use frequently. You'll find that most everything in this room has been modified one way or another to make it easy to quickly move about between scenes. Victor takes great pride in these props, and great care. He keeps this room locked so nothing walks away, if you know what I mean."

"More than you imagine."

Miss Darlyrope hit a lovely high note that carried to them from the hall, amazingly undistorted, and both Bradshaw and Mr. Fisher smiled.

"Marvelous," Mr. Fisher said.

"Quite," Bradshaw agreed.

A few minutes later, Mr. Fisher shook Bradshaw's hand with great satisfaction and returned to his office, and Bradshaw pressed open the heavy stage door into the alley. He wedged a wooden block in the jam to keep it from locking behind him. A single glance at the third floor window of the adjacent building told him all he needed to know. The blind was raised. His test had been successful. His devices had been overheard in each room, and the existence of the basement door in the prop room conveyed.

He turned his attention to the Sunset Telephone Company's forty-foot pole beside the building with its ten crossarms, each strung with a dozen lines. He followed the three theater lines. One provided telephone service, the second was the new musical service line, and the third was the slim cable heading off to his house. He followed its progress to the end of the alley and another forty-foot pole. There it dropped down to a large spool chained fast to the pole as a deterrent to thieves, who'd been known to attempt to roll away them away, and even climb poles to steal the wire right off the mounts. It came as a shock, in every sense of the word, when they sometimes grabbed hold of a live wire. Copper thieves didn't always know the difference between telephone and power lines.

But linemen were experts. Would the linemen who returned to continue the stringing notice the cable on the building across the alley? Would they wonder where it originated? Would they care? How would he explain if anyone began to ask questions?

He had his head tilted back, staring up the pole, when he heard, "Professor Bradshaw! That makes two places I never thought to see the likes of you."

Bradshaw lowered his gaze to find Patrolman Cox swaggering up to him.

"Good afternoon. I've entered the contest here at the Grand. Just checking the outbound lines. You going on duty?"

"On my way. I often swing by. These uptown theater people are a lively group, better trade than down in my district, if you get my meaning."

"No, I'm afraid not."

"Family man, eh? Well, I used to be. Got five of the blighters, but the Mrs. won't let me see'em. Won't let me see her either."

"Oh? Sorry."

Cox shrugged, then sniffed arrogantly. "Not sure I'm sorry. Frees me up. It's a dangerous job I've got. No room for worrying about the home front. She wants to live with her sister and put up with all the nonsense, let her, I say."

Bradshaw had no response to that. "You have an early shift tonight?"

"Putting in a few extra hours. There will be those individuals who try to take advantage of the official mourning time, while all the good citizens are at memorial services. Still, it'll be another dull night. Nothing like a national tragedy to put a damper on petty crime and drunkenness."

"I need to get going myself."

"Attending one of the services, are you?"

"I should be on my way."

He took his leave, and soon after, he was at the University, in the Administration Building's Denny Hall, with Justin, Mrs. Prouty, and Missouri Fremont, other members of the faculty, staff, and student body, their family and friends, paying their final respects to the twenty-fifth president of the United States.

Chapter Eighteen

The job was done, the listening devices installed, and O'Brien's stenographers trained and listening and scribbling. With McKinley officially laid to rest, Seattle and the nation breathed a sigh, and life was returning to normal. But Bradshaw felt at loose ends. Neither the theater's line nor his private cable had yet reached his house, and whenever he went down to the basement to focus on improving his loud-talker, his mind froze. Less than three weeks until the contest was held. Enough time, he told himself, to find a solution to the problem of distortion, or at least an improvement, if he could only get his mind to focus. He couldn't.

His concentration held better for the alluring prospect of Poulsen's wire recorder. He studied the concept, made a few sketches, gathered the basic materials, and began to build his own device. When he realized he couldn't, within reasonable time, complete a working model with the flexibility to switch between multiple telephone lines, he set the project aside to rig a telephone receiver to a sounding board and a Graphophone. A few experiments showed it to be a crude but effective way of recording short pieces of conversation, and it could be easily manually switched from one phone line to another.

His calendar held no inspiration, although he went through the motions, getting dressed, pedaling up to the University, organizing his teaching texts, and inventorying the laboratory equipment. He held office hours and met with students about the coming year and their future careers. He strolled the campus, pretending he didn't hope to catch a glimpse of Missouri, and he watched the surveyors and builders mark with small flags the footprint of the new Science Hall to be built over the coming winter.

Usually, this time of year brought him a deep satisfaction, and a pleasant sense of anticipation. The bluest skies in Seattle came in the fall, and often the fairest weather. The bite of the evening air, the fog rolling in from the Sound in the mornings, and the gusts of wind that sent the first leaves scuttling along the campus lawn all sang with the promise of the coming school year.

But this year, he felt robbed of the pleasure.

His outer life fell into an ordered pattern. His inner life was a disorganized mess. At night, he lay in bed awake, staring at the moon shadows on the ceiling, his mind unable to calm. He knew he should let go. Emily Hopper was not his child. He'd never even met her. She was ten years old, wise beyond her years from all accounts, able to survive, yet he felt as if his own child were missing and in danger. There was a nightmarish quality to the feeling.

He couldn't get hold of the reality of her, place her where she belonged, hear or see her properly. She was a ghost child, haunting him, taunting him for chasing her away. Even when he did manage to sleep, he'd find himself at the top of the stairs at his house in Boston, baby Justin in his arms, and his feet slipping out from under him. He'd feel himself fall, feel Justin slip from his grasp, and then he'd see Emily at the bottom of the stairs, fleeing from him as he reached out to her.

He'd get up at four and head down to the basement to tinker with a portable version of his listening device that he thought O'Brien might find useful in his police work. A secret, portable transmitting microphone would allow the detective to overhear conversations otherwise closed to him. And a microphone asked for no bribes.

After breakfast and seeing Justin off to school, he'd walk into town and check on the progress of the telephone lines. A mile from his house, he was able to distinguish his cable line, its journey slowed by the sheer volume of new phone and electric lines rising up the hill to the vacant lots waiting new owners. It was while on one of these early morning walks, eastward toward Lake Washington rather than into town, that he spied a traveling carnival setting up large tents in Madison Park.

The next morning, a Saturday, came dark and drizzly, but when Bradshaw woke Justin with the promise of a full day of carnival delights, the weather didn't dampen his spirits.

The drizzle had withdrawn to mere cloudiness by the time they arrived at Madison Park, now transformed into a wonderland of entertainments that beckoned with colorful tents, flags, and costumes, shouts and laughter and music. Mouthwatering fragrances greeted them as the smoke of roasting pits floated up to flavor the mist.

"Ben!" Detective O'Brien and his wife and three daughters had arrived minutes before and stood taking it all in. The sight of them, of O'Brien in particular, hit Bradshaw like a jolt out of a trance. He thought, at last, he could talk about what weighed so heavily on him to someone who understood.

O'Brien said, "You've never met my wife, Lorraine, have you?" She was a lovely woman, with shining black hair and eyes of light green, and skin that he'd heard described as alabaster. Her figure left no doubt as to her condition. O'Brien said it wouldn't be long now.

"A boy this time," said the lovely Lorraine, and was rewarded with a kiss on the cheek from her husband. She pushed him away with a laugh.

O'Brien introduced his children. Edith, aged two, and Clara, aged five, both had their mother's dark hair and fair skin. Lucy, the eldest at nine, had her father's looks, down to the freckles, and it seemed his courage.

"Professor," she asked boldly, "can your son go with me to see the tiger?"

Bradshaw wasn't about to force the boy to go off with a girl he didn't know, but Justin's face had lit up. "Can I?"

"Don't poke your fingers through the bars."

Lucy and Justin ran off to find the tiger, and Lorraine took the two little ones to see the ducks, which had nothing to do with the carnival, but were delighting the girls as they waddled across the grass.

"On duty?" asked Bradshaw.

"Not officially."

Bradshaw counted to ten, to keep from sounding too eager, then asked, "Hear anything useful yet?"

A gleam in O'Brien's eyes confirmed he had. "Victor isn't a fan of yours, Professor."

"No, I gathered that. I understand how the contraband must come in with the new actors, but how is it getting out?"

"You forget that Seattle isn't built on the ground. She sits on the ruins of the old city. That basement door in the prop room you told us about leads to Victor's distribution center."

O'Brien was, of course, alluding to the Great Fire of '89 that left twenty-nine city blocks ruined and smoldering. Before the fire, the tides had been a nuisance, always backing up the sewers and flooding basements. So rather than tear down the burned ruins, they buried them, and raised the city by several feet.

"The Seattle Grand and the Western Building next door sit on top of old basements. Some were completely filled in. Some bricked or planked over. No stretch of the imagination to think a man could find his way from one building to the other without ever being seen on the street."

"Who owns the Western?"

"The primary occupant, Cascade Accounting."

"I don't suppose they'd like a telephonic system installed in their offices?"

"Not necessary. One or two might be profiting from the use of certain passages, but the involvement doesn't go beyond that. Couriers come and go all the time, routine business. No one gives them a second glance. Everyone thinks they've got business upstairs, or downstairs, or the office down the hall." As O'Brien spoke, he continually scanned the crowd. Bradshaw noticed the sudden intensity of his gaze.

He looked where O'Brien was focused and saw nothing other than people having a good time.

"Excuse me a minute, Ben." The detective strolled to the crowd gathered around a raised platform where colorfully dressed fiddlers played an exotic tune. He stepped behind a man in an old brown wool overcoat and collared him unawares. The man struggled until O'Brien twisted an arm behind his back and pressed him into the waiting cuffs of a uniformed patrolman who'd quickly discerned the situation.

While the pickpocket was being dealt with, Justin came running, his face distraught.

Expecting to hear of some injury or trouble, Bradshaw dropped to one knee to be on Justin's level and he gripped the boy by his shoulders. The boy's cheeks were splotched red from exertion, but beneath he'd gone pale. Alarm filled his eyes.

"Brass buttons," Justin gulped. "Brass buttons, Dad. Emily saw them. I forgot. She said the man who killed her father wore brass buttons."

It wasn't what he'd expected to hear. He stood and looked around slowly, at the musicians on the stage with their dangling metallic buttons and bangles. At the brass-buttoned patrolman gripping the pickpocket, the gentleman in the audience in his military style brass-buttoned overcoat, the streetcar conductor in his brass-buttoned uniform grabbing a quick smoke at the edge of the park.

"I'm sorry I forgot." Justin's voice cracked, his face bunched up, near tears.

"It's OK, son. It's OK." He held Justin close, something the boy wouldn't publicly allow under normal circumstances. He was shaking. Lucy came running, slowing when she saw Justin in Bradshaw's arms. The puzzled look on her face told him she didn't understand what had made Justin run.

Bradshaw pressed Justin back to look into his face.

"What happened that made you remember?"

"We found a brass button on the ground, and Lucy said, 'dibs on the brass button' and I remembered."

"That's good you remembered, you don't need to feel bad that it took awhile. Memories are like that. Can you tell me about it? Do you remember now what Emily said?"

"Just what I told you before, she said someone killed her father, that's why she was alone and hiding. She said he had brass buttons and think I forgot because she was hungry and I was worried about getting caught going downstairs to get her something to eat."

"You've remembered now, and that's good. You don't need to be afraid."

"But Dad, there are so many men here with brass buttons. They're everywhere!" His voice pitched to near panic.

"Yes, there are. And none of them killed Emily's father."

"Are you sure?"

"Yes. You are safe here." He didn't want this memory, this knowledge, to make Justin fearful of men in uniform. He smiled, to show the boy that all was well. "Look, here comes Lucy." Bradshaw reached into his pocket for some coins. "Treat yourselves to some caramel candies." He pointed to the white-capped vendor in the red-and-white striped apron, just a few yards distant.

Justin hesitated. "Come with me?"

"I will wait right here for you. I can see you."

Justin showed Lucy the coins, and she followed him to the candy vendor. He looked once over his shoulder to be sure Bradshaw was watching.

As the children were choosing their treats, O'Brien returned, and Bradshaw quickly told him about the brass buttons.

The implication sat silent and heavy between them. O'Brien might not trust some of his fellow officers, but accusing a brass-buttoned patrolman of murder was something he would never do easily, or without substantial proof.

Accusing a detective's brother was only slightly less awkward. "Mr. Woodworth's driver was in the lane at midnight in his brass-buttoned uniform."

O'Brien arched a brow. "March's brother Albert. Yes, I know. I'm not completely without investigating skills. He's not our man. Albert left the Woodworths' at eleven to fetch his employer home and they returned together at midnight. Until then he was busy getting the carriage from the stables and driving into town. Your neighbor Mr. Stewart, four houses down from you, says the wagon was abandoned no earlier than a quarter past eleven, because that's when he arrived home and the lane was clear, and no later than half-past eleven, because that's when he heard the horse whinny and stomp. He went outside and shouted for whoever was there to move along, but the horse trotted a few feet and no one heeded his call. I'm surprised you didn't know that."

"The Stewarts don't have a housekeeper, just a daily."

O'Brien snorted. "We've found a flaw in Mrs. Prouty's gossip chain."

"What are the odds that there were two men in the alley that night wearing brass buttons?"

"Higher than expected, apparently. Take a look around. Brass buttons abound. It's not likely Hopper abandoned the wagon then hung around your back lane for thirty minutes waiting to be killed. Or it could simply be that the child confused details of that night. She might have seen the Woodworths' driver not long after her father died in that vacant lot. Trauma can mess with memories."

The children, each clutching a small brown bag, moved to a nearby park bench to inspect their treasures.

Bradshaw dropped his voice lower. "Could it have been a patrolman?" He thought about Patrolman Cox, who knew Ralph Hopper, who frequented the backdoor of the Seattle Grand. But to name names? No, he didn't feel strongly enough about Cox to do that. But his chest constricted painfully when he recalled Cox's surprised reaction to the news Emily might be hiding in his jurisdiction.

"I'll talk to the chief. He'll assign March to look into the possibility."

"Why not you?"

"My case load is full, remember? I wouldn't get this one anyway. I despise him, but March has the connections to find out if any of our men is involved without making a lot of waves. If he turns something up, there'll be another private council hearing and it'll get ugly. We're still not through the Considine trial. I'm not sure the department can take another scandal. The P-I would like to see us all fired. Did you see the cartoon in yesterday morning's edition? With the blind patrolman standing in the middle of the street with his cane? It's a wonder we get any respect at all."

"Does March know about your federal investigation?"

"No. And I don't intend to tell him. He can look into this without being told. The core of this ring is protected by outer layers of graft. That's how they work. Each ring is kept in the dark about the rest, and they like it that way. Just take the money and ask nothing is their motto."

"Hopper's death, the brass buttons, are connected with an outer ring? Not those at the Grand?"

"Maybe. Until I know for sure, I'm not risking this investigation. I'm too close to having the evidence I need."

Chapter Nineteen

Patrolmen, jailors, musicians, streetcar conductors, train conductors, ferrymen, state militia, college militia, army officers, bellboys, elevator operators, liveried drivers—

"Professor, you're wanted on the telephone."

"Please take a message Mrs. Prouty."

—costumed actors, private guards, ushers—

"It's President Graves from the university, and he says it's important."

Bradshaw threw down his pen, as annoyed at the abundance of brass buttoned professions as with the interruption.

He found the telephone receiver dangling on its braided cord.

"Bradshaw here."

"Aah, there you are, Bradshaw. I'm calling to extend an invitation to a ball. I'm on the organizing committee. You must come."

"A ball? No. No." The very idea turned his stomach. Had Graves gone mad?

"Did you hear my last three words? You must come."

"A ball, sir? It's not seemly. It's too soon." He couldn't possibly. The idea sickened him. He hated dances, and how could anyone think of anything so socially irrelevant so soon after McKinley's death?

"It's to celebrate President Roosevelt, Bradshaw. It's never too soon to stand up for what this country believes in and show those anarchists we won't be intimidated or subdued. A dance is just the thing. A red-white-and-blue affair. The women are to wear gowns of those colors, the men to wear formal attire with red-white-and-blue boutonnieres. It's to be on a barge out in the middle of the bay, with an orchestra and lights and food. You will be there, as will all the faculty and staff. Understood?"

"Yes, sir."

"Don't sound so forlorn. An evening of music will be good for all of us. I've given you enough notice to be properly dressed. You may bring someone, if you wish. Peggy in the office has mentioned your name on more than one occasion."

"How does one get to this barge?"

Graves laughed at Bradshaw's avoidance of Peggy. "Columbia Street dock. It departs at ten and a special ferry will be running back and forth all night."

Bradshaw hung the receiver on its hook and found Justin at his elbow.

"Are you going to the ball on the barge?"

"It seems so."

"Will you dance with Missouri?"

"She won't be there."

"Yes, she will. She told me today she's going with some other coeds to serve food and stuff."

"Oh, well then, she'll be working and not have time to dance."

"You should ask her anyway. Do you know how?"

"To ask her?"

"You write your name on her dance card."

"Oh, right."

"Do you know how to dance? I could teach you."

"Could you? And how do you know?"

"Paul taught me. He learned from his big sisters. Do you want to learn the waltz or the two-step? I like the two-step, 'cause you get to move faster, but you might want to start with the waltz. It's easier. You just make a square with your feet and go one-two-three, one-two-three."

"Not four? There are four corners to a square."

"You sort of slide between two of them," he said, and gave a demonstration. Bradshaw had to smother a laugh.

"I see." While he'd been buried in the basement, his son had been learning social skills next door. He wasn't sure how he felt about that. The boy was only eight. There was plenty of time for all that nonsense. "Don't you have homework to do?"

"I already did it. Want me to teach you to dance?"

"No, thank you. I think I remember how." And he had no intention of proving it to his son or anyone else.

Friday evening, when most sane individuals were already retired to their beds, and lucky inventors who didn't have orders from their bosses were down tinkering in their basements, Bradshaw dressed as ordered in his white-winged dress shirt, white bow tie, and dark tailcoat. The final indignity came with the silk top hat. It had seen better days, but he refused to throw good money at such a ridiculous article. And he refused to hire a taxi for the trip down to the waterfront. He headed out of his house quietly so as not to wake Mrs. Prouty or Justin, intending to catch the streetcar, when a polished carriage pulled up beside him, and the door opened.

"Professor! You could only be going to one place, dressed like that. Hop in, we'll make an entrance together like a pair of stray dogs and hope they take pity on us."

"Thank you, Mr. Woodworth." Bradshaw glanced up at the driver's seat, at the shiny brass buttons on the uniform, then at Albert March, meeting his eye, wondering if it were possible for a man with such a weary face to have prevented Ralph Hopper from rising from the mud.

He climbed in and shut the door. The carriage started off at a gentle pace. The interior of the carriage was as polished as the outside, with leather upholstery and paneled walls. Bradshaw noticed without actually comprehending. He was busy calculating the time it would take for a man to drive this carriage from the livery stable on Fifteenth Avenue to the Butler Hotel on Second and James, where Mr. Woodworth had attended the late dinner meeting on the night Hopper died. He pulled out his pocket watch and checked the time.

"Are we late?" asked Mr. Woodworth.

"No." Bradshaw slipped the watch back into its pocket. "Mrs. Woodworth is not attending?"

"Under the weather, I'm afraid. Has been ever since the day McKinley was shot. I've never known her to take anything so hard, unless it involved one of the children."

"I'm sorry."

"I have to go, of course, represent the business community and support our new president. I'd hoped to convince my wife to come. Thought it would cheer her up to see her friends and hear the music. She's always loved to dance and is as graceful today as the day I met her." Mr. Woodworth, missing his wife's company and worried for her health, was inclined to talk nostalgically, which suited Bradshaw. It meant he didn't have to add to the conversation.

He sat back in the plush seat to listen. Mr. Woodworth entertained Bradshaw with stories of his early days with his wife, their courtship, and how his heart still melted when she looked at him with tenderness. He was a happy man, a lucky man, and he had the good sense to know it. As the carriage approached Second Avenue coming down Columbia Street, Bradshaw checked his watch again. Twenty-one minutes to go a distance of just over two miles. The Butler Hotel sat two blocks south. He did a quick calculation, adding the time to cover the distance on foot to the livery and decided Albert was in the clear.

Mr. Woodworth lifted an eyebrow, and questions danced in his eyes, but he politely kept them to himself.

It was a fair, cool night, the dark sky revealing stars between patches of clouds.

At the dock, the barge was aglow with twinkling lights, the air filled with the patriotic marches from the lively orchestra, and the enormous temporary wood dance floor covered in all manner of red, white, and blue feminine fabrics on all manner of females, standing in chatting bouquets. Bradshaw and Mr. Woodworth were pinned with patriotic boutonnieres, and minutes later, the tugboat gave a few warning toots and began to gently pull the barge out into the bay.

The wind was a bit more than had been anticipated. The hanging lamps swung wildly, and the table cloths flapped, threatening the array of food trays. The gusts buffeted everyone so vigorously, squeals and guffaws rose above the noise as they all gripped their flapping finery. Two top hats went tumbling away and into the Sound, and the chase nearly sent their owners over the side with them. All was in a blustery state of convivial confusion until the barge was at last anchored and the wind settled down to the faintest breeze, warmed by blazing coal stoves.

Only then did Bradshaw and Woodworth part company to seek out their own friends and acquaintances. Bradshaw relinquished his top hat and overcoat to a roving waiter, then made his dutiful rounds, shaking hands with university faculty and staff, their wives and husbands and guests, conversing with Dr. Graves and his wife who were still laughing over the flyaway hats. Assistant Professor Tom Hill had brought the new teacher of women's physical culture and hygiene, a bubbly young woman with untamed hair and laughing eyes, and he seemed quite smitten.

Bradshaw was pleasantly surprised to find Mr. Daily in attendance, and they happily fell into a discussion of Marconi's latest wireless successes while avoiding the topic of the Seattle Grand contest, until Mrs. Daily, a plump, dimpled woman in regal blue, pushed her husband out onto the wood floor in time for the first dance on the program, a grand march to "Stars and Stripes Forever."

Both Detectives March and O'Brien were on duty, making the rounds, dressed like the other men in formal attire. Near the Pullman parlor car that had been hoisted aboard to serve as a ladies' lounge, Bradshaw found an out-of-the way corner where he intended to stay for the duration.

March spied him in his corner and sidled up to him. The golden-boy detective looked like a prince in his white tie and tails, and the eyes of the majority of ladies in attendance followed him like hopeful princesses, even the ones past their prime for the post. March said, "The chief didn't want an obvious police presence," as explanation for his attire.

"Of course. No one is noticing you at all."

March shrugged as if to say it wasn't his fault his looks drew attention.

"Any luck with your inquiries?"

March raised an eyebrow.

"Brass buttons?"

"Oh, right. It was your son who reported that tip. Nope, not a thing. Dead end, thank goodness. Department didn't need another scandal. This social ought to improve community relations. Mix and mingle, that's what the chief ordered. Yes, sir, I said. Oh, it'll be a hardship, but it's all in a good cause." His laughing blue eyes scanned the swirling silk and landed at the refreshment table.

Bradshaw's mood darkened as the detective's eyes lit up. "Have you ever seen anything more exquisite?"

No, Bradshaw thought. He hadn't. Which was precisely why he had been avoiding the refreshment table. It was there the coeds, and Missouri Fremont, stood smiling and doling out plates. He was about to inform the detective that as best friend of Missouri's uncle he felt obligated to act at times as her protector, when he realized March's eye wasn't on any of the coeds. He was gazing hungrily at Mrs. Hillyard, who was overseeing them. She was a lovely, full-figured woman in red silk that accentuated the paleness of her freckled shoulders and full bosom and the auburn tones of her upswept hair.

Bradshaw crossed his arms, almost smiling.

"She's married, detective. Mother of two, head of the Women's Cultural Committee."

"The very best kind of woman for a single man. No silliness, no ulterior motive or designs on one's future. Just a pleasurable dance, intelligent conversation, harmless flirting, and if one's lucky, later, a private afternoon."

"Aren't you supposed to be watching for anarchists?"

"How do we know she's not one? Excellent disguise. I shall have to interrogate her thoroughly."

He strode off, said something to make Mrs. Hillyard blush, and seconds later, held her daringly close as he swept her about the dance floor.

Bradshaw looked at his pocket watch and wondered if he'd stayed long enough to fulfill his duty and when the promised regular ferry runs would begin. Thirty-two minutes. Probably not yet.

"You'll have to stay at least until the speeches are through."

Bradshaw nearly dropped his watch. Missouri had appeared beside him, wearing a flag-patterned apron over a gown of white crepe de chine that clung to her slim figure. Her short hair framed her face, delicate curls tickling at her neck and temples. She was the only woman on the barge whose hair did not add six inches or more to her height. He greeted her with a nod, not trusting his voice, as he tucked his watch away.

"Justin said if you don't ask me to dance, I'm to ask you."

The presence of her apron told him she wasn't completely serious. He cleared his throat. "Highly improper."

"He also believes in a woman's right to vote, and that girls should be allowed to wear trousers, especially when climbing trees."

"I can't say as I disagree with either of those."

She smiled, her eyes gently searching his and moving their conversation, silently, to Emily Hopper. She said softly, "You're not sleeping."

"Not much," he agreed. As usual in her presence, he was baffled. How did she have the maturity and understanding to say just enough, to not ask him about details he'd rather not discuss. Her eyes told him she knew all. She knew he'd found Ralph's body, knew he was still terribly worried about Emily. Had she learned from Justin? Mrs. Prouty? Or did she simply look at him and know? She stayed quiet and merely gave him silent support. Her eyes said nothing of their last meeting.

"Did you know that Emily performed on stage before all this happened?"

"No—how do you know?"

"You can stop looking daggers at me, I haven't been doing anything dangerous, just talking."

Talking had gotten him a death threat.

"To whom?"

"Polly. She sits beside me at the switchboard. She told me this afternoon."

"Do you know where? In which theater she performed?"

"The Third Avenue, but she's not there now, I checked. Without leaving my post at the switchboard," she said before he could admonish her. "There are no children currently playing there. At the Variety, there are several boys playing in a new comedy, but no girls."

"Polly again?"

"Well no, actually, I got that from the playbills after work."

"She's in hiding, I doubt she'd be appearing on stage, not even disguised as a boy."

"You never know. I've heard that the best place to hide something is in plain sight. Everyone is so busy looking in drawers, they fail to see the letter on the desktop."

This bit of wisdom drew a smile from him. "The girl is just ten. I hardly think she's playing at anything so clever."

A frantic wave from the refreshment table caught their attention. "That's Millie. Her dance card's full and I promised to hold the fort, so you, Mr. Benjamin Bradshaw, can breathe a sigh of relief and tell Justin I was unable to dance because of my duties."

He watched her walk away and take her place behind the refreshment table, not sure if the tightening of his heart and the uneasiness in his belly meant he was relieved at having avoided holding Missouri in his arms, or disappointed, or that the miniscule motion of the floating dance floor was getting to him. He paced to the edge of the barge, but not too close, and stared at the lights of the city, his city, letting a feeling of nostalgia drift over him.

He hadn't been born here, but ever since he was a boy and had visited with his parents, he'd known this was where he belonged. It had changed much since then. In the past four years alone, the population had exploded, and every day, a new roof or high building altered the skyline. Yet Seattle's basic elements remained: the snow-capped mountains, Puget Sound, and the rugged shape of the Douglas firs rising into the sky.

"Not seasick, are you, Ben?" O'Brien stepped up beside him and took a long drag on a cigar. The smoke was pleasant, deep, slightly sweet.

"Just contemplating the view and wishing they'd stop tearing down the hills. Somehow, I don't think she'll be the same if all her curves are flattened."

"Heaven forbid," said March, stepping up them. The childish scent of Tutti-Frutti gum joined the cigar smoke. "Women? Roads? What are we talking about?"

"Hills," said O'Brien.

"Oh. It's a shame to do all that digging and not find any gold."

Bradshaw asked, "Did you step on Mrs. Hillyard's toes?"

"She's dancing with her husband. For appearances, you know. I don't mind; that clarinet is a half-note behind on the quadrilles and throwing off my timing."

"He's playing perfectly, Reggie," O'Brien goaded. "It's you that's off."

"Can't you hear it? Listen? There he goes again."

O'Brien, cigar held at the ready, said, "There's nothing our golden boy can't do, Ben. Even plays clarinet in his own band."

March grunted. "I've no time for that anymore, but I still expect a decent orchestra at these affairs. Don't you agree, Professor?"

"Me? Oh, I know little about music. It sounds marvelous to me."

"I envy your tone-deafness. Oh, say, he's caught up. Bless the man, he's back in rhythm. What a relief."

The three of them turned their backs on the city view to watch the swirl of patriotic colors on the dance floor. Bradshaw's eye wandered to the refreshment table, hovered on Missouri who was bobbing to the music as if itching to dance. A young man approached, said something, and Missouri smiled, then shook her head, and the young man turned away with an air of defeat. Bradshaw smiled at the dancers.

The approach of the promised ferry caught his attention. He watched it near, then disappear at the side of the barge. A hoist was employed, and a minute later, a late-arriving couple were swung aboard, clinging to the ropes and laughing. It was a spectacle Bradshaw hadn't expected and wouldn't relish when the time came to leave. He soon saw he had an alternative. A tail-coated young man came scrambling over the side, having climbed a rope ladder. The young man surveyed the crowd and on seeing Bradshaw and the two detectives, hurried over.

Bradshaw then recognized him as the clerk from police head-quarters. He greeted them politely, then addressed the detectives. "The Chief thought you might like to know Nell Pickerell's been arrested for the murder of Ralph Hopper."

"What?" asked O'Brien.

"Nell?" asked Bradshaw.

"Huh," said March.

"Oh, it's true. You know she was arrested the night he disap-peared. It was because she attacked Ralph on the street."

"She attacked a patrolman," said O'Brien.

"Patrolman Cox, wasn't it?" asked March.

The clerk nodded. "He says she attacked him when he tried to pull her off Ralph. Anyway, she's in jail, and if you haven't anything to report back about what's happening here, I'm allowed to stay. You don't have any trouble to report, do you?" He looked like Justin begging for candy.

"Dance your heart out," said O'Brien, and the clerk hurried off before the detectives could change their minds.

"It's got to be a mistake," said Bradshaw. "I can't see Nell committing murder."

"Or maybe that's why I had no luck with my inquiries," said March. "Brass buttons never came into it."

Bradshaw resisted the urge to defend Justin.

"Or Harry's got a military-style overcoat," offered O'Brien.

"Or the child later saw Albert in the lane that night and she's confused," put forth March.

"That was one of your theories," said Bradshaw to O'Brien and was rewarded with a disgusted scowl.

Bradshaw said to March, "You don't seriously think Harry could have done it?"

"Not really, but you know what they say, hell hath no fury...."

Bradshaw scratched his ear. "She did seem furious with that peddler still selling Ralph's. Scorn's not the right emotion, but I gather she knew someone sickened by it."

"Daisy," replied March.

"The blinded show girl?"

"Daisy's sweet on Harry," March explained.

"Oh?"

"She refuses to believe Harry is female."

"Oh."

Both March and O'Brien laughed, and Bradshaw felt a bit of a fool. He wasn't shocked by the information, just unsure of how to respond. He could see they read his awkwardness as unworldliness. "That certainly gives Harry sufficient motive, if someone she cared about was harmed by Ralph's tonic."

O'Brien said, "Except Harry doesn't feel the same about Daisy, at least that's always been her claim. Still, they're friends."

"Make a lovely couple," said March, and if he was being facetious, Bradshaw couldn't tell.

"Why is this all just being learned now? And why are neither of you taking it seriously? Patrolman Cox suddenly recalls Nell's attack on Ralph Hopper and has her arrested, and you behave as if you've just gotten news of a common pickpocket rather than murder."

"Well," shrugged O'Brien.

March snorted.

It was Bradshaw's turn to scowl. "What social undercurrent has swept over me this time?" He didn't like the fact that the first and only friendly exchange between the detectives was at his expense. Or that he'd jumbled his metaphors. "Is Patrolman Cox involved in a love triangle with Harry and Daisy?"

"He guessed it," said March in mock disbelief.

"Very near," agreed O'Brien, then took pity on Bradshaw. "Sorry, Ben. You aren't privy to the gossip like we are—you couldn't have known. He says the opposite, of course, but Cox is attracted to Harry. She hates him, and he hates himself for liking her, so he arrests her all the time on petty charges."

"But to accuse her of murder. That's not petty."

"No. He's taken it too far this time."

"Could there be any truth to the accusation?"

O'Brien shook his head emphatically. March shrugged. Out of accord again.

Chapter Twenty

Twenty-four hours later, with darkness pressing against the basement transom windows, Benjamin Bradshaw had had enough of waiting. There was just one full day left before the official start of classes at the university, and he didn't intend to waste it in forced idleness.

From a storage chest, he dug out his old lineman gear. Canvas carryall, climbing hooks, leather straps, thick gloves, and sturdy ropes. He changed into his blue denims and flannel shirt and old worn leather climbing boots. When dressed, he felt as if he'd stepped eight years into the past, to when he first arrived in Seattle, a widower, new father, a teacher with nowhere to teach because the university had not yet expanded to an engineering department. Rather than taking a post in an elementary or high school, he'd chosen to gain practical experience in electrical construction. For over a year he'd dug holes, set poles and climbed them, carried heavy crossarms, and, he thought with a smile, brought light to the city.

The smell of creosote had saturated his skin and clothes, and he'd returned home each night tired and satisfied. The sheer physicality of the work, he realized now, had helped him transition from the tragedy he'd left behind to a new, if sheltered, life in Seattle.

Tonight, if anyone asked what he was doing, he was going to use the truth as his excuse. He was completing the line to test the theater contest device. He hoped no one would ask. Technically, he was about to break the law.

He left the house by the basement door, and followed the telephone lines three blocks until he came to the spool of cable at the base of a Sunset Telephone Company pole in a dark neighborhood of empty lots. This was his cable, he knew not only from having watched the progress, but because a tag on the spool showed his address. As he'd seen elsewhere on his early morning forays, the linemen hadn't bothered chaining the spool in this quiet residential neighborhood.

He set to work.

For an hour, aided only by the lantern he'd brought, he unrolled, climbed, hoisted, and attached cable to the ceramic insulators on the outer edge of the bottom crossarms. It was hard work for a man alone, especially the task of pulling the slack between poles, but he got into a rhythm and was soon making good progress.

His vertigo remained quiet, and he wondered if it was because he felt safe in this familiar job, trusting the dig of the sharp climbing hooks into the wood and the strength of the leather pole strap.

By the third pole, he was sweating despite the coolness of the night air. He strained to pull the cable into position on the arm, and his leather glove slipped off his slick palm. The weight of the cable pressed the back of his hand hard against the rough edge of the wood, scraping the skin deep. Blood welled to the surface.

"Damn." He gave the cable a final heave and set it on the insulator, then was forced to climb down, remove his hooks, and trudge back home for a bandage.

In his basement sink, he ran stinging cold water over the wound, then found a clean cloth and applied pressure. The cloth quickly turned red and he realized the gash was long, extending to his wrist. The sight of it made him woozy. A fuzzy white cloud floated in his eyeballs.

His luck, he thought, trading fear of heights for fear of blood. No, not fear, just, oh, this dizziness. As the white cloud turned black and he felt himself slip into oblivion, he vowed to find a way to get more sleep and prayed he'd revive before Mrs. Prouty found him.

"Ben. Hey, Ben."

The gravelly voice, strangely familiar, penetrated the oblivion. Rough hands shook him, slapped none too gently at his cheeks. He pried open his eyes to find a great hairy beast swimming above him in a blur, growling and huffing.

My God, he thought, I've gone mad.

"Ben, you old dog, you look like hell! I've seen mugs on miners been froze that look better'n you. You're covered in blood."

"Henry?"

"Well, you're still alive anyway." Henry Pratt pulled him up to a sitting position. He felt like child being shifted by a giant. He blinked and looked around, saw the glaring basement lamps, the darkness still pressing against the high window.

"What time is it? And what are you doing here?"

"About two in the a.m., and I snuck in the back door. I was gonna hit the sack in my room—it's still my room, ain't it? I saw a light on down here and came to see what it was had you up so late."

Bradshaw looked down at his hand. It was still wrapped in the bloody cloth. He shifted it and saw that the wound had clotted.

"You'll live," Henry pronounced. "What you do?"

"Injured myself."

Henry grunted. "You always did like to state the obvious."

"You'd have given Mrs. Prouty heart failure if she'd caught you sneaking in."

Henry's eyes gleamed. "Still hoping to. Make her faint dead away." He chuckled happily.

They looked at one another silently for a moment, two old friends for whom the passing of time only meant they had more to talk about.

"You don't look like a millionaire."

"Ain't got a nickel to my name. It's not as fun up north as it used to be. Colder'n I remember from last time."

"It's not even winter yet. You've only been gone four months. You're getting old, Henry."

"You and me both. Sprained my back, truth be told. Doc says my digging days are over. Have to find another way to make my millions. How's Missouri? She start college yet?"

"She's studying to take the entrance exam."

"She's a bright girl. She'll get in, won't she?"

"More than likely."

Bradshaw got up and stretched his aching joints. "You want a job?"

"Sure. What's it pay?"

"I'll let you know. Come on, grab a pair of gloves. I'll explain once we're out of the house."

With Henry's limited help, the job went much more quickly. While they worked, Bradshaw explained what had been happening, leaving out no details, from the moment he'd found the abandoned wagon blocking the back lane, to O'Brien's search for smugglers at the Seattle Grand and the previous night's news of Nell Pickerell's arrest.

"Arrested Harry!" Henry bellowed, and Bradshaw, from fifteen feet above the sidewalk, shushed him.

But Henry kept on. "Ain't no way Harry killed Hopper."

Bradshaw climbed down.

"You know Harry?"

"Everyone in Seattle knows Harry."

Bradshaw didn't admit he'd been ignorant of her existence until recently. "I don't think she's guilty either, but she was very upset about Daisy being blinded by the tonic."

"Who's Daisy?"

"An actress at the Seattle Grand. She's sweet on Harry."

"But Harry's a girl."

"I know."

"I mean Harry doesn't like girls."

"How well do you know her?"

"Not very, but enough to know that."

"She's been in jail a full day and Emily hasn't come forward yet. O'Brien thinks she'll come out of hiding once her father's killer is locked up."

"Harry's seen plenty nights in jail. Still, it's no place for a girl. Not too nice a place for man, now that I think of it."

"It's a hell hole."

Henry grinned. "That's right. They locked you up while I was gone."

"Not a high point of my life."

Henry laughed throatily. As they'd talked, he'd been attempting to clamp a hook around the next length of cable. His movements were clumsy, and he didn't seem able to work the simple lock mechanism.

"I'll have to dock your wages for lost time," Bradshaw joked, but he was concerned. Henry appeared completely sober and yet was having difficulty with the simple task.

"Hand goes numb. It's the damndest thing."

"You should see a doctor."

"Saw one. Told me to come home. I came."

"Another doctor. If you're losing feeling in your hand, it's serious."

Henry grunted. He held a healthy distrust of medical practitioners. Bradshaw let the matter drop. For now.

He took the hook from Henry and with a flick of his thumb opened it. "How far did you get up north? Did you get to your old claim?"

"Nope, never made it. Lost it anyway. It's got to be worked annually. It's ugly up there, Ben. Place is run amuck with stakers. Soon as a sniff of gold is heard, off they go, hundreds of 'em, thousands, staking out their unproved claims then sitting back and waiting for greenhorns willing to pay two thousand, five thousand, or more. Then off they go again, staking another one. Some got tag teams going, one man goes out and stakes, his buddy stays in town to record. They got it all set up beforehand."

"I thought only the man who physically staked a claim could file it."

"How's the commissioner to know the man standing before him didn't stake the claim? Hard to prove he didn't. They can't keep up with it all. Neither could I. If my back hadn't give out, I would have come home soon anyway."

As the lightening of the sky announced an imminent dawn, they came to the house. Bradshaw had last week prepared the connection for the cable and it took only a few minutes to finish the job. They rolled the cable spool back to where Bradshaw had originally found it, leaving an unsigned note saying the job had been completed, then returned home, staggering in through the kitchen door together, laughing at an off-color joke Henry had supplied.

Mrs. Prouty, as predicted, slapped a hand to her heart and gasped, which made them laugh all the harder. Her face went red, not white, so Bradshaw knew the shock would do no lasting harm.

"Uncle Henry!" Justin came running, and Henry dropped to one knee to wrap him in a bear hug. "I can't breathe!" cried Justin happily.

"Aah, breathing's over-rated. You grew, son! Let me look at you!" He pushed Justin to arm's length. "Two inches if a foot, by gum."

"You're home!" the boy declared.

"Just like your old man, tell'n me what I already know. Wouldn't you rather hear about the whale that come behind the ship and nearly bit the stern in two?"

The tall tale of the whale was retold that evening when Missouri joined them for a welcome-home dinner. The reunion between Henry and his niece brought tears to all their eyes, even Mrs. Prouty's.

Henry had been rendered momentarily speechless at the sight of Missouri. They hadn't seen each other in seven years, and in that time they'd both changed much, and lost much. Henry's sister had been Missouri's mother, and it was her passing that had brought Missouri to Seattle.

"Spittin' image of your mother," Henry said at last. "And she was always beautiful."

"Oh, Uncle Henry," Missouri cried, and the hugs and tears continued.

But a gathering with both Missouri Fremont and her Uncle Henry Pratt could never stay somber long. Both optimists, both philosophers, both given to storytelling, soon they were all gathered around the fireplace, drinking cocoa and Postum and whiskey, according to age and inclination, and swapping stories with abandon.

Henry had given Justin a small leather pouch of gold dust, and the boy lay on his belly on the hearth rug with it, listening intently as Henry launched anew into his journey across the Bering Sea full of monster whales and islands of fur seals. His arms flung wide to demonstrate the raging rivers sweeping men and dogs away, his arms held fast with details of the frozen tundra and sleeping in a tent in the wilderness with wild animals sniffing and pawing at his supplies. True stories from the gold country were so outlandish it was impossible to tell exactly where Henry veered into exaggeration. It didn't matter. They listened with rapt attention. By that time, Missouri had relinquished the floor to Henry and sat curled up in an armchair, sipping cocoa, the fire and happiness glowing in her amber eyes.

Bradshaw sat back in his favorite wingchair, drinking Postum, savoring this temporary bubble of contentment.

"I shoulda gone to Nome where the digging's easy on the sandy beaches, but it's so cutthroat out there, nobody's sure who owns what, so you spend most your time at the commissioner's trying to sort it all out, no sport in it at all. Plenty of gold still in the Klondike creeks for men willing to put their back in their shovel. Course I put my back too far in my shovel, and here I am."

Bradshaw called him on that. "You said you never reached your claim."

"Well, no, figure of speech about my shovel."

Justin sat up. "How *did* you hurt your back, Uncle Henry?"

"Oldest way in the world, my boy. The downfall of all men, I'm afraid…"

Bradshaw tossed a warning glare at Henry and received a wicked grin.

"…stepped in a hole. Just like that. Fit as a fiddle one minute, marching along the trail on a fine summer day, snow melting all around me, little arctic flowers popping up for that few minutes of glory, my pack full of provisions, a few mates to share the long journey, my claim a few days hard tramping ahead with my gold just a waiting for me, and then poof."

"Poof?" said Justin.

"Poof. Down I goes, into a sink hole. Mud up to my knee-caps. I fell sideways and wrenched my back and it felt like a red hot knife plunging into my spine. My mates pulled me out. Nothing they could do to help. Left me there on the trail with my provisions. They went on their way, and I lay down in my tent till a party heading back to Dawson come along and took pity on me."

Justin was appalled. "They left you?"

"That's Alaska, my boy. Each man for himself, as it ought to be in those harsh and primitive conditions. I wouldn't have let them stay with me if they'd offered. No, they had gold to get, good solid claims they'd proved, and I'd not hold 'em back."

"Weren't you scared?"

"Oh, there were a few days that passed where I couldn't hardly move enough to feed myself, and then when the rains came, my tent leaked, and I got chilled to the bone and hadn't the strength to build a fire. I thought maybe that was it for me. Did a lot a praying that night. Always darkest before the dawn. And dawn brought help. That's the thing about Alaska. Greed and goodness go hand in hand. Men'll share every ounce of food and scrap of firewood, and if they're heading your way, they'll carry you on their back if they got to. Which is what they did for me."

"Wow," whispered Justin.

Bradshaw grinned and glanced at Missouri. She gave him a secretive, indulgent smile. He found it very difficult to look away.

Chapter Twenty-one

"Goldarnitall, I know that voice," Henry bellowed. "Play it again."

Bradshaw set the wax cylinder rotating again, and for two minutes they listened to stage directions and furniture being shifted. All week, while Bradshaw had been busy with the start of university classes, Henry had been down in the basement, eavesdropping on conversations and rehearsals at the Seattle Grand, occasionally setting Bradshaw's modified Graphophone in motion, and growing daily more agitated at recognizing yet not being able to pinpoint how he knew the stage manager's voice.

"Victor, you say? That's not ringing any bells, but I know that voice. I can see him. Short little fella, walks with a swagger, beady eyes, shrewd."

"Sounds like Victor. Where do you see him? Try to imagine him somewhere. Boston? Seattle?"

Henry scrunched up his face. "Bar, saloon, dance hall?"

Bradshaw snorted. "That narrows it."

"Tent."

"Tent?"

"Canvas tent, sopping wet, dripping ice water, him cussing up a storm. Goldarnit, I know his name, right there at the tip a my tongue."

"Alaska, the Yukon?"

"Dawson! Back in '97, first time I went. Met the feller in town. I liked his energy. He was like a dog, willing and eager, but not the sense to know where or how. I figured he'd make good company and not go on trying to tell me what to do."

"So what happened?"

"Ten days out, we're holed up in a tent and the rain won't quit unless it's turning into wet snow and he's missing a warm soft bed and a warm soft woman, not that I wasn't mind you, but he couldn't take it no more. Kept pacing the tent like a caged animal. Some men take it that way. They ain't got a clue how rough it can be until they're away from all they've ever known. City fellers, mostly, never done a real hard day's work in their lives until they decide to head up for gold. Then they find themselves in some icy, dripping tent with nothing but beans and bacon, tired and aching and feeling trapped cause the only way back is the way they just came, over mountains, across rivers, through mud and ice and rocks, and they can't imagine doing that ever again, and they know they got to because it's the only way back. Rudy, I says, you've got to buck up—hey, that's it, Rudy!"

"Just Rudy?"

"Hell, I don't know. Called him Rudy cause I couldn't pronounce his name. Too many letters, sounded Russian. Not Victor, but that coulda been his first name. Don't know what anyone else called him. Whining little pipsqueak. I had to take him back to town to get rid of him, and I never saw him again. Nah, I take that back. I saw him in town about six months later, livin' high. I didn't talk to him. I mighta been drunk. But he was definitely there. Seems to me someone said he was working for some shrewd swindler who was calling the shots. I remember thinking to myself that dog had found a master and would make good. There's more than one way to strike gold. It's a whole lot easier, not to mention warmer, to milk the miners than to freeze your arse digging and swilling."

Bradshaw recalled Henry's tales of that first trip. All around him, prospectors were finding ten or fifteen dollars worth of gold per shovel on their claims that winter. It was believed that in the spring, when it thawed enough for water to run and the dirt to be sluiced, the gold would pile up fast. And it did, for a few lucky claimants. For Henry and others, nature's twisted paths hadn't deposited gold between their stakes, at least not in quantities great enough to boast about. Just enough to pay for fresh supplies and keep the hope alive.

"Listen again. Are you sure it's Rudy?"

Henry listened. "Sure as I can be. Why don't I go pay him a visit?"

"No, if it's the same man, he might get suspicious."

"Won't know me if I get gussied up, go see a show. What's say you and I hit the town?"

Hitting the town included shopping for a new suit and shoes for Henry, and then dinner at a hotel restaurant because Henry declared he was lightheaded from hunger, all on Bradshaw's dime.

"Have pity, Henry. A professor's salary can only stretch so far," Bradshaw declared, as Henry ordered wine with their meal. Henry knew that it was income from Bradshaw's minor patents that actually gave him financial security, but their friendship had never been about money, and Henry was not a moocher, present circumstances aside.

"You owe me. I've been slaving in your basement all week."

"Napping is more like it."

"Just resting my back, Ben."

When they finally arrived at the Seattle Grand, a glance at the program for *The Folley on the Trolley* was encouraging. It told them the stage manager's full name: Victor Rudnikovich.

"That's not hard to pronounce," said Bradshaw, doing so.

"Not for you, mister college professor."

"Henry, why do you pretend you have no education?"

"Easier to live up to low expectations than high ones," he said with a wink. "I'll save all that highfalutin' nonsense to you and Missouri. I'm some proud of that girl. Passed those entrance exams with top marks; she tell you?"

"She told me." And he was some proud of her, too.

Henry jerked his head. "Feller over there looks like he knows you."

Coming toward them across the polished lobby was Detective March and a young woman in pale blue, her fair hair piled high above her forehead. Not a pretty girl, but handsome in a well-groomed sort of way. March introduced her as Miss Mabel Dodwell, daughter of State Representative Horace Dodwell. His preference for married women was apparently outweighed by his fondness for a good political connection.

"Henry Pratt? I thought you were up in Alaska."

"Just got back."

"Any luck?"

"Not a lick."

"That's too bad. Well, it's a game of chance."

"You're too modest, Reggie." Miss Dodwell gave him an adoring look. "He doesn't like to brag about striking gold. He did it through hard work and brilliance."

Bradshaw saw Henry's eyes narrow. He explained, "Detective March had success in '97, Henry. He was one of the lucky ones."

Miss Dodwell pooh-poohed that. "He was born to succeed. Some people are, you know. My father says he'll go far."

"Where'd you hit?" Henry folded his arms and thrust his chin.

"North of the Klondike, up toward Circle City.

"That's my territory. Whereabouts?"

"Oh, a small stream, not on the maps."

"Every trickle is on the maps."

"Now. Not then. Professor, did you hear about Harry? She escaped from jail this afternoon."

The sudden switch in topic took Bradshaw off guard a moment. "No, I didn't hear." And what did it mean? If Harry was innocent, why would she escape rather than wait it out to prove her innocence? He exchanged a look with Henry, who only pulled a face that said he didn't know what to make of it either.

"How did she manage it?"

March laughed. "She disguised herself as a woman. She borrowed bits and pieces of clothing from other inmates who were only in for one the night, the usual charges," he said tactfully, "and the guard didn't recognize her. She simply walked out with the others when they were released."

"Smart girl," said Henry.

"Shows how desperate she is." March shook his head. "She vowed she'd never be seen publicly in feminine attire. To put on a dress, well, looks like we had our man and she was a woman. The hunt is on to find her. Say, there go the lights. We'd better get to our seats."

Once settled in their plush seats amidst the murmuring crowd, Bradshaw leaned toward Henry and said quietly, "I can't believe it was Harry. It just doesn't feel right."

"I know what you mean. But you did say she was mad about what that tonic did to her friend."

"But Ralph Hopper wasn't beaten to death, it wasn't rage that killed him. He was weak and prevented from lifting his face from the mud. That sort of killing is cold. Evil."

The orchestra began to warm up and fill the auditorium with discordant expectant music. The stragglers in their finery filed to their seats. Bradshaw looked at his transmitters hanging discreetly above the dress circle. He'd tested his contest device and found the quality of sound delivered to the telephone headsets to be excellent. The loud-talker's output, as expected, disappointed him to the core. It soothed him not a whit to know that Daily and Smith's loud-talkers would be no better.

He tried not to think about it. He spied March a few rows over with his devoted date.

He said to Henry, "You didn't take a liking to Detective March."

"He's not my sort."

"Jealous, are you?"

Henry made a noise that sounded like he was gargling up a lung. "I know his type. Judge and jury and priest on the side."

"Pardon?"

"Makes his own rules, thinks he's ordained to lord over the rest of us. Must be nice to know you're superior. Born to succeed, my ass."

"Miss Dodwell said that, not March."

"Didn't deny it, did he?"

"He's not modest, I'll grant you that."

"Miner, hah! Hands are too soft."

"He's been back over three years. His calluses have had time to disappear."

Henry grunted.

"Look to your left, Henry, at the edge of the stage. Who is that?"

Henry looked, and smiled. "A little pipsqueak named Rudy."

"Good. Let's go." Bradshaw stood up.

"What about Miss Darlyrope and the trolley folly?"

"You can listen in the basement."

"I ain't seen a decent show in months, Ben. I don't want to sit alone in your damp basement when I could be right here. Sit yourself down, it won't kill you."

Bradshaw dropped into his seat, as the music swelled and the lights dimmed to darkness. He didn't hate it. He even enjoyed himself, when he wasn't puzzling over Nell "Harry" Pickerell and her escape from jail, and carefully considering each detail in the case of Hopper's death and Emily's hiding. As usual, he tried to line up facts and clues in a logical manner, searching for connections that eluded him.

Chapter Twenty-two

"Ben, listen to this."

Bradshaw had just returned home from telling O'Brien what Henry remembered about Victor Rudnikovich. He'd come in through the basement door and still wore his overcoat.

"Is it Victor?"

"No," Henry said. "I think it's your friend, O'Brien." He set the wax cylinder turning, and Bradshaw put his ear close to the Graphophone's tin amplifying horn. It was O'Brien, talking to a woman. They were speaking so low, his voice carried only because of its depth. Her gender could be distinguished, but not her words or identity. Since the transmitters could pick up whispers in the rooms below which they were installed, the conversation had to be taking place distant from those rooms.

Henry looked at Ben soberly. "Are they saying what I think they're saying?"

"Give me that cylinder."

"What are you gonna do with it?"

"Give it to me, Henry."

"Now don't go storming out of here all riled up, Ben. It might not be what we think."

Bradshaw elbowed Henry aside and removed the cylinder from the machine. He grabbed his hat, and as he flung open the basement door, Henry said, "Wait, I'll go with you."

"No. This is between me and O'Brien."

He found the detective where he'd left him not an hour earlier, in his office at police headquarters. He was at his desk, filling out some form. With his left hand.

Bradshaw ripped the paper out from under O'Brien's pen, tore off the official header, and slapped the rough square down.

"Let's see you perform your right-handed trick. You would have been smarter to find someone else to write your threat." He leaned down to shout the last in his ear, "Or was there no one you could trust!"

O'Brien flinched away.

"Ben, calm down. I can explain."

"You son-of-a-bitch."

"I've never heard you say that, Ben."

"Get used to it."

"I admit I used our friendship. Let me explain and then if you still want to hit me, I'll take off my badge and you can give it a go."

"I'm not going to listen to more of your fabrications. Just tell me where the child is."

"I don't know where she is. Not any longer."

Bradshaw tried to pull the wax cylinder from his jacket pocket. It caught on the fabric and he struggled angrily to free it. It took every ounce of his willpower not to fling it at O'Brien's head. Still, he dropped the fragile wax with more force than he should have on the desk.

He repeated the words gouged into the cylinder. *"Tell her it won't be much longer, she must be patient and stay hidden."*

O'Brien said quietly. "Wire to your basement. I should have guessed."

"You keep me in the dark, but you let your stenographers listen to you talk about Emily?"

"No one was manning the phones when I was there. I sent the girl off on an errand."

"Who were you talking to at the theater?"

"You didn't record that?"

"Tell me!"

"Miss Darlyrope."

"Where's Emily?"

"I don't know anymore. She's disappeared again."

"I'm supposed to believe you? How long have you known where she was?"

O'Brien dropped his eyes.

It was as if someone sucked the air from the room. "No. No. I haven't slept in weeks, I passed out twice, my housekeeper hates me, I've practically abandoned my son, and you stand there telling me this whole time I've been worried sick about the child you've known where she is!"

"Not the whole time, but soon after she fled your home, she sought sanctuary at Miss Darlyrope's apartment."

"At the Eskimo? I was there!"

"Quit shouting and let me explain. The hotel manager didn't know she was there. No one did. The girl is clever and snuck in unnoticed. You went looking for her and made some very dangerous people nervous. I warned you not to return. Detective March warned you not to return, he told me he even went to your house, but you wouldn't back off. That night, nerves turned deadly, Bradshaw, and there was a price put on your head."

"How the hell do you know? You haven't got any sources in the Tenderloin, or was that a lie, too?"

"March has sources."

"Oh? The same trustworthy sources that told him Ralph had gone off with the gypsies? Since when are you pals with March?"

"I'm not pals with Reginald March. He came to me at three in the morning with the news you were in the Tenderloin again and soon to be a dead man. We came up with the idea of the note, I wrote it, and he found someone to slip it to you an hour later."

"You should have told me."

"Be honest with yourself, Ben. That note scared you away from the Tenderloin. My warning wouldn't have."

"You threatened my son."

"I prevented your son from becoming an orphan. You see? You don't believe me. You saw Ralph Hopper dead in the muck with your own eyes, and you can't believe you were slated next."

Bradshaw paced. The windowless office was so small, he felt like the carnival tiger in its cage.

"How did you find her?"

"By accident. At Frederick & Nelson's. I was looking for a doll for my daughter's birthday. She was stealing one. She ran to Miss Darlyrope when I spotted her, claiming she was her aunt and would pay for the doll."

"And you just went along with the story?"

"Publicly, there at the department store. In private, Miss Darlyrope is my one and only informant inside the Seattle Grand. Besides you. She came to your rescue, I hear, when Victor noticed you crawling around above the dressing rooms. We both agreed Emily was safest with her, mostly because the child wanted to be with her. She never brought her to the theater, and only once did she bring her anywhere else. That was to the department store where I spotted her. Emily quit begging to go out after that, and stayed home with Daisy."

"The blind girl? The girl sweet on Harry? So Harry knew where Emily was?"

"Yes, but Harry didn't kill Ralph."

"Does Detective March know you found Emily? Has he been playing me for a fool, too?"

"No, March has never stopped looking for her."

"Why would you keep him wasting his time?"

"Same reason I didn't tell you. The fewer who knew where she was, the better."

"Maybe March would have more luck finding her now if he knew where she'd been."

"Telling March might upset my investigation."

"God forbid we should put a child's life ahead of your investigation."

"They're one in the same. I told you. Finding these smugglers finds Ralph's killer."

"You didn't want me nosing around in the Tenderloin, but you had no qualms about putting me in danger in the Seattle Grand, smuggling central."

"You were there legitimately. It was publicly known. You weren't there searching for Emily. I needed you to still be concerned about her, just like I needed everyone to know March was still looking for her. If you suddenly stopped being worried, someone might guess you knew where she was. I couldn't trust that your acting skills were up to that level of deception."

"You should have put her somewhere safer. Somewhere secure."

"She was happy with Miss Darlyrope, worships her a bit. I thought she'd stay."

"Did you at least discover where she's from or if she has family somewhere? Or what she saw on the night her father died?"

"I couldn't be seen going to the Eskimo. I never questioned the child. Miss Darlyrope tells me she wouldn't talk about her father or home. She's full of stories, but all of them are make-believe."

They faced off, Bradshaw glaring, O'Brien unapologetic.

So that was it. The child was missing. Nothing had been learned. And a friendship born of trust and mutual respect had been ripped to shreds.

Chapter Twenty-three

"Ben, you're a good judge of character," Henry said, "except one notable lapse, and even that was understandable."

"I was a young fool."

"Yep, but you ain't young or a fool anymore. You're mad, and you dang well got a right to be. Don't stop trusting your instincts. You're too upset to see it now, but O'Brien might have saved your life."

"He lied to me!"

"Yes, he did. Because he was afraid for your life. And he was right about your acting talent. Or lack thereof."

"How do I know what's the truth? How do I know O'Brien isn't behind everything. Maybe it was him that kept Ralph Hopper from rising from the mud."

"You don't believe that."

"I don't know what I believe."

Too angry to do anything but walk, Bradshaw had stopped home long enough only to get Henry. Together they now tramped the winding dirt paths of Volunteer Park. Henry gave an occasional grunt of complaint about his back. Bradshaw deliberately avoided the newly built reservoir that was sunk deep, rimmed by concrete, and looked like a bottomless black pit. He steered them through the woods of tall evergreens.

"I've got an idea, Ben. Here, wait a minute, have a heart. Let's sit."

Henry eased onto a park bench. Bradshaw stood, hands shoved in his coat pockets.

Henry said, "Now, I'm going to ask you some questions. Don't think about your answers, just tell me, quick. Do you trust O'Brien?"

"Henry, I'm in no mood for games."

"Don't be stubborn, I learned this from a wise man tending bar, and it works. Truth pops out when you don't give yourself time to think. Course it helps to be drinking. Bring any whiskey?"

"No."

"Me either. Mrs. Prouty must have confiscated my flask, darn her steely eyes. We can do it dry. Now, let's start again. Are you mad?"

"Yes."

"You trust me?"

"Yes."

"You trust O'Brien?"

His brain immediately said yes, but it took him a moment to fight through his anger to get the word out. He lifted his chin and stared at the clouds. "Yes."

"You trust that other one, March?"

"No."

"Hah! Me either. You trust Victor, Rudy, what's-his-face?"

"No."

"You love my niece?"

An exhalation escaped him before he could stop it.

"Thought I didn't notice? No, don't deny it. Can't lie to me, I've known you too long. You were mooning over her the other night. Damn firelight. Saddest sight I've ever seen. You gonna do anything about it?"

Bradshaw rubbed his face, not meeting Henry's eyes.

"Do me a favor? If you decide to do anything about it, you tell me first? I don't know how I feel, truth be told. I reserve the right knock you flat."

Bradshaw nodded faintly. "Fair enough."

"I say we leave the smugglers to O'Brien and his stenographers and go find the girl. Now, we can't go snooping around asking questions, you already tried that, and about got yourself killed."

"That note was from O'Brien."

"That don't make the threat any less real. He was doing you a favor. You trust O'Brien, so trust that note and don't go snooping around. We got to think like that little girl. She knows who to hide from, and who's safe. We need to know what she knows. So think. Who's she hiding from?"

"Who?"

"Hell, I don't know, I'm asking. You're the one with the sign in front of your house saying you're an investigator."

"I'm not a—" oh, why bother. He was an investigator of sorts. Who was Emily hiding from? That was the money question. He didn't know.

"Try algebra, Ben."

"You flunked algebra."

"That's why I said for *you* to try it."

It took him a few minutes to get his mind to calm enough to enter the rational world of mathematics. He paced before Henry, reciting simple equations in his head, mumbling a bit, until at last he could begin to put the problem of Emily Hopper into logical perspective. He needed to know who Emily feared. That was the unknown. On the opposite side of the equation were those people she didn't fear.

A local famous actress. Emily had felt safe enough to run to Miss Darlyrope, even accompany her to Frederick & Nelson, a major department store. She'd initially run from O'Brien, yet until recently, she'd stayed with Miss Darlyrope knowing full well that the detective knew she was there. She had felt safe with Justin, in Bradshaw's home.

What didn't fit? What factor in the string of events didn't balance? The child had witnessed her father's murder, but she hadn't come forward to point out the culprit or ask for help from the very people society is supposed to trust to protect them.

The police. Bradshaw had taught Justin to look for a uniformed patrolman if he ever found himself alone and in need of help.

"A patrolman," he said at last. He stopped pacing and stood before Henry. "She's afraid of a patrolman."

"Bingo. Brass buttons!"

"You said you didn't know."

"Didn't till you said it. Feels right. She leaves your house and goes to folks she knows and trusts, the sort of folks who know how to avoid the police. It's their way of life. But she's not hiding from O'Brien. Not the detectives, they're in plain clothes."

"Miss Darlyrope must have convinced her that O'Brien was keeping her hideout a secret."

"So why didn't that golden-boy detective find evidence against a patrolman? If he's so brilliant, got all these sources, why didn't he turn anything up? I don't trust him cause he's an arrogant ass. Why don't you trust him?"

"A gut feeling."

"Any reason he'd withhold evidence against a patrolman?"

"Maybe he's waiting for the timing to be right. So he can use the arrest and saving Emily to further his career."

"What else you got?"

"I don't know. Maybe he's protecting someone."

"Uh-huh, that's more like it? So who's he protecting? What doesn't he want anyone to know?"

What didn't March want anyone to know? March knew the game on the streets, he navigated the rules to nab thieves and keep some semblance of order in a place of complete disorder. He made compromises daily, choosing who to protect and when to protect them. Bradshaw thought of the book, *World of Graft*. "The copper tries to settle the squealer and the squealer tries to railroad the copper."

"Hell, Ben. You do surprise me. How many days you spend south of the line?"

"I read that in a book."

"You're on to something, with that lingo. It's the talk of the streets, and that little girl peddled on the streets with her old man. We gotta see those people, and the police, like that girl sees'em. She's heard that kinda talk, she's seen things a child ought not to see. Bound to make her different, not innocent like your boy, but still a child. She doesn't behave like a typical child, she, oh, what's the expression, she marches to a different drummer."

Bradshaw sat very still. He stared at Henry, and Henry stared back.

"You're a genius," Bradshaw whispered.

"I know," whispered Henry. "Why? What'd I say?"

Bradshaw dropped his head into his hands, his eyes shut. Henry started to speak, but Bradshaw flapped a hand to silence him. He was on the verge of something, he felt it, he *saw* it, and was dazzled by the visual and auditory display. Snippets of conversations, flashes of facial expressions, scenarios both real and imagined, formed and danced and fell into place like the most magnificent algebraic equation.

"What is it, Ben, you're kinda scaring me over here. You ain't gonna pass out again?"

Bradshaw shook his head, and pulled his hands away. They were trembling. He grabbed Henry by the shoulders. "I could kiss you!"

"Don't you dare! You've gone berserk!" Henry blustered and sputtered, but he was laughing, as he pushed Bradshaw away.

"March to the beat of a different drummer," Bradshaw said. "March. Dr. Drummer's Proven Elixir! That's what the killer has over March. Golden-boy's older brother all but put his name on the bottle! How much you want to bet Rudy's shrewd master up in Dawson was named Albert March?"

"No," Henry breathed.

"And that Seattle's smuggling mastermind is disguised as a mild-mannered man-of-all-work?"

"Damn it, Ben. Are you serious?"

"Dead serious. I should have seen it earlier! I was distracted by those brass buttons. Albert couldn't have killed Hopper, he didn't have time, so I never considered him. I failed to see how he might fit in. I failed to see there could have been two separate brass-buttoned men involved in the scheme. One provided the motive for Ralph Hopper racing up to my back lane, and the other committed the murder."

"What are we doing sitting here? Let's go tell O'Brien."

"No, we need proof. I've got only theory and tenuous conjecture."

"Tell me, let's have it, I'm in the dark."

Bradshaw closed his eyes and tried to describe his theory, a parade of images linked only by his imagination. "The smuggled phenacetin is being cut with acetanelid. Ralph's tonic was poisoned with acetanelid. I find Ralph Hopper dead, his tonic is off the streets, and Dr. Drummer's is left king of the corner. The corner is manned by a peddler who secures his prime spot with graft paid to a brass-buttoned policeman. Emily said her father was killed by someone wearing brass buttons, not far from my house. The Hoppers' wagon was abandoned behind my house, across the lane from the Woodworth's, where a man-of-all-work named Albert March toils in service and bitterness, forever in the shadow of a much younger, more successful brother. Albert March went up north to seek his fortune, but unlike his little brother, had no luck, but he did learn something, and that was how to milk miners and drifters and gamblers and businessmen with his friend Rudy aka Victor, who also failed in the gold fields only to find easier money in town. They got back to Seattle and set up shop, both of them hiding behind legitimate jobs, Victor at the theater and Albert with the Woodworths. All had gone well until Ralph Hopper showed up and put a dent in the tonic business. Hopper refused to pay up or leave town, even when Victor used the drugs in his supply to poison Ralph's tonic. Ralph figured out that Albert March was behind it all, and he got mad but he didn't know a cop he could trust, and he certainly couldn't go to Detective March. Sick from his own tonic, Hopper charged up Capitol Hill late one night to confront Albert at the Woodworth's, and that's why the blasted wagon was in my lane!

"Albert had gone out to fetch the carriage to bring Mr. Woodworth home, but someone else saw Hopper, or maybe Hopper announced his intention somewhere he shouldn't have, and he was followed. Who had a vested interest in shutting up Ralph Hopper? That brass-buttoned patrolman who's up to his eyeballs in graft, the very same patrolman who pointed a finger at Nell "Harry" Pickerell, the patrolman whose wife won't let him see his five children and who frequents the Seattle Grand where Victor works his smuggling operation, *that* patrolman gave chase and caught up with poor Ralph Hopper in a muddy empty lot."

He looked at Henry. "Our killer is Patrolman Cox."

"Hot damn, Ben, I *am* a genius."

Chapter Twenty-four

They went their separate ways, each with a mission. Henry eagerly took on the investigation of Patrolman Cox, and Bradshaw let him for the simple reason that Henry could go places and listen to gossip where he could not.

As they'd left Volunteer Park, Henry had asked, "You gonna tell O'Brien?"

"Not yet. I want something substantial to bring to him, and I don't want him giving me any orders that limit where we search."

Henry had stopped walking.

"But that means asking questions where you're not supposed to ask."

"I've been thinking about that. O'Brien said it was Detective March who told him my life was in danger."

"And that's as true as it ever was, Ben. March knows of what he speaks, don't he? Maybe he concocted that story he told O'Brien about a price being put on your head to protect his brother, but maybe there's more involved here. It might not just be Albert and Cox who don't want you nosing around. That part of the city, everyone's got secrets and they're all tangled up."

"The Tenderloin tangle."

"Sounds like a square dance, don't it?" Henry started whistling and dancing a jig, but he stopped when Bradshaw didn't laugh and put a hand to his back with a grimace.

"You're not thinking of going down there. Don't be an idiot. I'll go."

"I won't have you go in my stead, Henry."

"Who said anything about your stead? Hell, I'm expected down that part of the city. There's a few likely wondering why I haven't ventured down there since I got back. I won't ask a thing, just drink and carouse and visit a lovely gal I've sorely missed."

"You promise not to ask dangerous questions?"

"Only the kind that'll get me in a hard game or a soft bed."

"Can you subdue yourself enough to catch the streetcar home at about eleven?"

"Damn it, Ben, you do put a cramp in my style. I'm barely warmed up by then."

"That's about the time Cox would have followed Hopper up here, and I'm guessing he didn't walk the two miles, all up hill."

An hour later, Henry was on his way to the Tenderloin district, and Bradshaw, in an effort to keep his inquiries private, boarded the train heading up to the city of Everett where he wired telegrams to Dawson on the newly installed lines, asking the Gold Commissioner and the Northwest Mounted Police for information on Albert March and Victor Rudnikovich.

On his way home, he stopped into the newspaper offices to read back issues, searching for information on Albert's trip to the gold country. Lastly, he paid a visit to Mr. George Fredrickson of Seattle Printing.

At midnight, Bradshaw and Henry met in the basement to review their findings. Bradshaw sat on a stool at his workbench, and Henry lay on the floor, his knees up, trying to ease his back.

"I'll be glad to see Cox hung," Henry said. "Know why his wife kicked him out and refuses to let him see his kids? He beat her. Regularly. She never filed charges against him, but it's common knowledge on the streets that he's a mean son-of-a-bitch. Know why he's never been promoted?"

Bradshaw said, "He said he declined promotion to keep his experience where it's needed."

"Hah! A few years ago, they gave him a shot at detective. He made such a bloody mess of it, they gave him a choice. Back to foot patrol or find a new job."

"Did you learn where he was the night of Hopper's death?"

"Not yet. Soon as I steer the topic to that night, everyone gets yapping about McKinley, rest his soul, and what they were doing when he was shot, or where they were when they heard the news."

"On duty or not that night, we know he had on his uniform when he came up here to silence Hopper because we know Emily is afraid of brass buttons. Did the conductor remember seeing him?"

Henry sighed. "The man on duty tonight wasn't working that night. I'll try again tomorrow. What you learn about Albert?"

"He went north on the same boat as his little brother, but he came home less than a year later, penniless, with a few hundred other disillusioned men. He was asked about his brother and said only he hoped Reggie would smarten up and come home soon. Nothing else was written about him. But Mrs. Prouty came through."

"Aah, the gossip circuit." Henry's rough palms rasped like sand paper as he rubbed them together.

"The short of it is Albert has been in service since he was sixteen, in various positions from gardener to butler. He once took an entire year off to see the country by railroad, working his way from one town to the next. He says it cured him of wanderlust, and what little he had left he lost on the nauseating trip to Skagway."

"That'll do it. I tossed a few good meals over the side myself. Anything else? There's got to be more."

"He's never been married. He was in love with a young woman in San Francisco many years ago, the daughter of an employer, and they didn't approve the match. He has a small framed photo of her beside his bed."

"Stop, Ben, you're breaking my heart."

"He came to work for the Woodworths' when they moved to Seattle and his parents retired from service. The Woodworths' housekeeper, Martha, was in service when he arrived and has known him the longest. Whenever Reggie's name comes up, he gets all quiet and moody and starts barking orders at everyone. He used his entire life savings to finance his trip to Alaska, and he resented the Woodworths' backing his brother. They didn't offer to finance him."

"That's more like it."

"He was sullen and depressed after he returned, and started the habit of late night perambulations, as Mrs. Prouty called them, that continue even now, although not as frequently as in the beginning."

"Now we're getting somewhere. Where's he say he's going?"

"At first he said the docks, to wait for his little brother to return."

"Oh, how noble of him. Now where's he say he's going?"

"To the docks, just to think."

"Can't he come up with a better lie than that?"

"As soon as Reggie came home with his gold, Albert cheered up. Well, as much as a man of his temperament cheers up."

"Wait a minute there, Ben. That doesn't make any sense. His spoiled little brother comes home a millionaire, having succeeded where he'd failed, and it cheers him up?"

"It doesn't make any sense until you know who else was on that ship."

"Let me guess. Rudy."

"Yes, Victor Rudnikovich. And it was just about that time that Albert began leaving the house with mysterious thick envelopes, and returning home with others. No one in the house knows what's in them, or where he takes them."

"Money's in them, and he's taking them to the bank, or wherever he keeps his secret stash. Almost too easy, Ben."

"I know. I don't like it. He's not being secretive enough."

"Maybe he's more like his brother than we thought. Cocksure and full of himself. Thinks he's got the world fooled and doesn't need to hide."

"Maybe." Bradshaw handed Henry a flat Dr. Drummer's label. "And that brings us to the streets of Seattle. For the past year, there's been an active and paid account for Dr. Drummer's by Victor Rudnikovich."

"Hah!"

"He told Mr. Fredrickson that an honest man needs a side business to stay flush, and providing a healthful tonic for the bums and riffraff of Seattle's streets benefits the community."

"Honest man, my Aunt Fanny."

"Victor also said it gives his bum of a brother something to do. The peddler, Mickey, is Victor's brother."

"Hah!"

"The money finds its way from the peddlers, Mickey and others, to Patrolman Cox to Victor, then to Albert March. As far as I can see, calling the tonic Dr. Drummer's is the one and only bit of ego Albert's ever displayed, other than this business with the unexplained envelopes. He's keeping a low profile and has Victor doing all the front work and Cox protecting his territory. Cox might not even realize Albert March is behind it all. O'Brien said that smugglers like to know as little as possible about everyone else involved. Eyes shut and hands out to take as much as they can for their share of the job."

"It's hard not to go across the lane and pin Albert to the wall."

"I know. But finding Emily safely is our most important goal. We need solid proof about Albert and Cox and the rest so O'Brien can nab everyone at once. If any of these men get scared, it could put Emily at greater risk."

"So what do we do now?"

"Same as we did today. We keep digging."

"Till we strike brass, eh?"

But nearly a week went by with both of them following veins that glinted with promise only to reveal fool's gold.

From his forays below Yesler Way, Henry brought home stories and gossip and reports of petty crime. He learned of several patrolmen on the take, more who were honest, and that Cox held no one's respect. Detective March was beloved by the women, envied and admired by the men, and Detective O'Brien figured so little in their lives that opinions had failed to form. There was a general feeling of surprise over the police hunt for Nell Pickerell. Given her odd proclivity, it was believed she might be unbalanced enough to have killed a man. Mainly, everyone just wanted to see what she looked like in a dress.

While hunting evidence against Patrolman Cox, Henry kept an eye and ear out for Emily. The basement workbench began to fill with souvenirs from bars, and flyers from music halls and theaters, including one with a new company of child actors and a six-year-old Greek singing sensation named Cassandra, but no ten-year-old girl hiding from the law. Henry wasn't slipped any threatening notes, neither was he pulled aside to be told any secrets. The Tenderloin district, for all its openness, remained tight-lipped about the child.

Chapter Twenty-five

By Friday morning, Bradshaw was out of ideas. No one claimed to have seen Patrolman Cox charging or even slinking up Capitol Hill on the night Ralph died, and all week Albert hadn't left the Woodworths' house with a mysterious fat envelope or returned home with one or gone anywhere suspicious. Henry had exhausted himself following him.

Now Bradshaw sat gloomily in the kitchen with an untouched cup of coffee, dressed in his best suit, unable to muster enthusiasm for the contest that would take place in a few hours. He was confident his telephonic system would win, but this failed to cheer him. He could have done better, given the time, if he hadn't been so distracted, if he hadn't had to compromise his work, if O'Brien hadn't manipulated and lied to him. What had his secret listening devices brought him? News of Emily? No. Only news of deception. Was he any closer today to finding Emily or her father's killer than he had been a month ago?

No.

Was it possible his theory about Patrolman Cox was absolute claptrap?

Yes.

But who the hell else could it have been? Who else in brass buttons would have chased Ralph Hopper up Capitol Hill? Who else was mean and cold enough to drown a man in mud? Another patrolman, a musician, a bellhop, an elevator operator? Why would any of them do it? What motive would anyone else have? Hell, he couldn't open his theory to the entire brass-buttoned world, and besides, Emily was afraid of Cox. His whole theory rested on the belief that Emily was afraid of a brass-buttoned patrolman, and the patrolman tangled with smuggling and tonic and street corners was Cox.

Is that where he'd gone wrong? Had Emily been confused as both Detective March and O'Brien had so often conjectured? Had March concocted that death threat note scheme involving O'Brien to deflect attention away, simply to keep Bradshaw from stumbling on his brother's underworld connections?

Was there no evidence of murder because there was no murder?

Maybe he'd committed the cardinal sin of scientific investigation—seeking evidence to fit his theory rather than gathering evidence to see where it led.

But if that was the case, why did Ralph Hopper come up to this neighborhood? If his theory was nothing but the forced linkage of events, why did Hopper come down Bradshaw's back lane on the night of his death? Why was it *here* that he abandoned his wagon and his daughter? And why did he find it impossible to believe the location of the abandoned wagon to be random? Meaningless?

Bradshaw absent-mindedly took a drink of his now cold coffee as he examined his human equation that had so convinced him Albert March, and thus Patrolman Cox, was tied to Ralph's death. The key was Dr. Drummer's tonic. It was that name that had launched his theory, that tied it all together. *March to the beat of a different drummer.* There had to be a connection between Albert March and Dr. Drummer's!

A movement in the back lane caught Bradshaw's eye.

He got up and stepped out onto the back porch. Albert had arrived with Mr. Woodworth's carriage. A minute later, the coach door slammed shut, Mr. Woodworth stuck a gloved hand out the window to wave good morning, and Bradshaw waved in return as the carriage pulled down the lane and out of sight. He listened until he no longer heard the clomp of the horse's hooves.

The air held the scent of fall, of dampness, and sweet decay, much of it coming from Mrs. Prouty's vegetable garden and her system of compost piles. The back lawn would need cutting again soon, but the mower needed sharpening, and it would probably rain before he took the time to sharpen the blades. He glanced at the gray sky overhead as he passed through his gate and crossed the lane to the Woodworth's back yard, knowing his thoughts had strayed to avoid contemplating the awkward conversation he was about to force upon his neighbor, whom he hardly knew.

The housekeeper, Martha, answered his knock at the back door, surprised, and welcoming. She was a woman of smaller, softer proportions than Mrs. Prouty, with rosy cheeks and hair as white as her crisp apron.

The warm scent of baking and freshly ground coffee came wafting out to him, so comforting and domestic, he nearly changed his mind.

Martha said, "Professor! I thought it was your Gladys knocking, and that she was through with her Friday chores early and come for coffee."

"Gladys? Oh, Mrs. Prouty." He rarely heard her Christian name. She'd been with him so long, he supposed he should call her Gladys. But he couldn't. She would always be Mrs. Prouty to him. "She's cleaning upstairs, I believe."

"Then it won't be long. Friday's she cleans bottom to top, and it goes fairly quick as she's done her deep cleaning, top to bottom, on Wednesdays."

He'd never paid close attention to the pattern of Mrs. Prouty's housework. It was news to him that she had a system.

"Is Mrs. Woodworth at home?"

"She's in the sitting room. You come on in and wait here, and I'll let her know you're wanting to see her."

Bradshaw took off his hat and stepped into the warm embrace of the kitchen. Twice as large as his own, with the newest range and icebox, and a scrubbed wooden table loaded with two steaming pies and a fluffy-looking cake. He recalled plates of overcooked broad beans and had disloyal thoughts about Mrs. Prouty.

Martha returned to lead Bradshaw to a floral sitting room, and introduced him to Mrs. Woodworth, who remained seated with a quilt over her lap. She looked younger than her years, with little gray in her upswept brown hair. Lovely, but pale, and far too thin. She dismissed the housekeeper then looked at Bradshaw with a faint smile.

He said, "I'm sorry to trouble you when you're not well."

"It's no bother. Have a seat, please. What can I do for you, Professor?"

He sat in the armchair across from her, leaning forward beseechingly. "I'm not sure that you can do anything. It's about the peddler's wagon, Ralph's Restorative, that was abandoned in our joint lane."

She jerked her head away, turning her gaze to the small hearth fire. Its warmth filled the room and she had the quilt, yet she shuddered.

"You might have heard that I've been searching for the child, Ralph Hopper's daughter, Emily?"

He saw her throat work as she swallowed. She gave him a series of small nods, without looking at him.

"I've run out of ideas, and so I'm going back to the beginning, to that night."

Her nodding continued, and now her mouth was working, her lips pressing and biting softly.

"Can I get you some water?"

She shook her head, cleared her throat, and said, "No, thank you," as if trying, and failing, to put force behind the words.

"Have you ever heard of a tonic called Dr. Drummer's?"

She closed her eyes and sat perfectly still.

"March to the beat of a different drummer?"

Her intake of breath was shallow and sharp, telling him she had some knowledge of Dr. Drummer's being connected with Albert March. She placed a pale, trembling hand over her mouth. Alarmed, Bradshaw sat forward. She seemed unable to breathe.

"Shall I get your housekeeper?"

She shook her head and signaled him to wait. In a moment, she opened her eyes and gave him a trembling smile that held no joy.

He didn't want to press her, she was too fragile. Yet he needed to learn what she knew. Her reaction had been to his questions, he was sure of it, not her illness.

"You saw a patrolman that night. Patrolman Cox?"

She didn't deny it. She closed her eyes again.

"He followed Ralph Hopper because Ralph had come to confront Albert about Dr. Drummer's. Is that right?"

She shook her head.

"I know this puts you in a horrendous position, Mrs. Woodworth. Albert March has been with you a long time, and you're close to his family. I was hoping you'd give me permission to search Albert's room."

She blinked, her eyes narrowed, brow furrowed.

"I'm aware that he leaves home often with small packages, and returns home with them, but refuses to explain to the rest of your staff. I believe they might contain evidence of his connection with drug smuggling."

To his surprise, a true smile briefly flitted across her face. "No Professor, Albert isn't involved in anything illegal. Those envelopes contain stories."

"I beg your pardon?"

"He writes stories. Short stories that he sends off to magazines to be published. He began writing them a few years ago, when he came home from Alaska."

Surely, this was his cover. This was how he'd explained himself one day when she caught him with one of his packages. "Why is he so secretive?"

"Because they're love stories, Professor. He doesn't want to be teased. He carries a torch for a girl he loved long ago, and he pours that into his tales. They're very good, rather heart-wrenching."

He sat still, taking in her words. She had an opinion on the stories. She'd read them. They were real. But his writing stories didn't preclude more sinister activities. Patrolman Cox had come here the night Ralph died, she hadn't denied the fact. Neither had she confirmed it.

"Emily Hopper's life is in danger and you may be the only one that can help her. I believe she saw Patrolman Cox kill her father that night. She told my son the man who killed her father wore brass buttons."

Mrs. Woodworth had gone so still and pale, he was afraid she about to either faint or vomit. He withheld his questions, watching her to see if she would recover or if he should run for Martha.

After a long, silent moment, she took a deep breath and pressed the quilt aside. "Will you excuse me a moment, Professor?" He barely heard the faint words.

She left the room, walking more steadily than he'd thought her capable of. He got up and paced to the fireplace, feeling a bit sick himself. His shoulders ached. Love stories? Maybe he was wrong about everything. He'd manufactured a ridiculous theory with human variables. Human variables were not to be trusted. God, how he longed for the absoluteness of numbers.

He heard the soft swish of the door opening. He turned to see Mrs. Woodworth shut the door. She stood still for a moment, her back to him. When at last she turned to face him, he saw she held a carefully folded jacket. The scarlet material had satin trim, a square collar. And brass buttons.

Her voice trembled. "That night, the night you're asking about, Reggie asked me to store this for him. It's his band uniform."

"Reggie?" Bradshaw's voice carried no further than a whisper. But Mrs. Woodworth's eyes acknowledged him. "Detective March?" He asked again. To be sure.

She held his gaze, her eyes full of despair. "We gave him music lessons when he was a boy."

Chapter Twenty-six

Bradshaw didn't know what he said or did next, exactly, he'd gone numb, and then the opposite, his mind reeling with the implications of that brass-buttoned band uniform.

He found himself home again, in his own parlor before his own hearth, and looking into the blue eyes of Emily's doll. He picked it up and tipped it gently so that its eyes opened, closed, opened.

Reggie March had held this doll. He'd come to Bradshaw's home, knowing he'd killed Ralph Hopper. Knowing Emily was the only witness. And he knew that because Bradshaw had told him.

"Oh, God," he whispered.

Reginald March had played with his band the night Ralph Hopper died. Bradshaw heard him talking about it on the courthouse steps the next day. He must have seen Ralph Hopper going up the hill, heading for the Woodworths. Not Patrolman Cox, but Detective March. In his brass-buttoned band uniform.

Mrs. Olsen and Minnie had heard a thump or a clump or a bump. And then the wagon was abandoned. And a little girl was left shivering and alone, the only witness to a man in brass buttons keeping her father from lifting his face from the muck.

Bradshaw clutched the doll to his chest, suppressing a rising tide of anguish and remorse. He must find Emily. Now. Before Detective March found her.

"Where is she?" he whispered desperately to the doll. This doll was all that he had, the only tangible connection to Emily.

He'd told Missouri he'd not examined it closely. But March had, when Bradshaw had gone to the kitchen to pop the lid off the Coca-Cola.

Now, belatedly, he looked where March had looked. Under the doll's fur muff, inside the hat, inside the jacket. And there was a tag. A small silk tag printed with the name of the manufacturer, and the name they'd given this doll.

Cassandra.

Cassandra. Where had he seen that name? A thousand snippets of information flashed in rapid-fire succession and then he saw it, the flyer Henry brought home from a theater a few days ago. Cassandra, the six-year old Greek sensation. Missouri told him Emily had appeared on stage. She'd told him everyone always overlooked something hidden in plain sight. The letter on the table. The child actress on stage. Emily was small for her age. She could pull off six.

"Henry!" Still clutching the doll, Bradshaw spun on his heel and ran out of the parlor, up the stairs. "Henry, get up, I need you. Now!"

"What's all the shouting about?" Mrs. Prouty emerged from the bathroom with her scrub brush in hand as he hammered his fist on Henry's door.

"Telephone the police, Mrs. Prouty. Ask for Detective O'Brien and speak to no one else. It's vital you speak to no one else. Telephone his home if he's not at the station. Keep trying to get him. Tell him it's March. Detective March killed Ralph Hopper."

Henry's door flew open and he stood bedraggled in his bedclothes and nightcap.

"Detective March? That lily-livered liar!"

"Detective March?" echoed Mrs. Prouty with angry astonishment.

Bradshaw said her, "Tell O'Brien that Emily is posing as Cassandra at the Variety Theater. We're going there now to find her before March does. Henry, throw on some clothes and meet me out front in two minutes. Go!"

Henry hustled into his room and Mrs. Prouty dropped her brush to head for the stairs. Bradshaw beat her, flying down the hall to the kitchen and basement. He grabbed the flyer from the Variety Theater featuring the Greek child "Cassandra," his portable listening device, hat and overcoat, and when he reached the front yard, Henry was there, shirt tail flapping, bent over and trying to tie his boots, saying "ouch, ouch, ouch."

"Tie them later, let's go."

They ran two blocks, Henry yelping the whole time, and leaped aboard the streetcar just as it began to roll.

They dropped side-by-side onto a seat, gasping.

"What you bring that for?" Henry said, once his boots were tied and he'd caught his breath, nodding at the wire sticking out of Bradshaw's coat pocket. Emily's doll stuck out of the other pocket.

"I still don't have any evidence. Against anybody."

"You can use that to get evidence?"

"I don't know." He didn't have a grand plan, he had simply grabbed and run, motivated by instinct, hoping for a bit of luck for once.

They both examined the theater flyer. It was a mess of various lettering styles, and the drawing of the featured performer, Cassandra, gave little detail save a mop of black curls and an exotic costume on a pint-sized child. Opening night had been two days ago. Had March seen the flyer? Had he taken mental note of the doll's name? Were they too late?

The Variety was locked, the lights dark. They pounded on the doors anyway, hoping to find someone, a custodian, anyone, within. A window above the entrance opened and an annoyed voice called out.

"Go away, we don't open for another three hours!"

"This is official police business," shouted Bradshaw. The window slammed shut with a rattle, and a minute later, a haphazardly dressed pear-shaped man opened the door to them and squinted into the daylight.

"Are you the caretaker here?"

"Do you see a broom in my hand? I'm Mr. Thomas Peavey, the manager of the theater. Now what's this all about, and who are you? You're not one of the regular detectives." Mr. Peavey ran his squinted eyes over them. When he got to the doll's head peeking out of Bradshaw's coat pocket, his eyes flashed open, and he took a step back.

"I'm Professor Bradshaw. Detective O'Brien will be here shortly."

"I know him," Peavey said, jabbing a finger toward Henry. "Used to be a regular. Heard you come home empty-handed from Alaska."

"Hurt my back," said Henry defensively, putting a hand to his spine and pulling a face.

Bradshaw said, "We're here to find Emily Hopper. You'll know her as Cassandra."

"Now listen, I've already told the police everything I know about that. You got no call to get me outa my bed to ask the same questions again." He moved to shut the door.

"When did you tell the police everything?"

"Last night, of course, when Detective March came for her. Didn't even let her finish the show. She was none too happy. Neither was I. Right little star that girl."

Mr. Peavey's eyes darted between Bradshaw and Henry, who both stared at him in dismay. "Now listen," he said again, "I didn't know she was that Emily Hopper everyone was looking for. She said her ma worked nights and that's why she never came to the theater. She had those black curls. Told me her name was Cassandra. Course, I knew she was older'n six, but she was small enough to pull it off."

"Where did they go? Where did March take Emily? Did he say?"

"He took her home, of course. Where else?"

"How did Emily react? Was she frightened? Did she fight?"

"Course she were frightened, she'd been caught, hadn't she? She liked being here, liked being the star of the show. She went willingly enough, once her aunt had a talk with her."

"Her aunt? A woman was with Detective March?"

"We weren't formally introduced. It wasn't exactly a social call. Cassandra called the woman 'Auntie' and liked her well enough that she settled down, once she understood she'd have to go home. And before you ask, I'll tell you, it's New York City. The three of them left here for the train station."

"Some pluck, wouldn't you say?" asked the ticket clerk, a young man with pocked skin and a quick smile, who'd been on duty the previous night, and was back again in the booth just starting a new shift. "Only ten, and losing her father, and having the nerve to go it alone on stage. I've a bit of singing talent myself, but golly, I couldn't imagine at that age being bold as you please. That detective was as proud of her as if she were his own child, even though she did give him a chase. He bought two sleepers on the Great Northern, the luxury train. One for himself, and one for the lady and child. Taking her home on his own dime. Nice to see money don't spoil everyone. Generous as he is rich, that Detective March. Ever been on the Great Northern? She's a beauty."

Henry moaned, "They're half a day ahead of us."

"No," said the clerk cheerfully, "the Great Northern departs mornings so the passengers get the views going over the mountains. They pulled out about an hour ago."

Henry said, "Hot damn!"

Bradshaw knew it was too soon to celebrate. "Is there a train we can take to catch up?"

The clerk won Bradshaw's admiration for his reaction to the question. He was eager for the chance to find a solution and asked no prying questions. After a few minutes of consulting his time tables and maps and neat calculations with his pencil, he had the answer.

"A freighter, the Northern Pacific, leaves in twelve minutes, and she's scheduled to stop in Wenatchee just past noon. She's light and fast, got a new engine still breaking in, so only pulling half a load. Once in Wenatchee, they'll take on fuel and supplies.

If my calculations are right, the freighter will pull in behind the Great Northern about a half hour before she's due to depart."

"We'll trust your calculations and take two tickets, one way."

"No tickets needed for the Northern, sir. No accommodations either, mind, but the crew is always happy for a few paying passengers. No hobos. The company lets them keep the fare."

The accommodations turned out to be a space hollowed for them in a freight car loaded with fat, dusty flour sacks from the Everett Milling Company. They climbed in and the sliding door was slammed shut by the cheerful engineer in his blue stripes, and soon, the whistle blasted and the wheels began to roll. They were off, with only the clothes on their backs, two itchy wool blankets, a galvanized bucket for a chamber pot, two pints of water, and the ticket clerk's own lunch basket he'd generously donated to their adventure.

"Ben," Henry said, once the whistle had silenced and the train was moving at a steady pace that sent wind whistling through the wood slats. "I don't get it. Why'd he go and tell all and sundry where he was heading? Maybe we're on a fool's errand and he's heading anywhere but New York."

Bradshaw leaned back against the flour sacks, his eyes closed, letting the rhythm of the train rock him. A fool's errand? It was a possibility.

"He's taking her away, that's all I know for sure."

"So it was young Reggie not old Albert that milked the miners and came home to run a smuggling ring."

"No." Bradshaw frowned. "No, Reggie was protecting his brother when he killed Hopper." But he didn't believe that any longer, did he? Albert's secretive behavior hid only a clandestine writing career.

"You sure?"

For the sake of argument, because arguing with Henry often produced answers, he said, "Golden boy is rich, what would be the point?"

"You sure he's rich?"

"I know you hate the idea that he struck gold, Henry, but everyone knows he was one of the lucky ones. So I'm wondering, if he is the smuggling mastermind and not Albert, what would be the point?"

"Everyone knows? For a rock-solid fact? Isn't it you always spouting about *pre*sumptions and *ass*umptions? March struts around saying he's rich, he struck gold, everyone *assumes* he's telling the truth. If he's really rich, gold-rich, why be a cop? It's a lotta work. You gotta show up. You gotta *work*."

Henry had made a good point. To prod him onward, Bradshaw said, "Not everyone labors as hard as you to avoid work. March has ambitions. Politics, that sort."

"And being a cop helps how? Ain't it enough he can say he's living the American dream? Went to Alaska, a poor man, rolled up his sleeves, survived hardships, came home with buckets of gold? He's Rockefeller, Carnegie, self-made man, all that malarkey."

What *did* being a policeman do for Reginald March? Policemen were respected, mostly, sometimes. Policemen learned about crime in their cities. Policemen learned who was powerful. They could go anywhere they wanted, walk in and out of businesses, ask questions. It was the perfect job from which to run a smuggling ring.

"Didn't you read about him in the newspapers coming home with his so-called riches? Did anyone actually see him with any gold?"

Bradshaw had been mainly looking for details on Albert, but he'd read everything concerning the two of them. He now told Henry what he remembered. Both newspapers reported Reginald "Reggie" March was aboard the steamship *Rosalie* in July, 1897, with a few hundred other hopefuls, including Albert, and returned to Seattle, September, 1898, reporting a "substantial amount" in gold dust and nuggets, cash and securities. He'd refused to say exactly how much, but that was common with many of the passengers who kept their gold in grips and sacks and luggage, locked in their staterooms. The Seattle Assay office had newly opened for business, and while the others gladly traded in their gold rather than go on to California, Reggie March had opted to save his treasure for the San Francisco assay office. He wanted full bags to show his elderly, retired parents who lived in San Francisco, he'd said.

Henry grunted. "That's suspicious. Why haul all that weight and responsibility another thousand miles? He could have banked it all here, kept a bag of dust and nuggets to show off to the folks."

"He behaved no differently than many other lucky miners, keeping their gold close and their mouths shut," Bradshaw said, but he agreed whole-heartedly with Henry.

"How do we know he had any gold at all in his bags? Coulda been full of rocks."

They fell silent, the grumble and rocking of the train pulling them into their own thoughts. Bradshaw thought about the brothers. Albert, first-born son, following in his father's footsteps. Reginald, surprise child, welcomed like a little prince by his parents and the Woodworths. One served quietly in a small household. The other served prominently in a burgeoning city. One lived a modest life in a servant's room in another man's home, writing secret love stories. The other had been a spoiled child with the gift of charm who wore elegant new suits and escorted politician's daughters to the theater.

Reginald had laughed and joked on the courthouse steps the day after killing a man. He'd made small talk in Bradshaw's living room and convinced him he was genuinely concerned for the missing child. He'd convinced O'Brien to write a threatening note to a man he considered a trusted friend. Bradshaw brought to mind every encounter he'd had with Reggie March, analyzing them for deception and manipulation. He found plenty.

"Henry?"

"Ben?"

"I've been a fool."

"Again?"

"Reggie's the smuggler."

"Makes sense to me. What about Albert's perambulations? Where's he go at night?"

"I think he goes to the docks to wait for his little brother."

"What? You mean metaphorically? And yes, I know that word, I didn't sleep through all my classes. He knows, then? That his golden little brother is a fraud?"

"Or he suspects, and he's sick about it. And so is Mrs. Woodworth."

Fifty miles slid under them before Bradshaw spoke again.

"He's like a powerful magnet and those around him are conductors."

Henry snorted. "I'm sorry, Ben, go on. You talking about golden-boy March? How is March like a magnet?"

"Even you can see that, Henry. How is electricity generated? Induction. Move a magnet near a copper wire and electricity flows. March is the same. He uses his charm like a magnetic field to induce behavior, to generate action that benefits him. But that night—" Bradshaw paused, envisioning that dark night when March prevented Ralph Hopper from lifting his face from the muck. "I believe March realized he'd started something he couldn't stop. His attempt to run a competitor out of town had backfired. Instead of fleeing, Ralph Hopper had been induced to pry until he discovered the ugly truth of March's riches and threatened to reveal them. For Hopper, March's scheming became a fatal induction."

"I hate them sneak sneaky types. Fatal induction. Ha! Bet March never thought an electrical engineer would do him in. But what's to stop the child from telling the truth, once March brings her home or wherever he's taking her?"

What was to stop her? What had convinced her to go with March when she'd been so afraid of him all this time? He'd brought a woman with him, someone Emily trusted. Was it Miss Darlyrope? Was she involved in this? He'd bought tickets on a luxury train, with plush accommodations, the likes of which Emily had never seen, or felt, or tasted. In this new and wonderful environment, was March sweet-talking Emily? Was he now promising her great fame and fortune? What else would appeal to a child such as Emily? Was he promising her he was taking her to a place where her dreams would come true? Was he taking her somewhere so far away, so out of reach, her accusations could never be heard in Seattle? Or anywhere?

"Ben?"

"I believe he intends to take her to New York, with many witnesses to his heroic journey. After that—I don't know. Let's hope we catch up to them and never find out what was to come after that."

For an hour, they were silent again with their thoughts, lulled by the movement of the train and the cocoon of sound. The steady vibration leeched fine particles of white flour dust from the sacks that blended with the grittier black dust billowing from the engines and seeping through the slats. Bradshaw wrote "Missouri" in the layer of dust on his trousers, wiping the letters away when Henry opened his eyes.

"Ben, what did you learn that made you all fired up to go chasing March?"

Bradshaw smiled at Henry as it dawned on him he hadn't yet explained. He hadn't told him what he'd learned from Mrs. Woodworth, about Albert's love stories, the brass-buttoned band uniform, the doll named Cassandra. Henry had simply trusted him.

"I'm glad you're home, Henry," he said.

"Hell, I'm not home, I'm sitting on a hard flour sack heading for Chicago and all points east." He grinned. "But I know what you mean. I'm glad to be back. You're different now, you know that? Hard to believe the change. It's like being back in college. Only it hurts more. What happened?"

"What didn't happen? Professor Oglethorpe died and nothing's been the same since."

"You pined too long over what Rachel done to you. Glad to see a bit of life in you again."

"Glad to feel it." He explained to Henry what he'd learned from Mrs. Woodworth that had landed them here, now, on an eastbound freight train.

"Uh, Ben?"

"Hmm."

"Ain't today the eleventh?"

"I think so, why? Oh. Damn." The contest.

"Maybe they'll put it off if you don't show."

"No. It's been advertised. A hundred households are standing by to listen."

"Maybe they'll test yours anyway, without you there."

"My equipment in the electrical room is locked." He reached into his inner jacket pocket and retrieved a key.

"Maybe—"

"You're a hopeless optimist, Henry. It's over. Mr. Daily will win. It will be good business for his store."

"You're taking it awful well."

He thought of sitting in his parlor, with the sounds of the theater coming to him from someone else's telephonic system and his stomach churned and his chest tightened, as if it were something truly important. He was not proud of it, but there it was. His petty ego would not like having lost due to forfeit. His system, even with the less-than optimal loud-talker, was still superior to Daily's and Smith's and he knew it. The win should be his. And he'd lost it. "No, I'm not, Henry. No I'm not."

Chapter Twenty-seven

"This is Henry, one of our modernizing engineers. It's necessary for him to ride in here for a short time to test the wiring schema that transmits signals between the electric lighting fixtures and the main generator. If you could keep your voices down, he'll be able to better listen to the telegraphic signals and record whether the system is working correctly." Bradshaw managed to say this nonsense with a straight face to the three elderly women in the ladies' parlor aboard the Great Northern. Their uniform reactions were pursed lips and wrinkled noses.

The express freight train had caught up with the gilded passenger train in Wenatchee, a small, thriving farm town on the eastern side of the Cascades, as the young clerk had calculated. But he and Henry had had just twenty minutes to get aboard, and not enough money between them to buy even a single ticket. Their rough appearance, covered as they were in flour and soot, hadn't convinced the ticket master they were upstanding citizens and would make good on an I-owe-you, so they'd stood in line at the depot's express office to wire Bradshaw's bank. They'd watched the big hands of the station clock tick away precious minutes as they waited for a reply.

"Just tell them to stop the train from leaving," Henry had growled. "Haul March's sorry ass off the train and get the local sheriff to lock him up."

"We've got no evidence, Henry. We've got to catch him off guard, like we planned, or he'll talk his way out of any charges."

The rat-a-tat-tat of the bank's reply saved them, and they climbed aboard the luxury train armed with standard Pullman tickets, seconds before it pulled out. A porter had informed them they would find Detective Reginald March in the writing room adjacent the ladies' parlor.

Now, Bradshaw faced three stern matronly faces. "I apologize for Henry's dishevelment. He's near the end of his shift." Both of them had tried to clean up in the cramped gentleman's toilet, managing only to streak their clothing, smear the cakey soot deeper into their pores, and soil the pristine hand towels. "If you'd prefer to go along to the dining car, the railroad would be happy to extend their apology to the intrusion on your journey with complimentary drinks and appetizers." He held out a two-dollar bill enticingly.

"We'll stay here," declared one of the matrons, with a wary eye on Henry, as if to say, *and we will guard our parlor!* The other two nodded their support.

"As you wish. Henry—"

"And you may have the drinks and food delivered."

"Yes. Of course. As soon as I get Henry set up."

The women reluctantly arranged themselves together on one side of the compartment in the ornately upholstered chairs that matched the green Wilton carpet. Henry dropped down onto an upholstered chair, sending up a puff of gray dust. The women gasped.

"Try not to touch anything, Henry," Bradshaw muttered. A black smear already showed on the chair's arm. He pulled his portable eavesdropping microphone from his pocket, connected the dry cell battery, tugged the headset into position over his ears, and pressed the transmitter to the mahogany paneled wall. For two very long minutes during which sweat began to form at Bradshaw's temples, he heard nothing but the sounds of the moving train and distant clanks, distant voices. And then he heard, clear as if in the same room.

"Why, that's very good. I like the tree, especially." A woman's voice, young, cheerful.

"That's the tree I used to climb when I was a little girl." *Emily.*

"And who did you draw here? Is that you?"

"No, that's my baby brother."

Then came the sound of humming, two voices, perfectly harmonized, the woman's and the child's.

Bradshaw pulled the headphones off and placed them on Henry's head, then shoved a spare battery in Henry's coat pocket. Henry plunked Bradshaw's notebook on the small table beside the chair and held Bradshaw's pencil poised above it. He pressed the transmitter against the wall.

"Change the battery when the sound dims, about fifteen minutes," he whispered. "And don't try to write everything, just key words."

Henry nodded, his eyes distant, already listening. He wrote, "Bird Gilded Cage." The name of the song being hummed.

Bradshaw hurried along the narrow passage to the dining car to fetch the food, cursing himself for making the offer. The steward wanted to send a porter, but Bradshaw couldn't risk Henry's presence being questioned. He discovered why they'd been so insistent on his way back with the tray. The movement of the train made the silver rattle and the drinks clank dangerously as he weaved like a drunkard back to the compartment.

Henry was listening as if in a trance. Bradshaw slid the tray onto the table before the women and hurried out as they began to examine the shrimp salad, Paragon cheese and water crackers, and slices of spice cake with caramel frosting.

In the narrow passage, with stubbled farmland and rugged foothills sliding by the window behind him, he stood outside the writing compartment, debating a final question. Knock, or enter without warning?

He entered.

It was a large compartment, outfitted like a library, with shelved books, wide upholstered chairs and writing tables scattered with periodicals. Sheers over the wide window let in light but blocked the view.

Three faces turned to him.

One was young and painted, belonging to a woman with brown upswept hair. She smiled at him openly. Snuggled in the chair with her, face clean and innocent, curls dyed black, was Emily, unsmiling, tentative. She sat with a sketchpad on her lap, her feet not touching the floor. Yes, she could pull off six. She blinked at him, threw a glance at the woman beside her, then across to Detective March.

March's handsome face was smiling. He stood with a laugh and an outstretched hand. In welcome.

"Professor Bradshaw, as I live and breathe. This couldn't be a coincidence."

The sweet smell of Tutti-Frutti gum turned Bradshaw's stomach. He did not accept the extended hand. "No, it's not." He pulled a small burlap sack from his overcoat pocket and carefully removed the satin-dressed doll. Cassandra.

Emily gasped and reached out. Bradshaw put the doll in her hands, and she clutched it tightly. The climbing tree sketch slipped to the floor.

"Don't tell me you came all this way to return the doll. And did you travel by mule?" March chuckled, shaking his head as his eyes swept Bradshaw's grimy appearance.

Bradshaw held March's eye steadily.

March shrugged at Bradshaw's silence. "Have a seat, join us. It's such a strange feeling running into someone so far from home. I suppose you'll tell us eventually what the story is behind your sudden, disheveled appearance."

Bradshaw sat because the jostling of the train made standing awkward.

"Reminds me of the time I was in Alaska, trudging along a lonely, icy trail in the middle of absolutely nowhere, days from any town, when I saw a figure in the distance coming toward me, and after about ten minutes we met up, and he turned out to be the milkman I knew as a boy in San Francisco who used to deliver to the Woodworths' kitchen door twice a week."

Bradshaw remained silent. He'd been around students long enough to recognize nerves being played out in an overabundance of conversation.

Fifteen seconds of silence passed. Thirty.

"Well, I thought it was odd," said March. "Meeting the milkman in the Alaska wilderness." He laughed, and the young woman laughed. Emily stared silently at her doll.

Bradshaw asked, "Was that before or after you struck gold?"

"Oh, before. After I found gold, I avoided lonely, icy trails. I'd had enough of those to last a lifetime."

"And where was it that you struck gold?"

"North of Dawson."

"What creek? Henry's told me about every inch of that territory."

"Were you surprised to see your old friend return home so soon?"

"What creek?"

"I'll bet he has some stories to tell."

Bradshaw held March's gaze silently until the detective swallowed. "He told me a good one about a man named Rudy. That's his nickname. His full name's Victor Rudnikovich."

March didn't blink, but the young woman gave a small gasp. "Victor? He's the manager at the Seattle Grand. Isn't that a coincidence?"

Bradshaw turned to look at her astonished face. "We haven't been introduced. I'm Benjamin Bradshaw."

"Oh, I know who you are, Professor, but I don't suppose you know me. I'm not famous. No yet, anyways. I'm Daisy. Just Daisy. I dropped my last name for the stage. It's easy to remember, don't you think?"

Daisy! The young woman smiled at him prettily, her eyes perfectly focused on his.

"I thought you were blind."

"Oh, I was! For a whole day, I couldn't see a thing, not hardly at all."

"A single day?"

She shrugged and gave him a sheepish grin. "Well, it was blurry for a bit longer than that."

"Admit it, Daisy," said March teasingly, "you milked your condition to get Harry's attention."

"Lotta good it did me! Everyone told me he was a girl, but I just couldn't believe it, not until he escaped from jail in a dress and came to hide with me and Emily. Good heavens, she's even pretty! I don't know how I could have been so blind—oh! That's funny."

Bradshaw observed the interplay between Daisy and March, she blushing, he smiling, and he knew it hadn't been Daisy's idea to milk her blindness, although she believed it was. March had given her the idea, oh so skillfully. The art of induction. Had it been seduction as well? She was a single, young woman travelling alone with a single young man. Emily's presence, and separate sleeping compartments, didn't make the situation less compromising.

"You pretended to be blind to get attention?"

"I know it sounds bad, when you put it like that. But you must admit I was superb in the role. Even Ann believed me. Ann's my roommate, Miss Darlyrope. I had to stay in the apartment most of the time, and that was no fun, but presents kept arriving, and everyone was so kind to me."

"Including Detective March? He visited you on the day your vision began to clear."

"Why yes, how did you know? He was so concerned and attentive. When I tried to tell him I was getting better, he said I needn't pretend to be brave, that he would always look after me. That's when I got the idea to, well, delay my healing."

Oh, no, Daisy, thought Bradshaw, you didn't get the idea, he cunningly led you into it. Your blindness helped ensure the end of Ralph's Restorative and the success of Dr. Drummer's. Your blindness ensured Ralph Hopper's death would be considered a deserved fate and not investigated thoroughly. March also brought you here now, but you truly believe you've come of your own free will.

"Why did you hide Emily? You knew the police were looking for her."

"Of course I did, that's *why* we were hiding her." She put her arm protectively around Emily. "She was afraid of the police, but it was all just a big misunderstanding. Wasn't it, sweetie?" She looked down at Emily, who had buried her face in Daisy's sleeve. "I didn't keep my sight a secret from her, of course. She was with me all day—it would have been too tedious."

"What was the misunderstanding?"

"Detective March explained it all when he came asking for my help. I was tired of pretending to be blind by then and confessed to what I'd done. He thought I was a very clever actress," she threw a flirtatious smile at March. "He convinced me to go on a little longer, for Emily's sake. She was so safe with me, you see. But then the silly girl went and ran away again. Dyed your hair, too!" Daisy ruffled the top of Emily's black curls affectionately. "She wanted to be a great actress, like her Aunt Daisy. Well, she will. We both will, in New York."

Bradshaw said to March, "Detective O'Brien knew that Emily was at the Eskimo."

March's smile broadened. "No, he didn't."

Bradshaw imitated March's noncommittal shrug.

"Come now, Bradshaw. You know as well as I, that O'Brien would have sent Daisy and Miss Darlyrope to jail if he'd known they were hiding the child. That's why I said nothing while I continued my investigation. Surely you don't think they deserved to be locked up. They meant well, hiding her, their maternal instincts and all. Keeping quiet gave me time to investigate to be sure there was no murderer lurking about the city. It turned out the girl had been confused the night her father died, just like we thought. Understandable, under the circumstances, poor kid."

Bradshaw threw a concerned glance at Emily. Her face was still pressed into Daisy's arm. He looked again at March.

"Emily wouldn't have hidden with Daisy and Miss Darlyrope if she'd known you were a frequent visitor. She fled when you discovered her."

"She wasn't running from me, but to a life on the stage. She's got talent and ambition."

"You brought Daisy with you to the theater because you knew Emily would never leave with you alone."

"Daisy liked the idea of the adventure and wanted to come along."

"Where are you taking Emily?"

"Home of course." March's face turned earnest, and he leaned forward. "Listen, Professor, is that why you're here? Did you think I was taking Emily away to cover a crime? That I'm somehow guilty? Please, sir! I admire your deductive reasoning, but I'm afraid it has sent you on a wild chase for nothing."

"Dr. Drummer's? You couldn't resist the gag? Your name disguised on the label? You didn't really need the money, the phenacetin was so lucrative."

March laughed. "I don't know what you're talking about."

Bradshaw looked March in the eye, counting slowly to five before saying, "Emily was never afraid of the police, not the uniformed patrolmen."

"Oh, but she was, because of the brass buttons," argued March with another laugh. "Turned out to be Albert's all along. She confused details of that night. It's understandable."

"No, the brass buttons weren't Albert's, they were yours. What instrument is it you play? The clarinet?"

The blue eyes blinked at him. Time seemed to stand still. Bradshaw felt the power of March's personality, like a magnetic field, reaching out, seeking a way to force him to change course.

"Your band played the night of Ralph's death. I heard you being congratulated on your performance the next day, on the courthouse steps."

Daisy said, "He's a wonderful musician, and he has a great eye for talent. He says Emily and I are born to be stars of the stage. That's why we're going to New York—"

"New York isn't Emily's home," Bradshaw interrupted as he continued to study March. "That's not where the climbing tree or her little brother are."

March's expression remained amused, but Emily's reaction proved him right. She began to cry, and Daisy soothed her, saying, "Now, now, what's this all about, no need for tears."

March opened his mouth to speak, but Bradshaw had heard enough lies. "I've spoken with Mrs. Woodworth, Detective. I've seen your scarlet uniform."

For a few seconds, March was unable to mask his anger. It flashed in his eyes and wiped the smile from his face. He forced another laugh, but he seemed unable to phrase a lie, to find a way out.And then the corner of his mouth lifted in a smirk and he said in a pleasant tone, "Your son doesn't know about his mother, does he?"

The words hit Bradshaw with the full force of a belly blow. It was a weapon he hadn't anticipated, and the warning was crystal clear: take this any farther and the price would be his son's innocence. March would tell the world about Rachel's suicide.

Bradshaw looked into the cold, blue eyes, unable to breathe, or think, just feel the overwhelming ache in his heart.

Then March's face spread into a "gotcha" grin. And Bradshaw found his voice.

"I know you're guilty."

"You'll never prove it."

Without taking his eyes from March's, he said quietly, "Stop the train, Henry."

March's brow lifted in confusion, his grin fading.

An alarm whistle sounded in response to Henry pulling the emergency cord in the next compartment. Bradshaw wished he could relish the astonished look on March's face as they all braced for the sudden slowing of the train, the iron wheels squealing against the rails. But it had come at an unforgiveable price.

◇◇◇

By nine that evening, when Benjamin Bradshaw and Henry Pratt stepped off the streetcar on Capitol Hill in Seattle and began to plod wearily home, the sun had set, and the dark sky was spitting rain in cold gusts.

"I could use a bath," said Henry.

"Yes, you could," agreed Bradshaw. "As it's my house, I get to go first."

"Save me some hot water."

"Maybe."

They walked on, passing from the glow of one street lamp to another.

March had continued to claim his innocence and bemoan Bradshaw's "unfortunate mistake" once the train had stopped and the conductor, accompanied by several porters and a beefy baggage master, angrily demanded an explanation.

Bradshaw insisted Daisy and Emily be escorted to their sleeper before speaking of murder. Telegrams were exchanged with the Seattle police. A wire from O'Brien prompted the conductor to bind March's hands behind his back and soon after, the luxury train reversed direction back to Wenatchee. There, they caught a westbound train to Seattle, with March guarded by a Chelan County deputy. They'd been met at the Seattle station by O'Brien, the police chief, and several patrolmen. Miss Darlyrope had been there, sweeping little Emily and Daisy into her arms. And Harry appeared, dressed once more as a man, standing back from the women, biting her lip to contain a grin.

Outside the picket fence at 1204 Gallagher, Bradshaw and Henry hesitated, puzzled at the sound of music and laughter spilling from the open windows and through the screen door.

"We leave for a day and your household throws a party," said Henry. "That Mrs. Prouty is full of secrets."

They climbed the steps and entered the house to find Mrs. Prouty, Justin, Missouri, Assistant Professor Tom Hill, and Mr. Daily and his wife, all squeezed into the parlor, orchestra music pouring from Bradshaw's polished loud-talker. A blue ribbon graced the base of the horn.

"Dad!" shouted Justin, spotting them first. He pushed through the adults and ran into his father's arms.

"Did you find her?"

"Yes, she's back safely."

Justin hugged him fiercely.

Missouri presented her Uncle Henry with a hug, and then they all started to explain.

Bradshaw shushed them. "One at a time! Tom, tell me what this is all about."

"You won, old man! You won! Mrs. Prouty telephoned to tell me what was up. Said you'd forfeited your day at the competition to charge out of here like a knight on his steed. We took Justin out of school to help. Bright boy, don't know where he gets it," he said with a wink. "We all went down to the Grand and hooked up your device and you won, hands down, best all around."

He glanced at Mr. Daily, who smiled and shrugged, his palms up.

Justin said, "The people with your fancy loud-talker said it was just like being there! And it is. Listen, it's playing now, that's coming from the Grand. I called it the "Phone-a-Grand" and Mr. Fisher said he liked it so much he's going to use it."

"Excellent name, son. Well done." His invention, his contest-winning invention, now officially had a name. A toe-tapping ragtime melody swirled around them, and perhaps it was the dampness of the day or Bradshaw's exhaustion or the surprise of it all, but the sound was pure and full and only faintly touched by crackling distortion.

"How did you do it? My equipment was locked."

"Mr. Daily's a locksmith, don't you know," said Tom, and Bradshaw looked at Mr. Daily's satisfied face, proud as if he'd won himself. Tom went on, "He said he'd never feel right about winning if your invention wasn't tested. And he didn't try to examine your components, Bradshaw. Just hooked things up and turned away. He's a good man, our Mr. Daily."

"Yes, he is," said Bradshaw, and he shook Mr. Daily's hand, and that of his plump wife, who pulled him into a hug.

Then Mrs. Prouty pressed a glass of wine at him that he didn't really want, and he was astonished to see by the shine in her eyes that she'd already had a glass. Or two.

Henry pushed away the glass offered him, and said, "Where's the whiskey, woman!"

"Yes," agreed Bradshaw, "Where's the whiskey?"

The party continued, the music played, changing twenty minutes later to a musical comedy act that had them all laughing. Bradshaw stopped drinking after his first whiskey, feeling disconnected from the joviality around him. He stood at the threshold of the room, a smile pasted on his face, watching this small group of people he cared deeply about, watching his son's happy, carefree dancing and laughter with an ache that bordered too near tears.

When the knock sounded at the front door, only Bradshaw heard it. He found Detective O'Brien on his porch in the yellow glow of the lamp, Roosevelt hat pressed back. He wasn't smiling. His eyes were anxious.

Bradshaw stepped outside, shutting the door behind him.

O'Brien said softly, but urgently, "Have you spoken to Justin yet?"

"No."

"Don't. March is keeping his trap shut."

Had he had too much whiskey? "What?"

"March isn't going to say anything, to anybody, about your late wife."

"Why not?"

"I asked him not to."

"And he agreed? Just like that? I don't believe it."

"We dropped the murder charge."

He gasped. "In exchange for his silence? No, that's not right. He's dangerous. We can't let him get away with murder. No, it's wrong. I—"

"He'll be locked up a long time for smuggling, Ben. My stenographers took down enough to nail him on that, thanks to your transmitters. But he wouldn't have been convicted of murder. It wasn't enough. You know it wasn't enough. Henry is your friend, therefore a prejudiced witness. What March said to you, what Henry overheard, isn't proof. Your word against his. His word against a child's. Even Mrs. Woodworth's testimony, if she agreed to give it, wouldn't be enough. He never confessed to her. She put the pieces together herself. It's all circumstantial. His story is that Emily told him she lived in New York, that he had rescued her. And he has powerful friends. He's already trying to convince everyone he was working under cover, infiltrating the smuggling ring. Some will believe him, but Victor has been arrested, too, and he's spilling. And I mean giving dates, names, places, from the Alaska swindles to the phenacetin smuggling. Victor's got a mind like an encyclopedia. He'll get a break for his testimony, and March won't be able to talk his way out of the charges."

Bradshaw swallowed, but the lump remained in his throat. "You don't trade."

"Not for myself, no."

He exchanged a look with O'Brien, his friend. Yes, his friend. "I can never thank you."

"I can't promise forever, Ben. I bought a little time is all. For your son, and for the Woodworths. I'm heading there now. They didn't deserve to have their kindness returned like this. Oh, I almost forgot. We found Emily's mother. In Spokane. Emily told us where to look, finally. We wired. She fainted when she got the news. Seems she got a letter a few weeks ago saying her husband and daughter had been killed. She'd already had their funeral."

"March sent the letter?"

"No proof, but yeah."

"Jim, I—I don't know how…"

"I have three of my own."

Bradshaw nodded. "And one on the way."

"A boy, the wife says." A corner of O'Brien's mouth lifted, betraying his pleasure in the thought of a son, revealing, too, Bradshaw could see, his relief that their friendship had survived. He held out his hand, and Bradshaw accepted. The detective left then, heading around the house to cut through Bradshaw's yard to get to the lane behind, where a little more than a month ago Ralph Hopper had abandoned his wagon, and Emily Hopper had lost her father.

Bradshaw stood alone in the yellow light of the porch, eyes lifted to the horizon, to the dark silhouette of the lone Douglas fir in his neighbor's yard against an even darker sky. He listened to the music and the voices in his parlor. Ribboned throughout was his son's voice, pitched high with youth.

Not forever. A little time. O'Brien had given him a priceless gift. He took a deep breath and turned to go in, pretending the need to wipe the moisture from his eyes was a sign of how very badly he needed a bath.

Author's Note
and Acknowledgements

Real people, places, and events are woven fictitiously into this story, and as much as possible, I stayed true to the history of the University of Washington, Seattle, national events, and electrical invention.

The shoot-out between William Meredith and theater owner John Considine is a well-documented example of the power struggles in Seattle's Tenderloin district. Former friends and underworld cohorts, their relationship turned ugly when Meredith, as chief of police, began to crack down on Considine's illicit income. On June 25, 1901, Meredith wrote a letter of resignation, acquired a sawed-off shotgun, then strutted down the street telling everyone he was gunning for Considine. They met up at G.O. Guy's Drug Store. Meredith's shotgun pellets spread and strayed, only wounding, while Considine's handgun hit with deadly accuracy. Considine was later acquitted since several witnesses heard Meredith state his intention to murder.

Less known is the story of Nell "Harry" Pickerell, notorious for dressing as a man. Several young women did lose their hearts to her, to tragic ends. In 1902, Hazel Walters committed suicide by drinking carbolic acid, and in 1903, Pearl Waldron shot herself. Pearl was found alive and brought to a hospital, and a few days later the newspaper reported she was expected to recover. While Harry was never accused of murder, she was arrested for "charges ranging from disorderly conduct to highway robbery," according to her obituary in the *Seattle Daily Times*. After a brief illness, she died December 27, 1922 at the age of 40 at Providence Hospital, coincidentally, the same hospital where I was born.

The investigation into phenacetin smuggling began in the early 1890s and continued after the arrest of the mastermind Louis J. Fulmer on October 6, 1901, in Detroit. The investigations were led by the German company Bayer's United States agent, Faberfabriken of Elberfield. Before and after Fulmer's arrest, local investigators caught many more smuggling agents in the massive ring all around the country. An army of drummers sold the drug, which was often adulterated, directly to pharmacists who chose not to question the quality of the product in the face of the cheap price.

The fictional microphone Professor Bradshaw has filed a patent for in this book is modeled after K.M. Turner's Dictograph of the early 1900s. In 1910, the Burns Detective Agency began using a specially devised microphone called the "Detective Dictograph" to eavesdrop on criminal conversations, and evidence gathered by the agency was admissible in court.

Home delivery of telephonic entertainment was a hot topic in the late nineteenth and early twentieth century. In Europe, several services were established. Paris and London had systems that delivered music, plays, and dialogues to subscribers. Budapest's *Telefon Hirmondó* was the most developed system, working much like radio stations of the future with a broadcast-style office and on-air talent reading news and playing live music in a scheduled program. A few pleasure-telephone systems popped up in the U.S., but none survived long. This was an age of electromechanical devices that were limited in their ability to transmit signals and amplify sounds without distortion. The reality of a telephonic entertainment system never lived up to the dream. Then came Lee De Forest and his Audion vacuum tube, patented in 1907, eventually revolutionizing the methods of signal boosting and transmission. Telephonic dreams gave way to the amazing reality of radio.

My thanks to John Jenkins, President and CEO of the SPARK Museum of Electrical Invention, for reading the technical portions of the manuscript and for his informative book *LOUD TALKER: The Early History of Loudspeakers*. In the early stages of writing, Jonathan Winter, co-founder of the SPARK Museum, answered my questions and showed me numerous museum pieces—horns and sounding boards and music boxes—that inspired the development of this story. Another valuable technical adviser and reader was Bill Beaty, a research engineer at the University of Washington, who generously shares his broad knowledge and passion for the history of electrical invention, as well as his eye for editing.

Larry Karp and Tim Fabrizio provided advice on wax cylinders and historical dictation machines, and Marv Jahnke inspired me to investigate the history of wire recorders. Benjamin Helle of the Washington State Archives Olympia Regional Branch guided me to historical records. And I spent many happy hours immersed in The University of Washington Digital Archives and the *Seattle Times* archives.

Reading a manuscript critically is a huge undertaking, and I am indebted to my circle of writing friends who take on this role. For this manuscript I am particularly grateful for Jeannie Dunlap and Laron Glover, who both spent many hours reading and providing excellent comments, and my sister, Beverlee Burk, who gave the final version the final test lap. Thank you all!

I am grateful to have the guidance and support of my editor Annette Rogers, chief editor Barbara Peters, and the whole gang at Poisoned Pen Press, including Robert Rosenwald for his exquisite patience, and Jessica Tribble, a tireless publisher who never gets annoyed at my ceaseless questions and requests. My agent Jill Grosjean continues to be a treasured source of professional and emotional support.

In a happy moment of serendipity, I met two new friends. Art Davis, professor emeritus of electrical engineering and his wife Lalah, an electrical engineer, inspire me with their real life immersion in electrical matters, practical and theoretical. Much of this manuscript was written in the supportive company of The Sky Valley Education Center moms (Tracy, Marilene, Torie, Suzie, and Jennie, to name a few), and I treasure my friend Barbara Ekholm for her friendship and generous support. And finally, I'm thankful for my loving husband, who supports me in a thousand ways, and my son, who makes everything worthwhile.

To receive a free catalog of Poisoned Pen Press titles, please contact us in one of the following ways:

Phone: 1-800-421-3976
Facsimile: 1-480-949-1707
Email: info@poisonedpenpress.com
Website: www.poisonedpenpress.com

Poisoned Pen Press
6962 E. First Ave. Ste 103
Scottsdale, AZ 85251